Murder at Ardith Hall

A Redmond and Haze Mystery
Book 6

By Irina Shapiro

Copyright

© 2021 by Irina Shapiro

All rights reserved. No part of this book may be reproduced in any form, except for quotations in printed reviews, without permission in writing from the author.

All characters are fictional. Any resemblances to actual people (except those who are actual historical figures) are purely coincidental.

Cover created by MiblArt.

Table of Contents

Prologue 5
Chapter 1 8
Chapter 2 16
Chapter 3 24
Chapter 4 29
Chapter 5 34
Chapter 6 42
Chapter 7 49
Chapter 8 52
Chapter 9 59
Chapter 10 65
Chapter 11 69
Chapter 12 76
Chapter 13 82
Chapter 14 88
Chapter 15 93
Chapter 16 98
Chapter 17 101
Chapter 18 111
Chapter 19 113
Chapter 20 117
Chapter 21 128
Chapter 22 134
Chapter 23 139
Chapter 24 144
Chapter 25 149
Chapter 26 160

Chapter 27	165
Chapter 28	173
Chapter 29	178
Chapter 30	181
Chapter 31	195
Chapter 32	197
Chapter 33	201
Chapter 34	207
Chapter 35	216
Chapter 36	225
Epilogue	231
Notes	234
Excerpt from Murder on the Sea Witch	235
Prologue	235
Chapter 1	239
Chapter 2	243
Chapter 3	250

Prologue

A single candle in a silver holder glowed in the center of the table, casting a golden halo of light onto the tense faces of the people seated around it. The velvet tablecloth felt smooth and rich beneath her exposed wrists as Sarah joined hands with the guests on either side of her. The gold fringes of the cloth brushed against her thighs, sharpening her already heightened awareness.

The psychic, Mrs. Lysander, sat directly across, her dark eyes wide and her lips slightly parted as she took in the subdued group. She was younger than Sarah had expected, and more beautiful, her face and manner radiating an ethereal quality further enhanced by a low, melodious voice that Sarah found strangely soothing.

There were four others at the table: Mrs. Tarrant, their hostess, Lord Julian Sumner, Mr. Roger Stillman, and Mr. Nathaniel Forbes, a businessman from Barbados, all of whom had been introduced when they'd gathered in the drawing room before adjourning to the little parlor Mrs. Tarrant had designated for Mrs. Lysander's use.

Sarah shivered with anticipation, her reservations about coming tonight forgotten, as Mrs. Lysander asked them to close their eyes and remain silent for the duration of the séance. Mr. Forbes was on Sarah's right, his hand large and warm on hers. Mr. Stillman sat on her left, his fingers long and elegant but cold and unsteady as he took hold of her hand. It felt odd to hold hands with men who were virtual strangers, and uncomfortably intimate without the benefit of gloves to prevent such personal contact.

She had indirectly lied to Daniel by asking her mother to tell him that an old acquaintance had invited her to an evening of cards. He'd be surprised, since she rarely went out on her own, especially in the evening, but would not mind her going. Daniel wouldn't understand about the séance, however, nor would he approve, but this was something Sarah felt she had to do. And so here she was, trying to contact her darling Felix, who'd died four years ago at the age of three.

Mrs. Lysander closed her eyes and began to speak, summoning the spirits of the departed and urging them to show themselves. Sarah wondered if they were all meant to come at once, or would they take turns appearing to their loved ones? She shivered, suddenly frightened. Her earlier excitement had been replaced by gnawing fear, and she wished she could leave, but it was too late. The psychic's voice grew louder, turning into an almost inhuman wail as she called out to the deceased.

"Show yourselves," she implored.

Sarah allowed one eyelid to lift marginally. Mrs. Lysander sat with her eyes closed. Her head was thrown back, her face contorted with raw emotion as she opened herself up to the otherworldly presence that she claimed had entered the room and was ready to speak to them. By this point, everyone had opened their eyes. Their expressions were rapt, their gazes bright with longing, each one holding their breath in the hope that it was their loved one that was about to make themselves known.

"What is your name?" Mrs. Lysander moaned. "Tell us, O spirit." Her face had relaxed now that the spirit had made itself known to her, all emotion replaced by otherworldly calm.

As she sat still, listening intently for the spirit to fulfill her request, Mr. Stillman yanked his hand out of Sarah's grasp. His fingers clawed at the starched collar of his shirt, his eyes bugging out as his face turned a mottled red, the flush spreading to his neck. He opened his mouth, a croaking sound that might have been a call for help bubbling forth.

"Mr. Stillman!" Mrs. Tarrant cried. She sprang to her feet and rushed toward the man, although Sarah wasn't sure what she planned to do.

A torrent of blood erupted from Mr. Stillman's open mouth, the dark red fluid pooling on the velvet tablecloth and soaking into the fabric. He gasped for breath, his fingers desperately yanking at his blood-soaked cravat. When the noxious smell of loosened bowels wafted from the afflicted man, the other guests pushed back their chairs in shocked disgust, their horrified gazes flitting from one person to another as they tried to decide what to do. In his distress, Mr. Forbes knocked over the candleholder, extinguishing the flame and plunging the room into darkness.

Sarah heard a shrill cry, then realized it was coming from her. She was terrified, her hands trembling violently as she pushed away from the table, desperate to leave. Mr. Forbes grabbed hold of her hand, and together they groped their way toward the door, flinging it open to let in a faint shaft of light from the gas lamps in the corridor.

Despite her terror, Sarah turned back to see what was happening. Mrs. Lysander was on her feet, her beaded reticule in her hands. Lord Sumner seemed transfixed by the tableau playing out before him, his eyes wide with shock. Mrs. Tarrant was still working to loosen Mr. Stillman's cravat and unbutton his collar, but it was too late. His hands stilled and his gaze clouded as a soft sigh escaped his open mouth, his head tipping forward. Sarah's hand flew to her mouth as she realized the man was dead.

"Send for Dr. Parsons and the police," Mrs. Tarrant cried, her voice shrill with horror. "And don't touch anything!"

Chapter 1

Wednesday, December 18, 1867

Jason Redmond gazed at the imposing façade of Ardith Hall as the carriage rolled through the wrought-iron gates and made its way up the sweeping drive. Moonlight filtered through a flotilla of clouds that sailed lazily just above the twin peaks of the roof, illuminating the scene for several moments before plunging it into semidarkness once again. The house stood solid and stark at the edge of a snow-covered lawn and was surrounded by extensive parkland. According to Constable Pullman, who was driving the police wagon, the estate had belonged to the Ardith family for more generations than anyone could recall, but for reasons known only to himself, the last descendant of the proud old family had sold the house to a wealthy merchant from London about a year ago and decamped to the south of France with his mistress.

Jason had not had the pleasure of meeting Lord Ardith before his flight to France, but he had met the new owners last August at the annual fete in Birch Hill, the closest village to the Ardith estate. Mr. Tarrant had chatted to Jason for a few minutes and drifted away to greet someone he knew, but Mrs. Tarrant had talked his ear off until he finally found an excuse to extricate himself and go find his new wife in the tea tent, where she was lending a hand.

The carriage finally pulled up before the house, and Jason hopped down and strode across the frost-crusted gravel toward the front door, not waiting for Constable Pullman to join him. He'd be along in a few minutes, once he surrendered the horse and wagon to the groom. The butler silently took Jason's things and pointed him toward the library, where Mrs. Tarrant was pacing like a caged tigress in her distress.

She was in her mid-forties, a slight, nervous creature who reminded Jason of a magpie. Her dark curls bounced as she looked up at him, her cheeks and neck flushed above the lace-trimmed bodice of her mauve gown. She wore a necklace of jet beads and matching earrings that swung like two tiny pendulums, the black stones reflecting the light of the fire. Her attire proclaimed her to be in half mourning, but Jason didn't know whom she'd lost or how recently.

"Thank the good Lord you've come at last, your lordship," Mrs. Tarrant gushed. "I really am at a loss. I sent word to Dr. Parsons, but he refused to come. Told my man to summon you, since you are more knowledgeable in these matters and there was nothing he could do for the deceased. Such a tedious man," she complained. "Utterly inept at social discourse. Not that this is a social occasion, of course, but he could have been more considerate of my guests. Mr. Stillman might be beyond his help, but my guests are in a state of shock and might have needed seeing to."

She took a deep breath. "I pride myself on being a practical woman, Lord Redmond, but this is too much. Really it is," she blathered on. "To have a guest die in such shocking circumstances. The poor man. I can only hope I made his final moments a bit less frightening than had he been on his own. And John is not here," she moaned. "He's in Manchester on some wretched business. Always business," she said bitterly. "Even with Christmas right around the corner. I can't begin to imagine what Mr. Stillman's death means for the rest of us. Will we be able to continue, do you think?"

"I'm sure you did everything in your power to help Mr. Stillman and look after your guests, Mrs. Tarrant," Jason said, interrupting the flow of words. "Can you tell me what happened, and what is it that you wish to continue?"

"Yes, of course," Mrs. Tarrant said. "We were in the middle of a séance. The spirit had just made its presence known to Mrs. Lysander when Mr. Stillman went red in the face and began to cough. I was irritated at first, I don't mind telling you, since his coughing might have driven the spirit away. But this was no ordinary coughing fit. He was gasping for breath, his chest heaving as he struggled to draw air into his lungs." Mrs. Tarrant's hand flew to her breast as if she had trouble breathing herself. "And then the blood came," she whispered. "So much blood. It just erupted from his mouth, like a waterfall. Have you ever seen a waterfall, Lord Redmond?"

"Yes, I have. What happened then?" Jason asked.

"Well, he tried to say something, but it was impossible to make out the words, with the blood pouring out of his mouth. I suppose he was asking for help. He struggled in vain for a few more moments, then died. Just slumped in his chair, his eyes staring and his mouth open, blood dripping from his lips. It was horrid," she said, her eyes filling with tears. "And violent."

"Where's the deceased now?" Jason asked, hoping the dead man hadn't been moved. He wished to see him in situ.

"I left him just where he died. I knew we shouldn't disturb the scene, just in case there's something to be learned from the position of the body and the like. He's just this way. In the parlor. I had no idea you worked with the police, your lordship," Mrs. Tarrant said as she led him toward the room. "Imagine that, a man in your position assisting the police. Why, I don't quite know what to make of it. It's charitable of you, I suppose," she mused as she pointed toward the closed door. "I'll remain out here, if you don't mind. Lord knows, I won't be able to sleep tonight, not after what I've seen," she said. "Oh, I do wish John were here."

"When is Mr. Tarrant due back?" Jason asked.

"Not till the twenty-fourth, I'm afraid. You will take the body away, won't you?" she asked, her gaze pleading with Jason to say yes.

"Of course, Mrs. Tarrant. The body will be moved to the mortuary tonight."

"Well, that's something, I suppose," Mrs. Tarrant said. "I'll leave you to it, unless there's something you require."

"My colleague and I will need to speak to everyone who was present, but first, I would like to examine the body."

"Be my guest," Mrs. Tarrant said, and gestured toward the door.

Jason opened the door and entered the parlor. The curtains had been drawn, and a candle, which must have been used during the séance, lay overturned on the table, a solidified blob of wax stuck to the velvet tablecloth and the wick. The deceased sat in solitary silence, his face waxy in the light from the open door. Jason found the switch and turned on the gas lamps, flooding the room with mellow light. Setting his medical bag on the chair nearest the door, he approached the dead man gingerly, his gaze sweeping the floor and his nose wrinkling at the awful smell that emanated from the deceased. His bowels had let loose at the moment of death, and there was a noxious brown puddle beneath the chair.

The tablecloth was soaked through with blood, the stain nearly black on the burgundy velvet. Aside from smears of blood on the man's chin, cravat, and cuffs, there were no visible marks on the body. Jason studied the man before conducting an examination. Roger Stillman was in his mid-thirties. He had a thick head of fair hair and very blue eyes fringed by dark-blond lashes. His high cheekbones, fair skin, and straight nose put Jason in mind of the pillaging Norsemen he'd seen in history books. He had been an attractive man and, with his lean frame and toned muscles beneath his well-tailored suit, a physically fit one. Whatever had killed this man had not been an ongoing illness, Jason concluded.

He carefully combed the surrounding area, searching for any signs of poison or a concealed weapon, then maneuvered the dead man to the floor, carefully undressed him, and performed a thorough examination before dressing him again.

Jason left the body on the floor and exited the parlor to find Mrs. Tarrant waiting outside with a young maidservant, who had a folded towel slung over her arm and was holding a basin of warm water. Jason cleaned his hands, retrieved his medical bag, and turned toward the drawing room, where the remaining guests were assembled. It was at that moment that Daniel arrived with Constable Ingleby, who had been sent to fetch him.

Daniel's shoulders were dusted with snow, his face red from the cold, but his eyes were bright with anticipation, the question uppermost in his mind obvious as his gaze locked with Jason's. "Was he murdered?" Daniel asked.

"I won't know for certain until I perform the postmortem," Jason replied. "But the symptoms are consistent with arsenic poisoning. Given the man's violent reaction, I'd say that the arsenic was administered shortly before death rather than over a prolonged period."

Daniel nodded. "Let's interview the guests and see what we can learn," he said as he shrugged off his coat and handed it, together with his hat and gloves, to the butler hovering at his elbow. "Constable, make sure none of the guests leave," Daniel said to Ingleby. "I think it's best if you take up a position in the drawing room so you can keep an eye on the suspects while we interview them."

"Yes, sir," Constable Ingleby said.

Constable Pullman, who'd been standing near the drawing room door, his helmet under his arm, approached Daniel, ready to receive instructions from his superior.

"Constable Pullman, speak to the staff. Find out where everyone was this evening, if anyone had come in contact with the deceased, and who had been in the drawing room and parlor today. Were they privy to the identities of Mrs. Tarrant's guests? Also, I need to know who would normally be responsible for filling the decanters. Take everyone's statement, and let us know if there's anyone we need to interview in person."

Constable Pullman drew himself up, his eyes glowing with pride at the responsibility he'd been given. It was common knowledge around the Brentwood station that Constable Pullman was gunning for a promotion and hoped to be made inspector in the near future. He had been taking on more responsibility and was proving to be an invaluable asset to both Daniel and Inspector Peterson, who'd taken Constable Pullman under his wing and was teaching him the ropes.

"Oh, and Constable," Daniel said just as Constable Pullman made for the green baize door that separated the rest of the house from the servants' quarters. "Question Mr. Stillman's coachman. If he has nothing of value to impart, send him home. No sense keeping the man waiting in the bitter cold."

"Will do, sir," Constable Pullman said, and disappeared through the door.

Daniel walked toward the drawing room and opened the door. The four witnesses were spread about the room, the women sitting by themselves, the men engaged in quiet conversation, which ended abruptly when Jason and Daniel walked in. Jason had been curious to meet Mrs. Tarrant's guests, but the only person he saw was Sarah Haze, who sat staring at her hands folded in her lap.

Daniel froze when his gaze settled on his wife. He opened his mouth to say something but changed his mind, turning to Jason for help. Jason nodded his understanding and stepped in, giving Daniel a moment to compose himself.

"Ladies and gentlemen," Jason began. "This is Inspector Haze of the Brentwood Constabulary, and I am Jason Redmond, special advisor to the police. We would like to speak to each of you in turn to learn what transpired tonight. Once we are finished, you will be free to leave." His gaze slid toward Sarah, who looked like she wished the chair would swallow her whole. Jason would have dearly liked to speak to her first and send her on her way, but this was Daniel's investigation, and he would have to determine the order in which the suspects were interviewed.

Jason glanced at the men but didn't linger, allowing his gaze to settle on Mrs. Lysander instead. He'd heard of her, of course. There had been an article in the *London Times* about the renowned psychic and her uncanny ability to summon the most reluctant of spirits. Few people came away from her séances disappointed, and several past participants had been quoted, gushing about Mrs. Lysander's sensitivity and discretion. She never discussed her clients nor her methods for contacting the dead. There had been a grainy photograph of the psychic in the *Essex Standard* about a week ago, but it had failed to accurately depict the woman seated before him.

Mrs. Lysander was younger than Jason had expected, around twenty-five, if he had to guess. Her jet-black hair was artfully arranged about a face that was exotic and arresting in its beauty. Almond-shaped black eyes fringed with thick lashes stared back at him, challenging him to discredit her, and a ghost of a smile tugged at her sensuous lips, as if she were amused by what had taken place during her séance rather than horrified by Roger Stillman's sudden and violent death. Jason had to admit that he looked forward to speaking with her, if only to learn more about her origins. Few people aroused his curiosity, but Mrs. Lysander was without question one of them.

Jason suddenly realized that a pregnant silence had fallen over the room as the four witnesses awaited instructions. No doubt flustered by Sarah's presence, Daniel had yet to speak.

"Daniel," Jason prompted softly.

"Right," Daniel said, as if waking from a bad dream. "I'd like to speak to Mrs. Tarrant first. Is there somewhere we can talk in private?" he asked, his gaze still glued to Sarah's panicked face.

"We can use the library," Mrs. Tarrant said, and stepped forward to lead the way.

"Did you know Sarah was here?" Daniel asked under his breath as they made their way down the silent corridor.

"No. I'm as surprised as you are. Did you not know where she was tonight?" Jason asked softly.

Daniel didn't reply, but his expression said it all.

Chapter 2

The library at Ardith Hall was most impressive, with shelves upon shelves of books, a vaulted ceiling, and stained-glass windows that gave the room an almost church-like appearance. Several chairs were grouped around a low table before the hearth, and there were also discreet alcoves for those who wished not to be disturbed while reading.

No one had been using the library, but a fire blazed in the great fireplace, the room pleasantly warm and cozy despite its size. Mrs. Tarrant dropped into a seat and gestured for the two men to do the same. Daniel took the armchair closest to the hearth and pulled out his notebook, but his mind wasn't on the case. Sarah hadn't been at home when he'd returned from the Brentwood police station a few hours ago, and her mother had said that Sarah had been invited to an evening of cards at Chadwick Manor.

Daniel had been surprised, since Caroline Chadwick didn't normally make overtures of friendship to his wife, but had thought nothing of it, sitting down to an early dinner with his mother-in-law and then spending an hour in the nursery with his darling Charlotte before her grandmother put her to bed. He had assumed that Sarah had told him about the invitation and he'd simply forgotten, but now realized that she hadn't, probably because she preferred not to lie to him about where she was going. To think that she had made secret plans to attend a séance with the famed Mrs. Lysander left him not only speechless but deeply hurt.

Daniel flipped the notebook to a fresh page, wondering angrily why Sarah had felt the need to withhold the truth from him. Had she thought he wouldn't approve? Or he'd try to forbid her from going? Perhaps he would have. He didn't believe in the occult, nor did he condone the practice of trying to contact the dead. Psychics had sprung up like mushrooms after rain in the last few years. Feeding on the desperation of the bereaved and relieving them of their hard-earned money, they used obvious parlor tricks to convince participants at their séances that they had made contact with their departed loved ones. The psychic might go on to ask the spirits questions, instructing them to knock once for yes, twice for no. It was easy enough to counterfeit a knock, either with a foot or with a piece of wood tied to the psychic's knee. They'd raise the knee beneath the table and strike the underside, answering in place of the spirit. How gullible did a person have to be to fall for such claptrap?

Daniel refused to acknowledge the other reason desperate people waited for weeks to attend a séance with the psychic of their choice. They were heartbroken, unable to let go. He felt a dull ache in the vicinity of his heart but set his personal feelings aside and turned his attention to Mrs. Tarrant, who seemed to be vibrating with nervous energy.

"I really can't believe it," Mrs. Tarrant exclaimed. Now that the initial shock had worn off, she was as petulant as a child. "You don't know what it took me to secure Mrs. Lysander for this evening, and now everything's been ruined, and I'll never get another chance to make contact with my darling Hector. This really is unfair. I had such hopes for tonight," she moaned.

"Mrs. Tarrant, can you please tell us what happened? From the beginning," Daniel invited.

The woman sighed tragically. "Once everyone arrived, we proceeded directly into the parlor. Some hosts serve supper before, but I thought it would only delay what everyone had come for and asked Cook to prepare a light repast for those who wished to linger after the séance. Truth be told, I hoped they would leave so I could be alone with my thoughts. Who wants to make small talk after such an emotional experience?"

"When did Mr. Stillman arrive?" Daniel asked, trying to steer Mrs. Tarrant back to the events of the evening.

"He was the third to arrive. Mr. Forbes was the first, and then Mrs. Haze joined us. I invited them to have a drink in the drawing room whilst we waited."

"Did Mr. Stillman have a drink?" Jason asked.

"Yes."

"What did he drink?"

"Scotch whisky. He had a glass when he arrived and then accepted a refill once Lord Sumner had joined us."

"Did Mr. Forbes have a drink as well?" Jason asked.

"Mr. Forbes prefers rum, which I didn't have, so he settled for a glass of sherry."

"Did anyone else have Scotch?" Daniel inquired.

"No, only Mr. Stillman," Mrs. Tarrant said.

"I would like to examine Mr. Stillman's glass and the decanter," Jason said.

"The glass has already been removed, but the decanter is still in the drawing room," Mrs. Tarrant said. "I'll be sure to give it to your man as soon as I'm done here."

"Thank you. How did Mr. Stillman seem?" Jason asked. "Did his demeanor change after he drank the whisky?"

Mrs. Tarrant thought about that for a moment. "He was a little pale when he arrived, but I assumed he was just nervous. The whisky did seem to calm him somewhat, but then he grew anxious again and accepted another drink when I offered it."

"Whom was he trying to contact?" Daniel asked.

"I don't know. It's not customary to discuss such things before a séance," Mrs. Tarrant said with a small shake of her head, as if the men should really know better than to ask such questions.

"Who's Mr. Stillman's next of kin?" Daniel asked, his pencil poised to make a note.

"He lived with his mother. In Mayfair. I'll get you the address."

17

Daniel nodded his thanks. "And how do you know the people you invited tonight?" he asked, trying to sound nonchalant.

He tried to recall if Sarah had ever mentioned the Tarrants but couldn't bring up any memory of such an occasion. He'd heard of them, of course. There had been much talk when Lord Ardith absconded with his seventeen-year-old mistress and sold the family seat to a trumped-up merchant, but Daniel had never known them socially and assumed Sarah didn't either. The Tarrants had attended the church fete last August, as reported by his mother-in-law, but Sarah had been unwell that day, and she and Daniel had skipped the event.

Mrs. Tarrant smoothed down her skirts, even though there wasn't a wrinkle in sight. "I know the gentlemen through my husband. He's done business with them for years, and I've had the pleasure of receiving them at our London house."

"And Mrs. Haze?" Daniel asked, nearly choking on the name.

"I met Mrs. Haze several years ago, when we both belonged to a charitable organization for the improvement of London's orphanages. Those places are woefully overcrowded, and the conditions in which the children live are appalling," Mrs. Tarrant exclaimed. "Mrs. Haze and I had a lengthy discourse on the subject when I invited her to tea."

"In London?" Daniel asked. He couldn't recall Sarah taking tea with a Mrs. Tarrant, but then he had been busy with his work and hadn't paid as much attention to Sarah's needs as he should have. Nor had he been the best father he could have been, taking it for granted that his son would always be there when Daniel had time to spend with him.

"Yes, in London," Mrs. Tarrant replied. "It was only recently that I discovered that Mrs. Haze lives not too far from Ardith Hall. I wrote to her immediately, hoping to renew our acquaintance. You see, I had heard that she lost her precious boy several years ago. That's why she'd stopped coming to the meetings. I had sent a note of condolence but didn't wish to intrude on her grief. It wasn't long after that I lost my Hector," Mrs. Tarrant said, covering her mouth to stifle a sob. "I know Hector was practically a grown man, but a child always remains small and vulnerable to its mother. I suppose I was looking for someone who'd share my grief."

"Have you and Mrs. Haze been in contact long?" Daniel asked, afraid his chagrin was obvious. How had he not known that Sarah had belonged to the organization Mrs. Tarrant had mentioned and recently renewed their acquaintance? Why hadn't she told him?

"A few months. John and I came to Essex to escape the Season. It'd been more than a year since I'd come out of full mourning for my boy, but I simply couldn't bear the thought of attending anything more spirited than a musical evening or an intimate supper. And wild horses couldn't drag Flora to a ball," she added. "So, it's not as if we're doing her a disservice by keeping her away from all that rigamarole."

"And who is Flora?" Daniel asked.

"Our daughter. She's under the weather, so she remained upstairs tonight," Mrs. Tarrant explained. "Anyhow, Mrs. Haze and I had much to talk about, and when I put forward the idea of a séance, she agreed after a period of consideration. She did ask me to keep our plans confidential, since she didn't want her husband to know. Didn't think he'd approve."

"Mrs. Tarrant, you do realize that Inspector Haze is Mrs. Haze's husband," Jason said, clearly unable to keep silent any longer.

"What?" Mrs. Tarrant screeched, staring at Daniel with undisguised horror. "Oh, I do beg your pardon. I was so distraught, I completely missed your surname, but I thought it was all right, as long as I referred to you as Inspector." She cocked her head to the side, her dark eyes bright with glee as the implications of Daniel's presence sank in. "Do you not wish to speak to your wife,

Inspector? Surely she'd be able to tell you everything you need to know."

"I'll speak to my wife in due course," Daniel replied stiffly. "Right now, I'd like to hear your version of events."

"Well, as I was saying, we all met in the drawing room. Mrs. Haze and Mr. Forbes had a glass of sherry, and then we adjourned to the parlor once Lord Sumner arrived."

"Where was Mrs. Lysander?" Jason asked.

"Mrs. Lysander arrived a few minutes before Lord Sumner and was escorted directly to the parlor so she could set up."

"Did she come alone?" Jason asked.

"She has an assistant who sees to her schedule and acts as chaperone when the situation calls for it, but he didn't come inside. He took himself off to the Hound and Partridge to have a pint or two. He is due to collect her after the séance."

"And how does Mrs. Lysander normally conduct her séances?" Daniel asked. "I didn't see any implements, such as a crystal ball or a board for receiving messages from the dead."

"You see, Inspector Haze, that is the uniqueness of Mrs. Lysander's gift. She doesn't rely on any gimmicks. When a spirit makes an appearance, Mrs. Lysander goes into a trance and the visiting spirit speaks directly through her to their loved one. They hear the message, and so does everyone else, so there's no disputing the fact that a spirit has made contact."

"And does Mrs. Lysander bring forth the dearly departed of every person in the room?" Jason asked, sounding dubious.

"Oh no, my lord," Mrs. Tarrant replied. "If the attendees are lucky, then maybe two spirits will part the veil between this world and the next and speak to their loved ones."

"But from what I've read, no one ever leaves disappointed," Jason pointed out.

"Hearing the messages meant for others helps those who weren't as lucky to feel more at peace. They see for themselves that it is possible to contact the dead and that none of them appear to be suffering. That knowledge lessens their grief and gives them hope for the future. There are some who follow mediums like Mrs. Lysander from place to place, managing to secure an invitation to a séance more than once in the hope of their loved one coming to them at last."

"Did any spirits manifest tonight?" Daniel asked.

"We had just started when Mr. Stillman's coughing fit interrupted the séance, but Mrs. Lysander did say she felt a presence in the room. She never said who it was," Mrs. Tarrant said wistfully.

"Were you not supposed to keep your eyes closed during the séance?" Jason asked.

"Yes, Mrs. Lysander did instruct us to hold hands and keep our eyes closed, but I peeked just a little. I was curious to see what she'd look like when a spirit entered her body."

"And how did she look?" Jason asked.

"Blank," Mrs. Tarrant replied.

"Blank?" Jason asked in surprise.

"Well, of course," Mrs. Tarrant said, sounding exasperated. "She is a conduit, an empty vessel for the spirit to inhabit. How would you expect her to look?"

"Thank you, Mrs. Tarrant," Daniel said with a sigh. He dreaded working on this case, and not just because of Sarah's unexpected involvement. It was hard enough to get people to tell the truth and admit to their motives without dealing with restless spirits, heartbroken relations, and clever mediums. And Mrs. Lysander had to be clever, or she wouldn't be as sought after as she was. Empty vessel or massive fraud, she had found a formula that worked and would milk it until she either made enough money or was exposed as a charlatan.

"Would you kindly send in Mrs. Lysander now?" Daniel asked, bracing himself for the conversation with the psychic.

"Of course. Oh, I do hope she agrees to come back," Mrs. Tarrant lamented as she stood to leave, her small hands clasped before her. "I so want to speak to my darling Hector one more time."

Chapter 3

To say that Mrs. Lysander walked into the room would be like saying that a train exploded into the station or that an ocean liner crashed into port. Alicia Lysander's feet didn't appear to touch the floor. She glided. And when she took the seat Mrs. Tarrant had just vacated, she seemed to settle into it with the softness of a snowflake landing on one's tongue. She wore all black, but the absence of color did not take away from her beauty. If anything, it enhanced it.

"Mrs. Lysander, tell us about yourself," Daniel invited as he took in the woman before him. It was obvious to Jason that he felt uncomfortable, and if Mrs. Lysander was any sort of psychic, it had to be evident to her as well.

"What would you like to know, Inspector?" she asked softly, her gaze never leaving his face, which seemed to be turning pinker with every passing moment.

"Where do you come from? Where's your husband? Where do you make your home?" Daniel clarified, more forcefully than necessary, in Jason's opinion.

Mrs. Lysander smiled sadly. "I was born and raised in India, the daughter of a British major and a native woman he'd taken as his mistress. I never really knew my mother, since my father tired of her and sent her away, nor did I ever figure out why he didn't allow her to take me, since he never showed much interest in me. An English governess was engaged for me in accordance with my father's wishes and spent the next decade trying to turn me into a proper English miss, while my Indian *ayah* worked hard to help me retain something of my Indian roots. I married Captain John Lysander when I was eighteen and was widowed at twenty, shortly after arriving in England. I keep rooms in London, but I travel all over the country, helping those who can't come to terms with their bereavement contact their departed loved ones."

"And when did you realize you have this rare gift?" Jason asked, feeling an irrational desire to needle her.

"I can see you're skeptical, Lord Redmond, and I don't blame you. There's many a charlatan in my profession, but I assure you, I'm the real thing. I've been able to relay messages from the dead since I was a child. The first one was for my father from my mother, who passed when I was five. Her spirit couldn't rest because he'd separated her from her daughter. She urged him to love me and legitimize me so that I would have a chance at a respectable marriage."

"Indeed?" Jason asked, trying in vain to hide his amusement. *How convenient.* "And did he?"

"He did legitimize me, since he didn't have any other children, but asking him to love me was going a step too far."

"So, this appeal from the dead proved highly beneficial for you," Jason remarked.

"Yes, but had my mother wished for him to send me away, I would have passed on the message all the same."

"Would you have?" Jason taunted.

"You clearly don't believe me, my lord. Perhaps you'd like to join one of my séances," Mrs. Lysander suggested. She showed no sign of annoyance or anger. "There are those who wish to connect with you."

"Thank you, but no. I have no desire to commune with the dead."

"Not even to say goodbye to your parents?" she asked, a smile playing about her lips. "Tell them you love them?"

"My parents knew I loved them," Jason replied tersely. "They don't need to be reminded."

"I bow to your American pragmatism," Mrs. Lysander said. "But India is a very spiritual country, and I have great respect for the dead and their wishes."

"Are you a practicing Hindu?" Jason asked.

He didn't know much about Hinduism but thought it held a vastly different view of the afterlife than Christianity and didn't subscribe to the notion of heaven and hell. In fact, he'd heard that Hindus believed in reincarnation, but wasn't at all sure if everyone was reincarnated or how long after death the transference to a new body occurred.

"I was raised in the Church of England, but I don't practice any particular religion. I believe that the spirit lives on regardless of the faith one adheres to."

"Mrs. Lysander, I'm sure we could debate the merits of spiritualism until dawn, but let's concentrate on the here and now, shall we?" Daniel suggested. "Had you ever met Mr. Stillman before tonight?"

"I had not."

"Had you heard about him?" Daniel continued.

"No. When I arrive at a séance, all the guests are strangers to me."

"Except for your hostess, who made the arrangements," Jason pointed out.

"I had not met Mrs. Tarrant before tonight. She made the arrangements through my assistant."

"And how do you obtain your clients, Mrs. Lysander? Do you advertise in the papers?" Daniel asked.

"No. My clients come to me based on recommendations from others. I refer all inquiries to my assistant, so that I know nothing of the participants when I meet them on the day of the séance."

"Is there a reason your assistant doesn't accompany you inside?" Daniel asked.

"Mr. Moore's function is to deliver me safely and take me to my lodgings once I'm done. Rather than wait in the servants' hall, he prefers to take himself to a nearby tavern and have his supper. He's due to collect me at ten o'clock." She glanced at the clock on the mantelpiece pointedly. It was nearly ten.

"Did you see or hear anything out of the ordinary tonight?" Daniel asked. "Did you sense the impending death of Mr. Stillman?"

"I did not. I did, however, notice that he was unwell. I thought he had indigestion, but then again, I'm not a physician, only a medium."

"Do you know whom Mr. Stillman wished to contact tonight?" Jason asked.

"No. We were only a few minutes into the séance."

"Did you feel any spirits hovering nearby as Mr. Stillman breathed his last?" Daniel asked, a tad sarcastically.

"I did, as if happens. It was the spirit of a little boy. His name began with the letter F, and he was desperate to contact his mother."

Daniel blanched and looked away, but not before Jason saw tears in his eyes.

"That was unnecessarily cruel, Mrs. Lysander," Jason pointed out.

"I meant no offense. I simply answered the Inspector's question truthfully," Mrs. Lysander said. Given the look in her eyes, Jason was sure she had meant to cause offense, or more likely pain.

"That will be all for now, Mrs. Lysander. If you will provide us with an address where you can be reached, you are free to leave," Daniel said, clearly desperate to be as far from her as possible.

"I'm staying with Mrs. Evans at Bluebell Cottage near Elsmere. I will be there for three more days, as I have several engagements in Brentwood."

"And then?" Jason asked.

"And then I will leave for Colchester. Good evening, Inspector Haze. Lord Redmond."

Mrs. Lysander seemingly levitated from the chair and floated out of the library.

Chapter 4

Daniel removed his spectacles and pinched the bridge of his nose. It was growing late, and he was tired and more upset than he cared to let on. He was desperate to speak to Sarah, alone, but a part of him wanted to hold off on that conversation forever, fearful of where it would lead. Would she be honest with him? Would she try to make up some excuse? Would she apologize for deceiving him, or would she grow defiant and accuse him of not understanding how she feels? Some detective he was if he couldn't even detect his own wife's unhappiness.

Of course, he knew that she missed Felix dreadfully and felt responsible for his death, but he had been sure that she'd finally forgiven herself and begun to move on, especially since Charlotte's birth. Sarah seemed content, happy even. She was almost her old self, patient and loving with their daughter and affectionate with him. She no longer turned away from him in bed, nor did she refuse to speak to him about what was on her mind and in her heart. Or so he'd thought. The realization that he had misread Sarah's feelings so completely felt like a knife in his back, an assault he hadn't seen coming and would likely never recover from.

Taking out his handkerchief, Daniel cleaned the glasses and slid them back on his nose just as Mr. Forbes entered the library. For the moment, Daniel had to put his own feelings aside and concentrate on the case. If Jason was correct and Roger Stillman had been poisoned this evening, then this case shouldn't be too hard to solve. There were only five obvious suspects, one of them his own wife, unless one of the servants was to blame and the murder had nothing to do with the séance. Once he'd interviewed everyone in the house and Jason had determined the cause of death, he'd have a clearer picture of tonight's events.

Nathaniel Forbes was truly striking. He was tall and imposing, with the wide shoulders and muscular thighs of a man who clearly preferred physical pursuits to those of a more passive nature. His skin was a warm brown, a testament to his mixed parentage, and his eyes were a startling blue, his gaze intelligent and direct. He was elegantly dressed and clearly not averse to showing off his wealth. A diamond pin twinkled in the folds of his cravat, and a massive gold and ruby ring adorned the pinky of his left hand. When he spoke, his voice was warm and rich, the slight Caribbean lilt pleasing to the ear.

"How can I be of assistance, Inspector Haze?" Mr. Forbes asked as he took a seat across from the two men. He turned to Jason. "Lord Redmond, a pleasure. I've read something of your exploits."

"Have you?" Jason asked. He seemed genuinely surprised.

"Oh, yes. You were mentioned several times in the *Illustrated Police News*, especially after the case of the 'cleaved curate,' as they so tactlessly referred to it. I have certain London papers forwarded to me. I find them diverting." Mr. Forbes grinned at Jason, revealing straight white teeth. "You're quite the oddity, much like myself."

"You think me an oddity, sir?" Jason asked, sounding more amused than offended.

"An American surgeon who inherits a noble title and an estate and, instead of playing lord of the manor, devotes his time to performing autopsies for the police and investigating crimes on his own time is an oddity, indeed. I wish more people would challenge the boundaries of the position they were born into and choose how to live their lives rather than allow themselves to be defined and limited by the expectations of others."

Jason nodded in agreement. "You think like an American, Mr. Forbes."

"I suppose I do, but I've never had the pleasure of visiting your country. Perhaps now that the situation has changed, I might."

Mr. Forbes was referring to the abolition of slavery, of course, which made Daniel wonder if the man had been born a slave. Given his approximate age, it was likely. Countless men and women had been sired by plantation owners and visiting businessmen, but if they were born to a slave woman, they were treated as slaves, regardless of their paternity.

"Mr. Forbes, can you tell us how you came to be here tonight?" Daniel asked, eager to bring the conversation back to current events.

"You mean, how did a mulatto from Barbados find his way into the drawing room of someone like Mrs. Tarrant?"

"If that's how you choose to interpret the question, then yes," Daniel replied, somewhat put out by the defensiveness of Mr. Forbes' tone. He hadn't meant any offense, but he supposed it was a fair question on Mr. Forbes' part, given what Daniel had just been wondering about his background.

"John Tarrant and I met as young men. His father owned a sugar plantation in Barbados. After my situation changed, John wrote to me, offering me a partnership of sorts."

"How did your situation change? If you don't mind me asking," Daniel said. Even if Nathaniel Forbes had been born a slave, he would have been freed at a very young age, since slavery had been abolished in all areas of the British Empire by 1834. By the time of his meeting with John Tarrant, he would have been a free man.

"My mother was a slave. She worked as a housekeeper for Jeremiah Forbes, my father. He freed her as soon as he found out she was with child and asked her to marry him. She accepted, and I was born on the right side of the blanket, as you British like to say, although that's one blanket not many white planters would have cared to touch in those days. Once slavery was abolished, my father hired anyone who was willing to remain and kept the plantation going. When he died eight years ago, I inherited his estate."

"Do you visit England often?" Daniel asked.

"I come to England twice a year to meet with my business associates. I have plans to meet with John Tarrant after the New Year. Amelia Tarrant knew I was in London and invited me to the séance."

"Why did she think you'd wish to attend?" Jason asked.

"I recently lost my wife," Mr. Forbes said, his eyes misting with tears. He blinked them away. "She died giving birth to our first child."

"I'm sorry for your loss, Mr. Forbes," Jason said.

There was a slight tremor in his voice. The man's words had obviously struck a nerve. It had never occurred to Daniel that Jason might be worried about the impending birth of his first child. He was a surgeon. He'd saved a woman and her baby by performing an emergency cesarean section last year, and he'd delivered Charlotte, who was breech. The realization that Jason feared the birth of his own child came as a shock and filled Daniel with dismay. Not only had he failed to read the signs of Sarah's desperation, but he'd completely overlooked his friend's fears and worries. Was he really that oblivious to the feelings of those close to him?

Daniel sighed and turned his attention back to Mr. Forbes. "Mr. Forbes, were you acquainted with Mr. Stillman?"

"We met for the first time tonight."

"When did you arrive in England and on which vessel?" Daniel asked.

"I arrived on December fifteenth on *Caribbean Queen*. It docked in Southampton."

Daniel scribbled down the information. He'd wire the steamship line to confirm that Nathaniel Forbes was on their passenger manifest. "And where are you staying?"

"You can find me at Brown's Hotel in Mayfair if you wish to speak to me again."

"Thank you, Mr. Forbes," Daniel said.

Mr. Forbes did not wait to be dismissed. He stood and bowed from the neck before striding from the room.

Chapter 5

Lord Sumner came next. After Nathaniel Forbes, who'd filled the library with his presence, the best that could be said for Julian Sumner was that he was average. With a compact physique, medium-brown hair and eyes, a slightly too-long nose and too-thin lips, he was quite ordinary, except for his demeanor, which was anything but. He pulsated with impatience, his sense of entitlement pervading them room like a foul smell and instantly altering the atmosphere to one of charged expectation. Plopping into a chair, he glared from Daniel to Jason expectantly.

"Well, get on with it," he demanded. "I've no wish to sit here all night."

"Lord Sumner, thank you for your patience. I know it's been frustrating for you to be kept waiting. You will be able to leave as soon as we're finished here," Daniel said, doing his best to mask his dislike of the man with calm professionalism. In the end, he'd pay for being rude to a member of the nobility, and he had no wish to be reprimanded for his handling of the situation. Daniel flipped to a clean page in his notebook, wrote "J. Sumner" at the top, and looked up, ready to begin. "Who invited you to the séance tonight, my lord?" he asked.

"Amelia Tarrant. Who else?" Sumner retorted.

"And why did you decide to come?"

Lord Sumner stared at Daniel. "Why do you think I came?"

"Whom did you wish to contact tonight?" Daniel asked, striving to maintain a civil tone.

"That's none of your affair. That information can have no bearing on the case," Lord Sumner snapped.

"Perhaps it can," Jason interjected. He was visibly annoyed by the man's uncooperative demeanor and looked about to pull rank.

"How so?" Sumner demanded, but his tone was a trifle more deferential now that he was speaking to a member of his own class.

"The person you seek to contact might have had dealings with Mr. Stillman," Jason replied.

"Are you suggesting they managed to kill him from beyond the grave?"

"I'm suggesting no such thing," Jason replied. "But we do need to know the reason for your presence here tonight."

Lord Sumner let out a sigh of exasperation. "Fine. I wished to contact my fiancée. She died a few weeks before we were to be married. I wanted to ask for her forgiveness."

"For what?" Daniel and Jason asked in unison.

"It was my fault she fell ill. I had been out with a few friends and woke with something of a sore throat the following day. I gargled with salt water, then had several cups of tea with honey. My nanny used to swear by it. By noon, I felt well enough to leave the house and went to pay a call on Anne. I missed her and hoped to spend some time alone with her," he added sadly, showing a vulnerability Daniel hadn't expected. "I only stayed for a half hour, but I kissed her in parting," Lord Sumner said, hanging his head guiltily. "She came down with influenza the very next day. And it was all my fault," Lord Sumner added, his voice barely audible.

"Were you ill with influenza as well?" Jason asked.

"Well, no," Lord Sumner said. "But I'm rarely ill. I did have a slight fever that night, and the sore throat persisted for a few days, but that was the extent of it."

Jason listened to Lord Sumner's account carefully, his gaze thoughtful. "If it's any consolation, I don't believe you were responsible," he said at last.

"Why would you think that?" Lord Sumner asked, his tone hopeful.

"Because an infection usually takes several days to manifest itself, and if your fiancée showed signs of illness the following morning, it's quite possible she had been exposed to someone who was ill earlier in the week."

Lord Sumner brightened. "You really think so?"

"I do. It's highly unlikely that you passed the illness on to her," Jason said confidently.

"Oh, thank you. You don't know how happy that makes me. I mean, of course, I'm devastated that Anne died, but to know that I might not have been the one to pass the illness to her takes a load off my mind."

"If we might return to tonight's events," Daniel suggested, feeling once again that he'd lost control of the interview.

"Yes, of course. Ask me anything you like," Lord Sumner gushed, acting like a man who'd just been reprieved from the noose. "I'll help in any way I can."

"Had you ever met Mr. Stillman before tonight?" Daniel asked.

"No, I hadn't. Except for Mrs. Tarrant, everyone here tonight was a stranger to me."

"And you traveled from London to attend tonight's séance?" Daniel asked.

"Yes. Mrs. Tarrant had invited me to stay the night."

"Did you notice anything suspicious when you arrived?" Jason asked.

"Not at all. Everyone was in the drawing room. Amelia made the introductions and offered me a drink, which I declined, and then we adjourned to the parlor, where Mrs. Lysander was waiting for us. Mr. Stillman did look a bit fragile, but I thought it was just nerves. I felt a bit brittle myself, I have to admit. A part of me hoped Anne's spirit would make an appearance, but another, more cowardly part hoped she wouldn't show," he admitted sheepishly. "I suppose I would have been satisfied either way and wouldn't have tried to contact her again."

"Thank you, Lord Sumner. You are free to go," Daniel said.

"I think I'll go straight home. I have no desire to remain in this house a moment longer," Lord Sumner said as he sprang to his feet.

"The roads might not be safe at night," Daniel pointed out.

Julian Sumner waved a dismissive hand. "My coachman is armed, as am I. And as feeble as it sounds, I do prefer to sleep in my own bed."

"I suppose that's all we can do for tonight," Daniel said once the door closed behind the man. It was nearly eleven o'clock, and he was eager to get home. "I'll speak to Sarah at home. Incidentally, what do you mean to do with the Scotch?" he asked as Jason unfolded himself from the armchair.

"Roger Stillman was the only guest to drink the Scotch. It's quite possible that it was the murder weapon, since it was the only thing he'd ingested since arriving at Ardith Hall. Of course, he may have eaten or drunk something earlier, in which case the Scotch will prove irrelevant, clearing everyone at the house."

"How will you know if the whisky was tainted?" Daniel asked.

"There's a test used to determine not only if there's arsenic present, but how much. It's called the Marsh test. However, I would need to visit a chemist before I can determine if the whisky's been tampered with. I don't have the necessary compounds on hand."

"Are you available to perform the postmortem tomorrow?" Daniel asked as they walked toward the front door.

"Yes, I'm free tomorrow, and I will conduct the test on the whisky as well, but I'm collecting Micah from school the day after," Jason said.

"Of course. You must be looking forward to having him home."

"I am," Jason said. "The house feels awfully empty without him."

They had reached the foyer, where Constables Pullman and Ingleby were waiting for further instructions. Both men looked tired and hopeful that they would be allowed to go home soon. Constable Pullman gingerly held the cut crystal decanter in his large hands.

"The evidence, sir," he explained as he held up the decanter.

Jason took it and pulled out the stopper, sniffing the contents to make sure the correct receptacle had been provided. He seemed satisfied and replaced the stopper, holding on to the decanter to safekeeping.

"Constable Pullman, have you finished interviewing the staff?" Daniel asked.

"I have, sir. And Constable Ingleby and I took the liberty of removing the body and stowing it in the police wagon. I will deliver it to the mortuary on my way back."

"Thank you, Constable," Daniel said. "What were you able to learn from speaking to the staff?"

Constable Pullman squared his shoulders and puffed out his chest, visibly cognizant of the importance of the task he'd been assigned. "For a house this size, the number of staff is surprisingly small," he began. "There's just the butler, cook, housekeeper, and four maidservants: two upstairs, two downstairs. Except for Mr. Innes, the butler, no one had come in contact with Mr. Stillman this evening. He arrived in his own carriage and was escorted directly to the drawing room, where he was greeted by Mrs. Tarrant.

"None of the servants had entered either the drawing room or the parlor where the séance was to take place since this morning, when they cleaned the rooms and laid the fires, which were later lit by Mr. Innes. Mr. Stillman's coachman was sleeping inside the coach when I went out to speak to him. This was the first time he'd visited Ardith Hall, and he didn't know anything about the purpose of the visit or who else would be in attendance, only that his master would be returning to London around ten o'clock."

"Thank you, Constable. That's fine. Did any of the servants top up the decanters before the guests arrived?" Daniel asked.

"No, sir. It is Mr. Innes's responsibility to see to the spirits. According to his statement, the sherry decanter on the sideboard was still full, since the ladies rarely partake. Mr. Tarrant prefers brandy and keeps a decanter in his study. Mr. Innes took a clean decanter out of the cabinet and filled it with Scotch whisky from a new bottle he'd brought up from the butler's pantry. He keeps all spirits under lock and key, which he has on his person at all times, so none of the staff would have had access to it."

"Which means that if the whisky was the murder weapon, someone had added the arsenic just before Mr. Stillman arrived," Daniel said under his breath.

"Just so," Constable Pullman replied. "Same conclusion I had arrived at, Inspector."

Daniel was about to compliment Constable Pullman on his fine work when he was distracted by the opening of a door behind him. Daniel turned, following Jason's gaze.

Sarah stood in the doorway of the drawing room, her face pale, her eyes anxious as her gaze met Daniel's. She was the first one to look away, lowering her head like a frightened child. The hours of waiting had taken their toll, and she looked worn out with the strain, her curls limp and dark half-moons shadowing the tender skin beneath her eyes.

"I'll take Mrs. Haze home," Daniel said, glad that Sarah had taken the dogcart so they wouldn't have to rely on one of the constables to drive them.

"If someone will give me a lift," Jason said, looking from Constable Pullman to Constable Ingleby, who both had a conveyance at their disposal, having arrived separately.

"I'll be happy to take you home, sir," Constable Ingleby said.

Constable Pullman's relief was evident since he still had to return to the station to deliver Roger Stillman's corpse before going home for the night.

"Till tomorrow, then," Daniel said, wishing he could avoid the confrontation with Sarah but knowing it was inevitable.

"Till tomorrow," Jason replied as he followed Constable Ingleby out the door, the decanter held firmly in his hand. Daniel thought he'd detected a note of sympathy in his voice.

Chapter 6

Daniel was relieved when Sarah asked him to refrain from discussing her involvement in tonight's events until they returned home. He needed time to calm down and organize his thoughts, and she needed to process the unexpected way the evening had ended. As they set off, soft snow was falling from an overcast sky, and a chill wind had picked up, making them both shiver as the dogcart exited Ardith park and entered an open stretch of land beyond the ancient trees that was unprotected from the elements. Daniel's feet were numb, but his face was burning, partly from the bitter sting of the wind and partly with anger.

What had Sarah been thinking? he kept asking himself as he stared straight ahead at the snow-covered lane. Why had she felt the need to summon Felix's ghost? Daniel had genuinely believed that Sarah had accepted Felix's death at last. She had seemed happy and fulfilled this past year. So why this, and why now? Did she still feel guilty about what had happened? Did she feel the need to ask for forgiveness?

Letting out a deep sigh that came out as a vaporous cloud, Daniel felt the anger drain out of him, replaced by deep sadness. Perhaps he did understand. What he wouldn't give to speak to Felix one last time, to say a proper goodbye, to tell his son that he'd loved him more than life itself and that his love hadn't diminished after Felix's death. Perhaps Sarah had needed that too but had been afraid Daniel wouldn't understand and would ridicule her need for closure. He'd have to tread carefully once he got home, speak to Sarah kindly, and not demand answers but simply hope that she would wish to talk of what had happened and explain herself willingly.

Halfway home, the snow stopped and the sky cleared, a nearly full moon floating in the night sky and bathing the landscape in a silver glow. The scene was achingly beautiful and might have been romantic had Sarah not been huddled next to him, her face buried in the folds of her woolen scarf, her gloved hands clasped in her lap. She refused to meet his gaze when they finally pulled up before the house, and ran inside while Daniel surrendered the cart and horse to a sleepy Tom.

Tilda threw Daniel a baleful look as she silently took his things. Normally, she went up to her attic bedroom by eight o'clock, leaving the master and mistress to fend for themselves should they need anything, but tonight, she'd been forced to wait up. Daniel ignored her pique and hurried toward the parlor, hoping Sarah was finally ready to talk to him.

She hadn't bothered to turn on the lamps. The room was illuminated by the glow of the fire, Sarah's form a dark silhouette. She stood with her back to him, her hands held out to the flames, her spine rigid. Her eyes shone with unshed tears when she turned at the sound of his footsteps.

"I'm sorry, Danny," she whispered as soon as he shut the door behind him "I…" Her voice trailed off. She met his gaze shyly, imploring him to understand.

"You wanted to hear his voice one more time," Daniel said softly. "And maybe to know that he forgives you."

Sarah nodded miserably. Silent tears slid down her cheeks, her eyes filled with the kind of sadness Daniel hadn't seen in a long time, not since they'd reconciled after he was nearly beaten to death after leaving Redmond Hall one evening last year.

Daniel pulled Sarah into his arms, and she rested her forehead on his shoulder, her body trembling as she cried. "I just can't let go, Danny," Sarah moaned into his chest. "I just can't let him go. I know I can't bring him back, but I wanted to make things right."

"Sarah, it wasn't your fault. It was a tragic accident," Daniel whispered into her hair.

"I know, but I can't help going over the ifs again and again. What if we'd left the park a few minutes later? What if I'd managed to hold on to his hand? What if the driver of the carriage had stopped in time? What if it had rained that day and we hadn't gone out at all?" she cried.

"Sarah, there are so many different variables to every situation, but things happen as they do, and there's nothing you can do to change the outcome. Felix is gone. You must accept that and allow yourself to be happy. He would want that for you. He loved you," Daniel said. "If he could tell you so himself, he would let you know that he forgives you." Daniel felt the weight of his words between them. "Was that what you were after? To hear that he forgives you?" he asked gently.

"Yes," Sarah whispered. She wrapped her arms around his waist and pressed closer, holding on to him as if he were a life preserver that could keep her from drowning.

They remained like that for a long time, Sarah crying softly and Daniel just holding her and whispering words of comfort and love. How could he have thought of berating her? What a fool he was, utterly oblivious to what she was going through, as usual.

"Sarah, we have Charlotte now," Daniel said at last. "Will she ever be enough, do you think?"

Sarah looked up at him. Her lashes were wet with tears and her face looked puffy, but to Daniel, she was the most beautiful woman on Earth, and all he wanted to do was protect her from pain.

"She's enough, Danny. She's perfect, but a mother can't replace one child with another. I will never stop loving Felix or missing him. I suppose I wanted to know that he was happy, wherever he is."

Daniel sighed. He didn't think Felix was anywhere. He might have believed in the concept of heaven and hell when he was a child, but having been first a Peeler and then an inspector, and having seen the uglier side of life, he had long since abandoned the idea of life everlasting or divine justice. People were born, they lived, and they died. He didn't believe for a moment that their spirits lived on or that they could be summoned at will to comfort their loved ones.

"Would you have believed Mrs. Lysander had she told you he was?" Daniel asked, testing the extent of Sarah's commitment to her cause.

"Yes, because I wanted to," Sarah replied. "I know she's probably a fake, but some small part of me hoped she wasn't and she'd act as a conduit between us. I just wanted to believe, Danny. Can you understand that?"

"Yes, I can," Daniel replied as he led Sarah toward the settee and pulled her down beside him. "Can I get you a drink?"

Sarah nodded and sniffled. "Yes, please."

Daniel walked over to the sideboard and poured Sarah a glass of sherry and a tot of brandy for himself, which he tossed back before refilling his glass. He returned with their drinks and sat back down, waiting for Sarah to take a sip of sherry before questioning her.

"Sarah, tell me what happened tonight. There'll be a reckoning once CI Coleridge finds out my own wife was present at the scene of a crime. I need to assure him that I can be objective despite your involvement."

Sarah looked at him, her dark eyes watching him intently. "Are you sure a crime has been committed? Could Mr. Stillman's death not be a result of an accident, or an illness?"

"Jason believes Mr. Stillman was poisoned with arsenic. Tonight."

"But how can he know that for certain?" Sarah asked.

"There are the symptoms Mr. Stillman experienced just before his death and the manner of the death itself. I won't know the particulars until Jason completes the postmortem, but I trust his judgement. Tell me what happened," Daniel urged again.

Sarah took another sip of sherry. "I don't know what happened. I arrived at Ardith Hall around seven. Mr. Forbes was already there, talking to Amelia Tarrant in the drawing room. Amelia introduced us and offered me a glass of sherry. I didn't really want it, but accepted because I was terribly nervous," Sarah said, looking at her sherry with distaste. She set the glass down. "Mr. Forbes asked for rum, but there was none, so he accepted a glass of sherry instead."

"What happened then?" Daniel asked softly.

"We made small talk until Mr. Stillman arrived a few minutes later."

"Did he look ill? Was there anything odd about his behavior?"

Sarah considered the questions. "He did not look ill. In fact, he practically glowed with good health. His cheeks were pink from the cold, and his eyes were clear and bright. His hand was cool when he took my hand in greeting." Sarah's brows furrowed as she continued. "He did seem taken aback by Mr. Forbes' presence."

"Did they seem to know each other?" Daniel asked.

"I couldn't say. Perhaps he hadn't expected someone of Mr. Forbes'… eh… background to have been invited," Sarah explained diplomatically.

"Did the two men speak to each other?" Daniel asked.

"Nothing beyond a polite greeting. Amelia then offered Mr. Stillman a drink, and he asked for whisky. She poured him a glass, and he downed it in one."

"And then?"

"Lord Sumner arrived. He refused the offer of a drink, but Mr. Stillman accepted a refill. A few minutes later, we were invited to move into the parlor, where Mrs. Lysander awaited us."

"Did you notice any tension between Mr. Stillman, Mr. Forbes, and Lord Sumner once you were in place?" Daniel asked.

"I was so nervous, I barely registered anyone else's mood. All I could think of was Felix," Sarah said.

"Were you told where to sit?" Daniel asked.

"Not specifically, no. Mrs. Lysander only said that we shouldn't sit next to someone of our own sex. Once we were seated, Mrs. Tarrant turned out the gas lamps and took her seat at the table. She sat between Lord Sumner and Mr. Forbes. We were asked to join hands."

"Can you describe the atmosphere in the room?"

"Tense. Mr. Stillman squeezed my fingers so tight, I nearly asked him to loosen his grip but was afraid to interrupt."

"Go on," Daniel prompted.

"Just as Mrs. Lysander began to speak, Mr. Stillman coughed. Then he coughed again and again, the coughing escalating into a fit. He pulled his hand out of mine and grabbed for his collar. I suppose he couldn't breathe because he turned very red, and his eyes bulged. And then the blood spurted forth, and his bowels let loose," Sarah said, shivering despite the warmth of the room. "It was all over rather quickly. Amelia tried to help him, but it was too late. He was already dead."

"And Mrs. Lysander, what did she do during this time?"

"She just sat there, watching. I think she realized there wasn't anything anyone could do."

"And then what?" Daniel asked.

"Amelia asked everyone to move back into the drawing room and sent for the police and Dr. Parsons. Dr. Parsons never came, so Jason was the first on the scene. And then you arrived," Sarah said softly, her expression grim in the firelight.

"I think you should go to bed now," Daniel said gently. "It's been a trying evening."

"Aren't you coming?" Sarah asked as she pushed to her feet and held out her hand to him.

"I need a few moments to go over what I've learned this evening," Daniel lied. "I'll be up shortly."

Once Sarah left, Daniel buried his face in his hands, allowing the feelings that had been building within him all evening to finally find their release. He hadn't cried when Felix died; he hadn't been able to. But now the tears flowed, years of grief and loss spilling forth as he finally let go and allowed himself to feel what Sarah must have been feelings all along. He wept for the unfairness of it all, for the loss they still grieved every day, and for the boy and man Felix might have grown into had he been allowed to live.

Once the torrent of emotion passed, he felt lighter, and stronger. The fire had burned low, so Daniel positioned the fire screen before the hearth and made his way upstairs, glad to see that Sarah was already asleep. Daniel undressed and climbed into bed, but sleep wouldn't come, not for a long time.

Chapter 7

Once Jason finally arrived at home, he divested himself of his coat, hat, and gloves, handing them over to Dodson, and walked directly toward what had been his grandfather's study, where he locked the decanter in a tallboy that had a side compartment high enough to accommodate the crystal container. He never used the study and didn't think anyone else did but needed to make sure that no one helped themselves to the contents, especially his valet Henley, who'd drink anything alcoholic at any time of day or night. With the decanter safely stowed, he retreated to the drawing room, poured himself a large drink, and settled before the fire.

"Do you require anything, sir?" Dodson asked as he stepped into the room, his face eager. He probably hoped Jason would tell him about the case, but Jason was in no mood to talk. He was hungry, though, and would have liked one of Mrs. Dodson's ham sandwiches but had no wish to disturb her at this late hour. If his hunger got the best of him, he'd go down to the kitchen and help himself.

"I'm fine, Dodson. Go on to bed. I'll see to the fire when I'm ready to go up."

"Very well, sir. I'll just lock up, then."

"Dodson, how long ago did Lady Redmond retire?" Jason asked.

"About an hour or so, my lord."

"Thank you," Jason said, and glanced at the clock. It was nearly midnight, and he hoped Katie was fast asleep. If she wasn't and he went up, she'd interrogate him about the case and make him recount every gruesome detail. Normally, he'd be happy to talk things over with her, but she was in her seventh month, and he'd be damned if he planted images of violent death in her mind, especially this late at night, when she'd be sure to dream of them. No, he'd wait an hour to make sure she was asleep.

Jason stretched out his legs, enjoying the warmth of the fire on his cold feet, and took a sip of brandy. What had happened tonight had been a first, and he couldn't help wondering what tomorrow would bring. The death itself was routine enough. Countless people died from arsenic poisoning every day. It was a national crisis, but what made this case different was that Sarah Haze had been present at the séance. If the whisky proved to be pure, then her involvement would be dismissed as a mere coincidence, but if he found traces of arsenic, Sarah would immediately become a suspect in the death of Roger Stillman. Jason didn't think for a moment that Sarah had anything to do with it, but CI Coleridge might not see it the same way. He was a highly experienced copper who would instantly recognize the conflict of interest should Daniel remain on the case.

Jason had seen the shock and hurt in Daniel's eyes when he'd realized his wife had lied to him, and Jason had felt sorry for the man. Everyone lied from time to time, no matter how honorable a person, but what had happened tonight was sure to test Daniel and Sarah's marriage. Jason hoped Daniel would be kind to her. She had suffered a tragic loss and clearly hadn't been able to let go, regardless of what Daniel believed. To attend a séance would not have been an easy decision for her, more so because if Daniel got wind of her plans, he wouldn't understand and would demand an explanation and quite possibly an apology for being less than truthful with him.

Daniel attended church regularly, but Jason didn't think of him as a particularly spiritual person. Daniel felt more comfortable with statistics and facts, organizing them into well-defined areas of black and white and never allowing shades of gray to creep in. As a policeman, Jason supposed that made it easier for him to analyze people's actions and motives, but as a husband, it probably made him difficult to live with.

Jason tossed back the rest of his brandy and set the glass on the low table at his elbow. He glanced at the carriage clock on the mantelpiece. It was only twelve thirty, but he was tired, and tomorrow would be a long day. He pushed to his feet and took himself off to bed.

Chapter 8

Thursday, December 19

Jason woke early. He washed and dressed quietly and made his way downstairs.

"Good morning, Fanny," he said to the maidservant, who was setting the table for breakfast in the morning room. Katherine preferred to take breakfast there instead of the dining room, which could accommodate a dozen diners and fit as many chafing dishes on its massive sideboard. The morning room faced east and was sunny and bright on fine days.

"What would you like for breakfast, your lordship?" Fanny asked. Mrs. Dodson no longer prepared food in advance, making it as needed instead.

"Just coffee today, Fanny. Have a postmortem to perform."

"Of course, sir," Fanny said, nodding in understanding.

Jason unfolded the newspaper she'd prepared for him and settled in to wait. He rarely ate breakfast before a postmortem, finding it easier to work on an empty stomach. Fanny returned with a pot of coffee, a jug of cream, and a bowl of sugar cubes and set the tray on the table before pouring Jason a cup. He thanked her and returned to the article he was reading.

"If I didn't know better, I'd think you were trying to sneak out," Katherine said as she walked into the room.

Jason jumped to attention and pulled out a chair for her before giving her a kiss on the cheek. "I didn't want to disturb you," he said as he resumed his seat. He didn't offer her any coffee, since she preferred tea in the mornings.

"Are you going to tell me about last night?" Katherine asked.

"No," Jason replied, hoping he sounded playful rather than cantankerous.

"Oh, come on," Katherine said, smiling at him winsomely. "Spare me the gory details, but do tell me what happened."

"Mrs. Tarrant of Ardith Hall—you remember her—hosted a séance. One of the guests died a few minutes after the séance began."

"And?" Katherine asked.

"And I think he was poisoned," Jason said, wishing she wouldn't ask him any more questions.

"Was it intentional or accidental?"

"I believe it was intentional."

Katherine fixed Jason with an inquisitive look, one eyebrow raised like an exclamation point. "What are you not telling me, Jason?"

"Sarah Haze was there."

"What?" Katherine exclaimed. "Are you serious?"

"Yes."

"Did Daniel know she'd be there?" Katherine asked.

"No, he didn't. Look, Katie, I don't know how late I'll be back today," Jason said, desperate to change the subject.

Katherine looked like she would have liked to ask more questions but took the hint and didn't persist. She knew he'd tell her everything sooner or later anyway. "That's all right. I have plans of my own today."

"Oh?"

"I'm going call on the Chadwicks, then stop by the vicarage for tea."

"Didn't you call on the Chadwicks only last week?" Jason asked.

"I promised Arabella I'd come," Katherine said. "Now that they're out of mourning for Imogen, she's longing for company. With Harry gone and her mother in the throes of planning Lucinda's wedding to Sir Lawrence, Arabella has no one to talk to. She's lonely."

Jason nodded. "Give her my regards," he said. Being one of the few people who knew what had transpired after Arabella's sister-in-law was murdered, he felt a deep sympathy for her but had no desire to pay a call on the Chadwicks himself. He saw them in church; that was enough. But Katherine and Arabella were good friends, and Katherine was too kind-hearted not to go where she was needed.

"I hope you don't mind, but I invited Father for Christmas dinner," Katherine said, smiling at him sheepishly.

Jason did mind, but he could hardly refuse to invite his father-in-law, throbbing boil on the backside of humanity though he was. "Of course I don't mind," Jason said, forcing a smile to his face. "It will be my pleasure to spend our first Christmas as a married couple with the reverend."

"Oh, Jason," Katherine said, fixing him with a reproachful stare before bursting into a merry giggle. "I know he can be difficult, but he's my father."

"And thank the Lord you're nothing like him," Jason replied. "Now, I really must be going."

"I will expect a full report when you get back," Katherine said haughtily. "And no evasive maneuvers this time."

"*Oui, mon generale,*" Jason replied, and saluted her playfully. He kissed the top of her head and headed to the study to retrieve the decanter of whisky he'd so cleverly hidden.

Once in Brentwood, Jason asked Joe to stop by Linnet's chemist shop and went inside. Mr. Linnet greeted him like an old friend. "Ah, Lord Redmond. It is good to see you. Do you require medical supplies to replenish your stock?"

"Not today, Mr. Linnet. I am actually in need of sulfuric acid and zinc, as well as several beakers, a very narrow copper tube, and a stopper, I think," Jason replied, considering what he'd need for his experiment.

"Are you planning on performing the Marsh test?" Mr. Linnet asked, his eyes twinkling with amusement.

"Yes, I am," Jason said, glad the chemist was familiar with the procedure. It would make it easier to explain what he'd need.

Mr. Linnet nodded. "If you like, I can help you. I'm quite familiar with the process and have all the necessary components. We can do it right now if you have the substance you wish to test with you."

"Thank you, Mr. Linnet. I do. I would very much appreciate your help. I've never had an occasion to perform the test, but I have seen it done several times at the hospital in New York where I worked."

"Just give me a moment to set up," the chemist said, rubbing his hands together. "Is this for a police case you're working on?"

"It is. The results will influence the course of the investigation," Jason explained.

"Let's get on with it, then."

Jason went out to the brougham and retrieved the decanter of whisky, then returned to the shop. Mr. Linnet turned the sign in the window to CLOSED and invited Jason to join him in the back room, where he opened the window to vent any toxic gasses that might be produced by the experiment. Jason was glad the man knew what he was doing, since it would have taken him a while to set up the test on his own and double-check the results.

Jason removed his coat and hat while Mr. Linnet lit a candle stub. He then added about an ounce of whisky and some sulfuric acid before dropping a piece of zinc into the beaker. Mr. Linnet swirled the contents, then stoppered the beaker with a cork and inserted a bent copper tube through a circular opening in the cork before setting the beaker on an elevated stand that fit over the short candle. It took several minutes for the solution inside the beaker to heat, but once the chemical reaction began, the liquid began to bubble, producing a cloudy gas that filled the stoppered beaker and began to escape through the copper tube. The chemist handed Jason an enamel circle the size of his palm.

"Here, hold that, your lordship," Mr. Linnet instructed.

He removed the candle from beneath the beaker and held the flame to the end of the tube, igniting the gas that was hissing as it passed through the narrow opening. After a few seconds, Mr. Linnet blew out the candle and removed the tube, pressing the heated end against the enamel in Jason's hand. Several black spots appeared on the clear, white surface, the residue a silver and metallic deposit that was only produced when there was arsenic present in the solution.

"That's the murder weapon, then," Jason said as he studied the spots intently to make sure they weren't merely soot.

Mr. Linnet shook his head as he extinguished the flame. "The whisky is most definitely laced with arsenic, but the victim would have had to consume the entire amount in order for it to kill him. How much did he actually drink?"

"He had two drinks the night he died," Jason replied.

"So, unless he'd been ingesting arsenic on a regular basis, this is not your murder weapon," Mr. Linnet said.

Jason set down the enamel circle and stoppered the decanter. He'd have to dispose of the whisky and return the expensive item to Mrs. Tarrant.

"I'm about to perform the postmortem," he said as he put his hat and coat back on. "I'll have a clearer picture once I've finished."

Mr. Linnet nodded wisely. "No doubt your man was killed with arsenic, but most likely it was done over a period of time. That's how it's usually done. I think at the rate people are poisoning each other with arsenic, most police stations will soon have an apparatus set up for checking the contents of the victims' stomachs."

"Sadly, I think you might be right. I really think the poison should not be so readily available."

"Where there's a will, there's a way," Mr. Linnet said. "If not arsenic, they'll find something else. The law rarely stands in the way of murder."

That was all too true, but Jason had no time to engage in a lengthy discussion. "Mr. Linnet, I thank you for your help."

"Do let me know how it turns out," the chemist said as he followed Jason back into the front of the shop. He turned the sign over, unlocked the door, and wished Jason a good day.

Upon arriving at the Brentwood police station, Jason dismissed Joe and went around the side of the building directly to the privy located out back. He poured the tainted whisky into the smelly hole and entered the station by the back door. He was greeted cheerfully by Sergeant Flint, whose sole purpose seemed to be to man the front desk. He was rarely called upon to do actual police work, an arrangement he didn't seem to mind.

"Your man is ready and waiting," Flint said. "Pullman brought him in last night. I nearly bust a gut laughing as he dragged him inside. Looked like they were dancing."

"You might have helped him," Jason said.

"Oh, I did, guv," Sergeant Flint said, feigning offense. "I held the door," he said, and laughed uproariously.

Jason chose not to engage and headed toward the stairs that would take him to the basement mortuary. He was surprised to encounter Ned Hollingworth, the on-call photographer for the Brentwood Police. Ned was a weasel of a man who sold photos of the dead to the newspapers in order to supplement his income, but as there weren't many photographers in Brentwood, he still managed to keep his position. Ned was just leaving the mortuary, his camera slung around his neck, the tripod gripped in his hand.

"Couldn't come out last night," Ned explained. "Doesn't really matter though, does it? Not like he had a knife sticking out of him or a bullet wound between the eyes. This one looks like he's sleeping." He sounded bored and walked away without expecting an answer.

Jason sighed with exasperation and pushed open the door to the mortuary, ready to face Roger Stillman at last.

Chapter 9

The mortuary was silent and cold, the white-tiled walls reflecting the weak winter light that shone through the narrow window set high in the wall. Jason finished stitching, tied off the thread, and breathed a sigh of relief, glad to be finished with the postmortem. A char woman would clean the mortuary and prepare it for the next victim after Roger Stillman's body was collected by an undertaker.

Jason pulled off the linen cap he used to keep the hair out of his face and washed his hands thoroughly before removing the leather apron he wore to protect his clothes and pulling on his coat. He longed to get home and lounge by the fire with Katie but didn't think the fire would warm him through. He was cold from the inside. Jason had seen his share of corpses over the past decade. Some deaths had been the result of wounds sustained in battle, others brought on by malicious intent, but he'd never seen anything like this and hoped never to again.

Jason stepped out of the room, his greatcoat slung over his arm, his hat in his hand, to find Daniel lurking in the corridor. Daniel rarely ventured inside the mortuary, his stomach not strong enough to take the sight of a butchered body, but he peeked around Jason's shoulder, curious to see the body, nonetheless. Daniel looked tired and irritable, his demeanor likely the result of the conversation he'd had with Sarah last night.

"Well? What's the cause of death?" Daniel demanded impatiently.

Jason shook his head, words failing him.

"Jason?" Daniel prompted.

"I don't know, Daniel. I've never seen anything like it."

"How do you mean? What did Stillman die of?" Daniel persisted.

"The cause of death is poisoning by arsenic, but the dose wasn't lethal."

"I don't understand. You just said he was poisoned."

"He was, but had he been in good health, the dose that was administered last night would have made him ill but would not have killed him."

"You're not making any sense," Daniel complained, eyeing Jason anxiously.

"Let's go speak to CI Coleridge. I don't want to have to explain this twice."

The two men ascended to the ground floor and headed toward their superior's office, followed by Sergeant Flint's curious stare. He craned his neck in the hope of overhearing the conversation, but Daniel made sure to shut the door behind them.

CI Coleridge sat behind his desk, a fat cigar dangling from his lips. Noxious plumes of smoke curled toward the ceiling, shrouding the man's head in a gauzy cloud.

"Well?" he asked as he pointed toward the guest chairs placed before his desk. "Out with it," he barked, glaring at Daniel.

He was noticeably angry, and with good reason. By now, he would have heard that Sarah Haze had been present at last night's séance, no doubt informed of the circumstances of Roger Stillman's death by Constable Pullman first thing this morning. The constable's desire to make inspector was beginning to cloud his judgment. Or maybe just the opposite. By undermining Daniel, he was hoping to make himself appear more valuable, ready to take on the responsibility of an investigation.

"What did the autopsy show?" Coleridge asked, fixing Jason with a belligerent stare.

"Roger Stillman ingested a quantity of arsenic-laced whisky last night," Jason began. "I tested the whisky using the

Marsh test, which is remarkably accurate, and was able to determine that arsenic was indeed the murder weapon, or the attempted murder weapon, in this case," Jason corrected himself. CI Coleridge and Daniel looked mystified, so Jason went on. "Also, he had little in his stomach, so he hadn't eaten or drunk anything in the hours before arriving at Ardith Hall."

"Everyone who was present at the séance is a suspect, then," CI Coleridge boomed, evidently satisfied to have narrowed the field.

"That's not all," Jason interrupted. "When I opened him up, I was shocked to discover that his esophagus and the lining of his stomach were heavily lacerated."

"What's that mean?" CI Coleridge asked, his gaze narrowing. "What's an esof—whatever you said?"

"The gullet," Jason explained. "Both his gullet and stomach were lacerated from the inside."

"I don't follow," CI Coleridge said.

"The abrasions were caused by ingesting ground glass," Jason said. "There were numerous particles still clinging to the lining and some mixed into the half-digested food I found in his stomach. I've no doubt that if I were to examine the inside of the intestines, I would find similar damage."

Daniel and CI Coleridge stared at Jason, uncomprehending.

"Ingesting glass?" CI Coleridge demanded. "Intentionally?"

"I highly doubt it was intentional," Jason said. "I think someone tried to kill Roger Stillman slowly. Had he been a physically weaker man, he might have already succumbed. If not for the arsenic, he might have lived for a few more weeks, possibly even months."

"So, it was the arsenic that killed him?" CI Coleridge asked, his brows knitting in concentration as he tried to narrow down the cause of death.

"The arsenic was the final straw. Roger Stillman began to cough, quite possibly because the poison had irritated his throat and already-compromised esophagus. The spasms brought on severe internal bleeding, which led to his death."

"Good Lord!" CI Coleridge exclaimed. "What are you saying, man?"

"I'm saying that someone tried to kill Roger Stillman last night, but their attempt was preempted by someone else," Jason explained.

"So, someone fed Roger Stillman ground glass, hoping that he would go quietly. Then, the same person or someone entirely different poisoned his whisky, which brought on the internal bleeding that would have happened sooner or later anyhow?" CI Coleridge asked.

"Correct."

CI Coleridge turned his less-than-friendly gaze on Daniel. "And your wife was there for the final act, was she?"

"Yes, sir," Daniel muttered.

"And how do you explain that, Inspector Haze?"

"Mrs. Tarrant knows my wife from our time in London, sir. She invited Sarah to attend the séance, thinking she might wish to—" Daniel's voice trailed off and he bowed his head, staring at his hands splayed on his thighs.

CI Coleridge's expression softened. "Ah, yes. Your boy," he said quietly. "Well, regardless of the reason she was there, I don't think you should be the one to investigate this case, Haze."

"My wife had nothing to do with what happened, sir," Daniel exclaimed. "She simply happened to be at the wrong place at the wrong time. I can retain professional objectivity, if that's your concern. Please, don't take me off the case, sir." A pleading note had crept into Daniel's voice, giving CI Coleridge momentary pause.

"DI Peterson is rather busy at the moment. He's got his hands full with the Carmichaels and their opium shipments, and Constable Pullman, eager as he may be, isn't ready to take on a case of this complexity."

Daniel breathed a sigh of relief. As there were no other detectives at the Brentwood police station, he'd be the only one left to investigate the case if DI Peterson wasn't available. But CI Coleridge hadn't quite finished.

"Of course, I could always pass this case over to Scotland Yard," he mused. "Roger Stillman lived in London, and the initial attempt on his life would have happened there. Except for your wife, Inspector Haze, all the suspects come from London," he added acidly.

"Roger Stillman died in Essex, sir," Daniel argued. "This is a matter for the Brentwood police."

CI Coleridge looked annoyed. "Just say it straight out, Haze. You are terrified your wife will be branded a suspect, and that's why you're so eager to take the case. Well, I'll tell you what. Given the circumstances and my personal regard for you, I would like Lord Redmond to take the lead on this, as a special advisor to the police. I will permit you to assist him, but he's in charge."

Jason stared at CI Coleridge, taken aback by his decree. He was just a surgeon who lent his expertise to the police, mostly because he enjoyed the process of solving a crime, but he wasn't an inspector. He didn't even have a warrant card. Jason sucked in a deep breath. It wasn't the lack of a warrant card that kept him from taking this case, and he knew it. He didn't want the responsibility, not when Sarah was involved. How could he treat her as one of the suspects when Daniel would undermine him at every turn? And he would. Daniel would do everything in his power to protect Sarah from any undue scrutiny, just as Jason would protect Katie. No, he couldn't possibly agree.

"Sir, I—" Jason began.

"If you refuse, then I will have no choice but to call in Scotland Yard," Coleridge stated, his voice flat.

Jason could almost feel Daniel's pleading gaze boring into the side of his head. He was probably terrified, and with good reason. One of the people in Mrs. Tarrant's drawing room had administered a dose of arsenic to an unsuspecting Roger Stillman, which had ultimately led to his death. A detective from Scotland Yard would not go easy on Sarah. There would be no reason for him to discount her just because she was married to Inspector Haze. If anything, that would probably prompt him to look at her involvement even more closely. Sarah Haze would remain under suspicion until she was either cleared or charged.

Jason nodded. As Daniel's friend, he couldn't allow his family to suffer, nor could he knowingly cut Daniel out of the investigation, leaving him to helplessly await the outcome and pray that the Scotland Yard man was a competent detective and wouldn't bungle the case. "All right," Jason acquiesced. "I'll do it."

"Good man," CI Coleridge said. "Now, go and find Stillman's killer. Oh, and have Sergeant Flint make you a temporary warrant card," he added, his mind seemingly already on something else.

Chapter 10

"Daniel, I'm sorry," Jason said once they boarded the London-bound train and settled into an empty compartment. It was the first chance they'd had to speak privately since leaving CI Coleridge's office half an hour before. "I didn't mean—"

Daniel held up his hand. "I'm grateful to you for taking the case, Jason. If Coleridge brings in someone from Scotland Yard, I will not be allowed anywhere near the investigation. I won't be able to protect Sarah," he added miserably.

"Do you believe Sarah needs protecting?" Jason asked carefully, wondering what exactly Sarah had told Daniel last night in the privacy of their home. Jason would have to question her, but now wasn't the time to bring that up.

"Someone gave Roger Stillman a lethal dose of arsenic last night," Daniel replied. "Sarah was there—first in the drawing room, then seated at the table where he died. Any detective worth his salt will count her among the suspects until she can be definitively ruled out."

"Did Sarah know Roger Stillman?" Jason asked, trying to make the inquiry sound like a casual question.

"No, of course not. She didn't know anyone except Amelia Tarrant," Daniel snapped. "And before you ask, no, she didn't see or hear anything."

"Okay," Jason said, hoping to pacify Daniel. He could understand Daniel's defensiveness but hoped he would calm down, and soon. It would be difficult to work with him when he was so overwrought.

"What's your plan?" Daniel asked, looking contrite.

Jason considered the question. He hadn't had time to formulate a strategy, not that investigations ever went according to plan anyway. In a successful investigation, one clue led to another, and more often than not, the suspects unwittingly revealed hitherto unseen connections that made it easier to fit the pieces of the puzzle together.

"We'll start with the victim's mother, then question the staff," Jason said.

Daniel nodded in approval. "Yes, that's a sound strategy. Do you mind if I pose questions of my own?"

"Of course not. Daniel, we're a team. We have been since the very start. Just because CI Coleridge has decided to put me in charge doesn't mean I'm going to lord it over you," Jason said, smiling at his own joke. "No pun intended," he added when Daniel raised an eyebrow at his unfortunate turn of phrase.

"Thank you, Jason," Daniel said. "I appreciate that."

It was nearly two o'clock by the time they arrived in London. Daniel hailed a passing hansom as soon as they stepped out into the street and gave the cabbie Roger Stillman's address. The hansom lurched forward and came to a stop not two minutes later when a dray wagon blocked its path, the unwieldy contraption taking up most of the street as the driver pulled up before a nearby tavern to unload the casks from the back. Jason sat back, resigning himself to the delay. It was to be expected. This was London, after all.

The cab finally moved about ten minutes later, but it was slow going. There was the usual traffic, consisting of delivery wagons, fine carriages, horse-drawn omnibuses, and pedestrians. Ragged children darted around, skinny limbs clearly visible beneath their inadequate and often tatty clothing. They were lucky if they had shoes, much less a coat to keep out the winter chill. A crossing sweep ran out into the street and cleaned up a steaming heap of manure before collecting a few pence from the coachman of the carriage whose path he'd cleared and returning to his post. A girl of about ten stood hunched under the weight of the tray slung around her neck, a mound of oranges a bright splash of color against her pale face and faded brown shawl.

There were aspects of London that Jason loved, but the ever-present poverty wasn't one of them. This part of the city reminded him of Five Points in New York, an area he'd often visited while still at medical school. He and his friends had offered free medical assistance to those in need, taking the opportunity to practice their newly learned skills. Jason hoped he'd helped some of those people, but in reality, his contribution had been about as weighty as a drop in the ocean, their lives following a roadmap that inevitably led to a harsh existence and an early death. In that respect, London wasn't so different from New York, where only the well-to-do could afford competent medical care, pricy cures, and the ability to leave the city during the hottest months to avoid annual outbreaks of illness.

Jason tore his gaze away from the orange seller and stared at the back of the burly driver, his mind turning to Roger Stillman. What he'd seen this morning had disturbed him deeply. Once he'd finished the autopsy and gone about the task of stitching the corpse back together, a task that didn't require great mental effort, he'd tried to comprehend the frame of mind of a person who'd feed another human being ground glass. The individual had to have known that the internal damage would not only prove fatal but be so extensive that the victim would not benefit from medical help even if he realized something was terribly wrong. This wasn't a crime born of passion or murderous anger.

This was a premeditated, well-thought-out plan that would take weeks, if not months, to achieve its goal, an act perpetrated by someone who burned with hatred and intended for their victim to die only after a period of prolonged suffering. Given the condition of Roger Stillman's esophagus and stomach lining, he must have begun to experience discomfort, but there was no way to gauge how much. The man might have mistaken the burning in his chest for heartburn and ignored the gripes in his belly caused by damage to his intestinal tract, thinking the pain was caused by something he'd eaten that didn't agree with him. Had he consulted his physician? Jason wondered as the carriage moved at a crawl toward its destination. Had he realized that his condition was worsening, or had he felt nothing at all and gone on with his life? A dead man walking.

Was that why the killer had resorted to arsenic? Had he or she grown desperate and decided the initial plan wasn't worth the wait, or had there been a second, unconnected attempt on Roger Stillman's life? Did whoever had laced the whisky wanted to be there to watch him die? If that were the case, then the murderer had been in the same room with the victim, and with Sarah Haze. Jason offered up a silent thanks to God for keeping Sarah safe. The poor woman had suffered enough when her son was run over by a carriage, his body broken beyond repair. It would have been a blessing had the child died instantly, but Felix held on for several days, the drawn-out end resulting in unbearable suffering for the child and his parents.

It had taken Daniel and Sarah years to rebuild their life and find their way back to each other after a prolonged period of grieving and self-blame. And now this case had the power to destabilize their newfound contentment. Jason stole a sidelong glance at Daniel, who looked worried and tense, his jaw clenched with frustration as the hansom slowed yet again.

I'll do everything in my power to solve this case and erase any suspicion that might be cast on Sarah, Jason thought. *It's the least I can do for Daniel and his family.*

Chapter 11

The hansom finally deposited them in front of a three-story red-brick house with a white portico and black railing to separate it from the street. It was attached on both sides and identical to the rest of the houses lining the street, the uninspired architecture of the buildings giving the impression of uniformed soldiers standing shoulder to shoulder. Daniel lifted the brass knocker and announced their presence, his gaze traveling to the tall windows of the front parlor that stared blankly onto the street. Perhaps no one was at home.

Daniel knocked again. A few moments later, a flustered maidservant opened the door. She looked from one man to the other, her eyebrows lifting in a silent question.

"Please inform Mrs. Stillman we're here to see her on an urgent matter," Daniel said. "Inspector Haze and Lord Redmond of the Essex Police." He held up his warrant card for the woman to see.

Her mouth opened in astonishment, but she quickly closed it and invited them into the foyer.

"We're clearly not expected," Jason said under his breath. "Perhaps Mrs. Stillman is unaware that her son is dead."

"How could she not be? Surely the coachman would have informed her," Daniel said, wondering if perhaps Jason was right.

"The mistress will see you in the drawing room," the servant said once she returned. She held out her hands for their things, but her curious gaze was fixed on Jason, whose unexplained presence often took people by surprise. Jason smiled down at her and she blushed, instantly looking away.

The drawing room was elegantly and expensively furnished, with a rather fine painting of a hunting scene hanging above the mantelpiece and a lovely arrangement of fresh flowers displayed on a small table between two windows. A thick carpet covered most of the floor and perfectly complemented the chairs and settees upholstered in sea-green damask. Matching curtains hung at the windows and were tied back with tasseled silver cords.

A woman of about sixty occupied the chair closest to the fire. She wore an exquisite gown in a lovely shade of slate blue accented with a cream-colored fichu and lace cuffs. Her fair hair was elegantly dressed, and her skin was surprisingly smooth for a woman of her years. She must have been a beauty in her day, Daniel decided as he accepted the offered seat.

"How can I help you, gentlemen?" Mrs. Stillman asked, raising her pince-nez to examine them more carefully.

Daniel turned to Jason, mutely inviting him to take the lead.

"Mrs. Stillman, I am very sorry to inform you that your son died suddenly while attending a gathering at Ardith Hall last night," Jason said, his gaze watchful.

Mrs. Stillman paled, her hand flying to her breast as the pince-nez dropped to her lap. "What? Are you certain it was Roger?"

"We are. We are deeply sorry for your loss," Jason said.

Mrs. Stillman looked from one man to the other, her eyes clouded with confusion. "But I don't understand. Roger was in perfect health. He was always so sturdy, so strong. Was he taken ill?"

"I'm afraid not, Mrs. Stillman. Your son was murdered," Jason said softly, probably wishing he could soften the blow.

"Murdered? By whom?" Mrs. Stillman cried. Her cheeks had become alarmingly red, and her breath came in shallow gasps, her chest heaving with emotion. Jason was on his feet immediately, reaching for her wrist.

"What are you doing?" she cried.

"I'm afraid your blood pressure is dangerously elevated, Mrs. Stillman. Daniel, get Mrs. Stillman a glass of sherry."

Daniel sprang to his feet and hurried over to a sideboard that held several decanters and glasses of various sizes. He poured some sherry and brought it over to Mrs. Stillman, who was breathing heavily and trembling.

"Take a sip, Mrs. Stillman," Jason urged her.

"I don't want any sherry," she rasped, but Jason wouldn't back down.

"You need to calm down in order for your blood pressure to return to normal. Please, drink the sherry. It will help."

Mrs. Stillman shot him a resentful glance but accepted the glass and took several dainty sips.

"Finish it," Jason instructed.

She did and handed the glass back to Daniel. A few moments later, her breathing eased and her cheeks, although still pink, lost that volcanic flush.

"What happened to my son?" she demanded, her gaze fixed on Jason. "You seem to have some medical knowledge. You tell me."

"Mrs. Stillman, someone poisoned your son with arsenic," Jason replied, leaving out the more harrowing details.

"Why?" she wailed, her grief getting the better of her again. "Who'd want to hurt my Roger?"

"That's what we're here to find out," Jason replied.

Mrs. Stillman slid lower in the chair, as if the act of sitting up straight had sapped her remaining energy. "I don't understand," she moaned. "Roger was a good boy. So kind to everyone."

"Mrs. Stillman, we need to ask you a few questions," Daniel said gently. "Do you think you can manage that?"

She gave an almost imperceptible nod. "Go on," she said at last. "Ask."

"Did you not realize your son hadn't returned home last night?" Jason asked.

Mrs. Stillman shook her head. "I assumed Roger had already left for the day. He liked to get to the office early."

"Did no one mention that they hadn't seen him last night or this morning?" Jason asked.

"No."

"And the coachman said nothing?" Daniel asked, astounded that the man would keep such news to himself.

Mrs. Stillman shook her head. "He's a useless oaf. I told Roger so on several occasions. I don't know why he didn't dismiss him and hire someone with a bit more sense."

"Did your son have any enemies?" Daniel asked, leaving his questions about the coachman for later. He'd speak to the man in person.

Mrs. Stillman looked startled by the question. "Not that I know of. I'm sure there were people who might not have liked him, but I can't imagine they'd try to kill him with arsenic." The woman suddenly sat up, her gaze growing more alert. She turned to Jason. "He attended a séance last night. He told me he was going. Is that where it happened? Why are you here questioning me when you should be interrogating the miscreants who were there? I told him not to go. It was silly at best, idiotic at worst. Who believes in such nonsense?" she exclaimed. "Only fools and charlatans. I've heard of this Mrs. Lysander. She's nothing more than a jumped-up trollop trying to make a living off gullible people who can't cope with the loss of their loved ones. It's an outrage. People like her should be arrested and tried for fraud."

"Mrs. Stillman, whom was your son trying to contact?" Jason asked, disregarding her tirade.

"I don't know," she retorted bitterly. "He wouldn't tell me when I asked. He said it was private."

"What did your son do?"

"Do?" Mrs. Stillman echoed.

"For money. Or did he make it the old-fashioned way and inherit it from his father?" Jason asked.

"No, he did not make it the old-fashioned way," Mrs. Stillman replied archly. "Roger was a respected businessman. He was an importer."

"What did he import?" Jason asked.

Mrs. Stillman made a vague gesture with her hand. "Spices, rum, silk."

"From where?" Daniel chimed in, suddenly feeling redundant.

"From the places where such things are made, I imagine. We never talked about the particulars of his work."

"Have you ever met any of his associates?" Jason inquired.

"No. Roger never brought any of them home. He preferred to invite them to his club."

"Are you familiar with the names Nathaniel Forbes or Julian Sumner?" Daniel asked, intentionally leaving out Sarah's name.

"I've heard of Lord Sumner, of course, but I don't know this Forbes person."

"Do you trust your cook, Mrs. Stillman?" Daniel asked.

"What's that got to do with it?" she exploded.

"We have reason to believe your son was being systematically fed ground glass," he replied, inwardly bracing for Mrs. Stillman's pain.

Her eyes rounded with shock, her mouth dropping open. "Ground glass?" she whispered. "Who would do such a thing? What sort of monster would do such a thing?" she cried, her face becoming dangerously flushed again.

"We don't yet know," Jason said. "But we mean to find out."

Mrs. Stillman's hand was on her bosom, her breathing labored as she tried in vain to calm herself. "I can't take this," she moaned. "I simply can't bear it."

"Mrs. Stillman, we need to question the staff," Daniel said.

She nodded, as if unable to speak.

"Perhaps you should lie down for a little while," Jason suggested. "May I help you to your bedroom?"

Mrs. Stillman looked like she was about to refuse, then acquiesced. "Yes, please," she whispered. "Send Martha to me when you're done questioning her."

"Of course," Jason promised as he helped the woman to her feet and led her from the room.

Chapter 12

Daniel and Jason decided to start with the cook, since she was solely responsible for all the meals in the house. They found her down in the kitchen, rolling out dough, her hands covered in flour. Mrs. Murray was a woman of about forty, rail thin, with dark hair and deep-set brown eyes. Her skin had the sallow tinge of someone who rarely set foot outside. She looked up in surprise, her hands stilling.

"And who might ye be?" she asked.

"Good afternoon, Mrs. Murray," Daniel said as he held up his warrant card. "I'm Inspector Haze, and this is Lord Redmond. We're here to talk to you about the death of Mr. Stillman."

The woman looked dumbstruck. "Wha'?" she asked, her eyes darting from Daniel to Jason and back again in obvious panic. "Mr. Stillman is dead?"

"Mr. Stillman was a victim of arsenic poisoning. He died last night at a house in Essex," Daniel explained, watching her closely for a reaction.

She blanched, her face going slack with shock.

"Why don't you sit down, Mrs. Murray?" Jason suggested solicitously.

"I'll remain standing, if it's all the same to ye," the cook replied, squaring her shoulders as if preparing for a verbal assault.

"All right. Can you tell us how long you've worked for the family?" Jason asked.

"Nigh on ten years now," Mrs. Murray replied.

"And was Mr. Stillman a kind employer?" Jason kept his tone even and friendly, and Mrs. Murray began to relax somewhat.

She shrugged. "I hardly ever saw 'im, truth be told. 'E never came down to the kitchen. 'E summoned us to the drawing room once a year on Boxing Day," she added sadly, clearly realizing that Christmas would be a melancholy affair this year.

"Mrs. Murray, does anyone else in the household have access to the food?" Daniel asked.

"Not during preparation. Martha brings the dishes upstairs and serves at table."

"Do you have a scullery maid?" Jason asked.

"Neh. It's a small 'ousehold; I make do on me own."

"Have you ever seen anyone in your kitchen who shouldn't be there?" Daniel asked.

"There's tradesmen as come to call," Mrs. Murray said. "Like in any 'ouse. But I know them one and all. Why?" she asked, her eyes narrowing in suspicion. "The master wasn't killed 'ere, so what difference do it make if anyone's touched 'is food?"

"Mrs. Murray, Mr. Stillman had particles of ground glass in his stomach," Jason said, his gaze never leaving the cook's face.

She looked blank. "What ye mean, then?" she asked, looking from Jason to Daniel in confusion.

"His insides were all cut up," Jason clarified.

"And ye think I done that?" she cried, finally comprehending the relevance of the questions she'd been asked. "Why would I want to 'urt Mr. Stillman? 'E's been good to me. 'E pays me a fair wage."

"I'm not suggesting you were the one to add the glass, Mrs. Murray," Jason said in his most soothing tone. "I'm only trying to establish if anyone had access to the food."

"Well, they 'aven't. In this 'ere kitchen, no one touches the food but me. And what makes ye think the glass came from 'ere?

74

Mr. Stillman dined out all the bleeding time," she exclaimed, bright spots of color blooming in her sallow cheeks. "I won't be blamed for something I ain't done. I take pride in me work."

"No one is blaming you," Daniel rushed to reassure her. "We're only trying to establish who, if anyone, might have had an opportunity to tamper with the food without your knowledge," he stressed.

Mrs. Murray relaxed slightly, but it was clear she was still frightened.

"Now, if we may continue. How often did Mr. Stillman dine at home?" Daniel asked.

"At least three times a week," Mrs. Murray replied.

"Did he normally have breakfast?" Jason asked.

"Not downstairs. Burns—that's the master's valet—took up his chocolate and a slice of buttered bread every morning."

"And who made that?" Daniel asked.

"I did," Mrs. Murray replied. "But I never added no glass or arsenic to it," she added.

Jason nodded in understanding. "And where did he eat the rest of the time?"

"'Ow should I know? Not like 'e shared 'is plans with the likes of me," Mrs. Murray sputtered.

"What happens to the leftovers from the dining room?" Jason asked.

"They get eaten, o' course. Down 'ere, by us."

"And how many of you are there?" Daniel asked, trying to get a clearer picture of the household.

"Well, there's me, Martha, the parlor maid, Judith, the maid of all work, Burns, and Jack, the groom. Just the five of us, and we all eat together once they've finished upstairs."

"Has anyone been unwell recently?" Jason asked.

"Jack had a chesty cough last week," Mrs. Murray said. "And Martha had a toothache last month."

"I mean, did anyone suffer from any stomach pains or spit up blood, for instance?" Jason clarified.

Mrs. Murray shook her head. "If they did, they didn't tell me."

"Thank you, Mrs. Murray," Jason said. "I think we'll interview the rest of the staff in the drawing room."

"Shall I send up some tea?" Mrs. Murray asked in a conciliatory tone, obviously relived to be finished with the interview.

"Thank you, but there's no need," Daniel hastened to reply. He'd be damned if he put anything in his mouth in this house.

They returned to the ground floor, where they found Martha anxiously waiting for them.

"Is it true, then?" she asked, looking to Daniel, who was closer to her social status. "Is the master dead?"

"He is. Please, come into the drawing room, Martha. We'd like to speak with you," Daniel said.

Martha looked like she was about to faint but meekly followed them into the room. She didn't sit down when invited to but stood with her head bowed and her hands clasped before her.

"Martha, how long have you worked for the Stillmans?" Daniel asked.

"'Bout three years now."

"Have they been kind to you?" Jason inquired.

"Yes."

"Have you seen or heard anything suspicious over the past few weeks? Anything that might have had to do with Mr. Stillman's death?" Daniel asked.

"Like wha'?" Martha asked, looking stupefied.

"Like an argument, or a threat. Surely you served refreshments when Mr. Stillman had guests. Was there anyone who seemed threatening to you? Or angry?" Daniel added, hoping Martha would produce at least one name.

"No. Mr. Stillman rarely 'ad company," Martha said.

"He never invited anyone to dine?" Jason asked.

"Mr. Standish comes to dine once a month."

"And who's Mr. Standish?" Daniel asked.

"The mistress's brother. Recently widowed, 'e is."

"Does Mrs. Stillman ever have visitors besides her brother?" Daniel asked. "What does she do with her time?"

"Mrs. Stillman receives morning calls on Mondays and Wednesdays and goes out to pay 'er own calls on Tuesdays and Thursdays. She plays bridge on Friday afternoons at Mrs. George's 'ouse, and takes her morning constitutional nearly every day, weather permitting, at eleven o'clock," Martha said, her brow furrowing with concentration. "There was a small dinner party in May when Mrs. Stillman turned sixty. Four couples 'ad been invited."

"Do you recall their names?" Daniel asked.

"Mr. Standish came with 'is wife. That were before she passed," Martha clarified. "And there were Mr. and Mrs. George, the Elliots, and the Goodmans. All friends of Mrs. Stillman and 'er late 'usband. Mr. Stillman never brought 'is friends 'ome, as I've already said."

"Martha, have water closets been installed in the house?"

"No, sir."

"Who takes out the chamber pots?" Jason asked.

"That would be Judith, sir," Martha replied, clearly grateful to be spared that most unpleasant task.

"Thank you, Martha. Can you please send in Mr. Burns?" Jason asked.

"'Course," Martha said, her relief at being dismissed evident.

"Oh, and Martha," Jason called out to her. "Please check on your mistress and let me know if she requires a doctor."

"Yes, sir."

Chapter 13

Alfie Burns was a lanky man in his twenties. His dark hair was carefully pomaded and his pale-blue gaze alert. He wore the customary attire of a gentleman's valet—black suit, white shirt, and black tie—but there was something debonair about him, an inborn elegance and self-awareness. He took a position before Jason and Daniel, shoulders back, feet slightly apart, as if standing his ground.

"Mr. Burns, how long have you worked for Mr. Stillman?" Daniel asked, pen poised over his notepad.

"Two years come February, Inspector." By now, word had gotten out, and Burns knew exactly who Daniel and Jason were and why they were there.

"Did Mr. Stillman ever confide in you?" Jason asked. He was rarely tempted to confide in his own valet, Henley, but he presumed some men did and spoke freely while being shaved or getting dressed. And with his elegant appearance and educated speech, Burns might seem more like a friend than an employee.

"Mr. Stillman wasn't the chatty sort," Burns replied. "But I knew him well enough to anticipate his moods."

"Did he seem worried or scared these past few weeks?" Daniel asked.

Alfie Burns thought about that for a moment. "He'd been a bit anxious lately, but he didn't tell me why. Just seemed on edge," Burns said, his expression earnest. "I was worried about him."

"Mr. Burns, presumably you saw to your master's wardrobe," Jason said. "Did you notice any garments that might have been bloodstained?"

"Which garments do you mean, sir?" Burns asked.

"Undergarments," Jason replied. "Or handkerchiefs."

"No, sir. Mr. Stillman was in good health. He ate sparingly and took regular exercise."

"What sort of exercise?" Jason asked, clearly intrigued.

"He went to a fencing club twice a week."

"Name of the club?" Daniel asked, hoping it might be a lead.

"Gordon's Fencing Academy," Burns replied. "In Chriswell Street."

Daniel made a note of the name and address.

"What would Mr. Stillman's typical day look like?" Jason said.

"Well, he normally rose at seven, had his morning chocolate and toast, and set off for his office in the City. He went to work every day except Sunday, when he took Mrs. Stillman to church. He remained at his office until around five, sometimes a bit later. He dined at home on Mondays, Wednesdays, and Fridays, since he visited the fencing club after work on those days and liked to have a bath before changing for dinner. He dined out the other four days."

"That's very precise," Jason said, nodding in approval. "Where did he go on the days he dined out?"

"Mostly, he went to his club. Sometimes he was invited to a supper at someone's home or to a musical evening. He was very fond of music," Burns said sadly.

"Which club did he belong to?" Daniel asked.

"The East India Club in St. James's Square," Burns said.

"Had Mr. Stillman worked for the East India Company before starting his own venture?" Jason asked.

"Indeed, he did, sir. And made many useful connections along the way."

"Mr. Burns, did Mr. Stillman keep a mistress or visit brothels?" Daniel asked, feeling it was the right time to introduce the topic. As a valet, Burns would be sure to know what his master got up to, if only from seeing his soiled garments.

Alfie Burns' cheeks colored. "I really don't think I should say, sir."

"This is a murder investigation, Mr. Burns," Daniel reminded him sternly.

"So it is," Burns said, nodding sadly. "I suppose it no longer matters, does it?"

"It matters a great deal, young man. Your assistance can lead us to the killer," Daniel reminded him.

Mr. Burns nodded again. "Mr. Stillman wasn't fond of brothels. He was a fastidious man and found the notion of…well, you know, used goods, repellent. He did, however, have a mistress when I first began working for him."

"Do you know the lady's name?" Jason asked.

"He never openly discussed her with me, my lord, and she certainly never came to the house. I only know that he visited her two to three times per week."

"How do you know it was the same woman he went to see?"

Burns smiled. "It was the perfume, sir. Always the same smell on his clothes."

"That's hardly conclusive evidence," Jason replied.

"I'd also seen several letters from her in the wastepaper basket in his study. The paper smelled of that same perfume."

"Was there a signature?"

"Just Elise," Burns replied. "No surname."

"Was Mr. Stillman still seeing this woman?" Daniel asked.

"No, sir. He hadn't visited her since June, which was when the letters came. I suppose she was trying to change his mind, but he wasn't having it."

"Do you have any idea why Mr. Stillman stopped seeing her?"

Burns shrugged. "He tired of her, I suppose. Why else does a man stop seeing his mistress?"

"Perhaps she had hoped he'd marry her, and that led to a row," Daniel suggested.

Burns gave him a contemptuous look. "Men don't tend to marry their mistresses, Inspector. It's not the done thing."

"Did Mr. Stillman ever express a desire to marry?" Jason asked.

"Not to me, sir, but he did say once, quite recently, that it would be nice to have a son to carry on the family name and inherit the business."

"So perhaps he was considering marriage," Daniel speculated. "In which case, Elise would have a sound motive for murder."

"Hell hath no fury like a woman scorned," Jason intoned dramatically.

"Did you just come up with that?" Daniel asked, surprised at the poetic response.

Jason chuckled. "No. It's from a play by William Congreve."

"Right," Daniel said. He wasn't much for reading plays, but he heartily agreed with the sentiment.

"Mr. Burns, did Mr. Stillman keep a social diary?" Jason asked.

"No, sir. He had a remarkable memory. Always kept everything in his head. He did always warn me ahead of time when he had an engagement, so I'd prepare the right clothes for him."

"And where did he keep his personal correspondence?" Daniel asked.

"He didn't," Burns replied. "Mr. Stillman never held on to anything of a personal nature. Once he'd read a letter, he'd dispose of it. If it held little significance, he tossed it in the bin. If he wished to keep the content private, he threw it on the fire. It was the fact that he didn't bother to burn Elise's letters that told me he was through with her for good."

"Did Mr. Stillman employ a clerk at his office?" Daniel asked.

"Yes, he did. Mr. Percival Osbourne. You'll no doubt find him at the office, as he most likely hasn't heard the sad tidings yet."

"Do you have the address for Mr. Stillman's office?"

"Yes." Mr. Burns recited the address and looked at the men expectantly.

"Thank you, Mr. Burns. You've been most helpful," Jason said. "Please ask Judith and Jack to come speak to us."

Chapter 14

Judith was a young woman of about eighteen. Fair, blue-eyed, and utterly unhelpful. She knew nothing, had seen nothing, and had not noticed any blood or other secretions on Mr. Stillman's laundry or in his chamber pot. She rarely saw the master, and the only time he had spoken to her had been last Boxing Day, when he'd given her a small gift.

Jack, who had driven Roger Stillman to Ardith Hall last night, might have been a more promising prospect, had the man had any natural curiosity or a gift for observation. He was about forty, heavyset, with thick brown hair liberally streaked with gray, dark eyes, which were bloodshot since he'd just been woken by Martha, and tobacco-stained teeth. He didn't come too close, but the odors of stale sweat and alcohol hung heavy in the air, making Daniel wish he could open the window to let in some fresh air.

"How long have you worked for Mr. Stillman, Jack?" Jason asked.

Jack shrugged. "Can't remember."

"Five years? Ten?" Jason persisted.

"Close to five, I reckon," Jack said.

"And what were your duties?" Daniel asked.

"I look after the brougham and the 'orses."

"And you also acted as his coachman?" Daniel prompted.

"Aye, that I did," Jack replied.

"Where did you take him?" Jason asked.

"'Ere and there," Jack said with an indifferent shrug.

"Can you be more specific?" Jason tried again.

"'E liked to walk, Mr. Stillman did. Didn't take out the brougham too often."

"But when he did, where did he go?"

"To the docks, to balls, and such."

"What did he do at the docks?" Daniel asked.

"Went to 'is warehouse in Limehouse," Jack replied, looking at Daniel like he was daft.

"And was he invited to many balls?"

Jack shrugged. "A few."

"Did you ever take him to see someone named Elise?" Daniel asked.

Jack's eyebrows lifted in astonishment. "D'ye really think 'e'd say, 'Take me to see Elise, Jack'?" He cackled.

"Surely you'd know if he went to see a lady. Observant fellow such as yourself," Jason added smoothly.

Jack seemed to like that. "Aye, I did. Kept a bird near Golden Square."

"Kept?" Jason asked. "As in supported financially?"

"I don't know nothing 'bout that," Jack replied. "All's I know is that 'e stopped going there come June."

"Do you remember the address?" Daniel asked, trying hard to control his frustration. The man was the epitome of an oaf.

"Aye. Thirty-six, Bridle Lane."

"Thank you," Daniel said, feeling gratified. At least they now had an address for what he believed to be Elise.

"When was the last time Mr. Stillman took out the carriage before going to Ardith Hall?" Jason asked.

"Monday. 'E went to the warehouse."

"Had Mr. Stillman met with anyone at the docks?" Jason asked. It was evident he was also growing increasingly frustrated with this buffoon of a man.

"Dunno. 'E might 'ave."

"Right. Thank you, Jack. You've been *very* helpful," Daniel said, but the sarcasm was clearly lost on the groom, who lumbered out of the drawing room without uttering a word of farewell.

"Let's search Roger Stillman's bedroom and study," Jason said as he heaved himself to his feet and headed for the door.

Alfie Burns, who was still lurking downstairs, showed them the way and remained nearby, keeping a proprietorial eye on the proceedings.

A quarter of an hour later, they were done. Burns hadn't been exaggerating when he'd said Stillman had been a fastidious character. The bedroom was completely impersonal. There were no photographs, no books, not so much as an item out of place. The library that doubled as the study was much the same. There were dozens of books, but they all looked brand new, as if they had been bought simply to fill the shelves. The mahogany desk was bare except for basic writing implements, and a search of the drawers revealed nothing but writing paper, envelopes, a stick of old-fashioned sealing wax, and several bottles of ink. There wasn't a single letter or note, not even an old invitation or a calling card.

"I think we're done here," Jason said as they stepped out into the corridor, where they met Martha, who was coming out of Mrs. Stillman's room.

"How is Mrs. Stillman, Martha?" Jason asked.

"Sleeping, sir."

"We'll be going, then," Daniel said, eager to leave this cold, impersonal house.

"Very good, sirs."

Martha fetched their things and saw them out. As they walked down the walkway toward the street, Jason went quite pale, swayed, and grabbed on to the railing to steady himself. His gaze was fixed on the streetlamp, but Daniel didn't think he actually saw anything since his pupils appeared to be dilated. Jason closed his eyes and took several deep breaths.

"Jason, are you all right?" Daniel asked anxiously. Perhaps Jason was sickening for something. Thank God they hadn't accepted any refreshments, or he might have thought Jason had been poisoned.

Jason took another deep breath and opened his eyes. His color was slowly returning to normal, but he was still holding on to the railing, seemingly not trusting himself to let go.

"I need to eat," Jason said. "I haven't eaten anything since last night."

"Did you not have breakfast this morning?" Daniel asked, scandalized. He never missed a meal if he could help it and knew that Jason was a big proponent of breakfast He seemed to think it was more important to furnish the body with fuel in the morning rather than in the evening, when all one would do afterward is go to bed with a full belly and possibly suffer from indigestion as a consequence.

"I had a cup of coffee, but I don't usually eat before performing an autopsy. And then we left for London immediately after our meeting with CI Coleridge," Jason said. He sounded weak and tired, and quite unlike his usual self. "I think my blood sugar level has dropped."

Daniel didn't need to consult his watch to know it was well past lunch. He was quite hungry himself, truth be told, since he hadn't had anything to eat since his eggs and kippers that morning.

He didn't think he'd be able to eat after the heart-rending conversation with Sarah, but he'd been ravenous when he woke up, possibly because the emotional toll had left him depleted. Sarah had been surprisingly hungry as well and had joined him for breakfast before he set off, asking detailed questions about how he planned to investigate the case.

"Is this the first time this has happened?" Daniel asked as he waited for Jason to indicate that he was ready to proceed.

"No, but this was the worst episode by far. I had really left it too long this time."

Daniel raised a hand just as a hansom turned the corner. "Come on. We're going to get you steak and kidney pudding and a pint of ale," he announced. "That ought to set you to rights."

"No!" Jason exclaimed, clearly horrified by the prospect. "I don't want any kidney pudding. A beefsteak will do nicely."

"A beefsteak it is, then," Daniel said, using the kind of soothing tone one would take with a hysterical woman or a fractious child.

Jason nodded and meekly followed Daniel toward the hansom, his gait somewhat unsteady.

Chapter 15

Daniel took Jason to a chophouse just off Leicester Square and led him toward a table by the window. He instructed the waiter to bring bread and butter, beefsteaks with potatoes and buttered peas, and pints of ale.

Daniel buttered a piece of bread and shoved it toward Jason. "Eat," he ordered, looking for all the world like a worried mother.

Jason accepted the bread, hoping Daniel wouldn't notice the tremor in his hand. He felt so weak, black spots danced before his eyes and all sounds were muted, as if he were underwater. Jason ate the bread and drank half the ale before beginning to feel marginally better. Daniel didn't say anything, but his dark eyes followed Jason's every move as if he were preparing to perform lifesaving procedures should Jason faint dead away.

Jason reached for another piece of bread, even though bread by itself wouldn't fix what was ailing him. He was angry with himself for allowing this to happen. Low blood sugar could be easily controlled with regular protein-based meals. He should have taken the time to eat something before heading to London, but the disturbing results of the autopsy and the emotional blackmail CI Coleridge had resorted to in order to get him to take the case had left his stomach in knots, his need for fuel forgotten. He supposed he'd just wanted to get started, to feel some sense of control over the situation and do what he could to help Daniel. And now Daniel felt the need to help him.

"Does this happen often?" Daniel asked.

"Only when I don't eat for a long stretch of time. A souvenir of my time in prison," Jason said. "I'm fine now. Really," he assured Daniel. "Nothing to worry about."

"Do you want to go home?" Daniel asked solicitously.

"Stop fussing, Daniel," Jason replied, a tad too irritably. "I'm fine."

The waiter placed the food before them. "Enjoy your meals, gentlemen," he said cheerily, and left them to it.

They ate in silence for a few minutes. With every bite of steak, Jason felt stronger, the debilitating weakness he'd felt outside Roger Stillman's house receding as soon as the food hit his stomach.

"Sorry about that," Jason said sheepishly.

"You've nothing to apologize for. Do you feel up to discussing the case?" Daniel asked.

"Of course. What are your thoughts?"

"I don't know what to make of it," Daniel said, shaking his head, the steak momentarily forgotten. "Someone hated Roger Stillman enough to want him to suffer a prolonged, painful death, an attempt that failed, since the man seemed to experience no ill effects from ingesting the ground glass. Either the killer thought his plan had failed and tried again with the arsenic, or Roger Stillman had inspired more than one person to attempt to snuff him out. I had hoped that Mrs. Stillman and the servants would be able to shed some light, but it seems they know as little about the man's private life as we do. He seemingly had no wife, no current mistress, no close friends, no business associates that they know of, and no enemies."

"Yes, that does seem to be the case, doesn't it? Unless they're simply not telling us all they know."

"Why wouldn't they? I would think Mrs. Stillman would want to see her son's killer apprehended and hanged."

"I doubt Roger Stillman would have spoken to his mother of his business affairs or romantic trysts, but I had hoped that the valet and coachman would be able to tell us more, being the two people privy to his comings and goings. And Mrs. Murray seemed genuinely shocked. I don't think she's responsible."

"Then who is? How did the killer get the glass into Roger Stillman without him realizing it?"

"He dined out four times a week," Jason pointed out. "Perhaps his food was tampered with then."

"How many times would he have to ingest the glass in order for it to cause a fatal rupture in his stomach?" Daniel asked.

"That depends. I highly doubt that whoever tried to kill him simply dumped a pile of glass particles into his food and hoped the man wouldn't notice. My guess would be that the glass was administered in miniscule doses over a period of days, weeks even."

"So, whoever devised this plan was in no hurry. They had thought it through, figured out a way to administer the glass, and found someone willing to help them," Daniel mused.

"Which doesn't really square with what happened last night," Jason said. "Either the killer grew tired of waiting for his initial method to take effect and found a way to feed Roger Stillman the arsenic, which would mean that this person was at the séance last night, or there was an unrelated attempt on Stillman's life, which would also mean that the perpetrator had to be present at the séance.

"According to Constable Pullman, none of the servants went near the drawing room last night. A new bottle of whisky was opened by Mr. Innes and poured into the decanter on orders from Mrs. Tarrant. As of now, I see no reason the Tarrants' butler might have wished to kill Roger Stillman, so we're back to the five people who attended the séance."

Daniel winced but made no effort to protest Sarah's innocence. "According to our initial interviews, no one had known Roger Stillman except Mrs. Tarrant," he said instead.

"Mrs. Stillman said her son imported rum," Jason pointed out. "He could have had some business dealings with Mr. Forbes, who owns a sugarcane plantation."

Daniel considered this. "Supposing he did know Forbes. You said yourself that it would take days, possibly weeks to administer enough glass to kill the man. Forbes said he arrived on the fifteenth, which is only a few days ago."

"He might have had an accomplice. He said that he comes to London twice a year. Surely he knows people here. He may have arranged with someone to carry out the plan and arrived just in time to see his handiwork."

"Yes, he may have," Daniel said thoughtfully.

"Daniel, the killer might have been a woman," Jason said carefully. "Men tend to be more action-oriented in their killing. They shoot, stab, bludgeon, and so on. Men don't generally resort to methods that call for patience and imagination."

"You think this was a woman's doing?" Daniel asked.

"I think it's likely. There were three women at that séance," Jason said softly.

"Don't you dare include Sarah in the list of suspects!" Daniel cried. "You hear me?"

"Would you immediately discount my wife in the same situation?" Jason demanded with more heat than he'd intended.

"Yes, I would. Katherine is no more capable of murder than Sarah is. What possible reason would she have to kill a man she'd never met?"

"Are you certain they've never met?" Jason asked.

"Yes, I am," Daniel snapped. "But you can ask her yourself. Tomorrow morning. Ten o'clock. My house. Now, if you're finished, perhaps we should head back."

"I think we should try to speak to Elise and call on Mr. Osbourne before we return to Essex," Jason said. "As we're already here."

"Fine. It's your decision, since you're in charge," Daniel said acidly.

"Then I say we do. I also think we should call at Roger Stillman's club. Perhaps we can obtain a list of individuals he's dined with over the past few months."

"Why, because you think someone was feeding him glass at his club?" Daniel asked, clearly opposed to the idea. "That would take some doing."

"Anything is possible. Shall we go?" Jason threw some money on the table and pushed to his feet. He was in no mood for Daniel's outrage. CI Coleridge was right; Daniel should not be on this case, not even in a peripheral capacity. He was too emotionally involved, but saying so would almost certainly bring about the end of their friendship. All he could do was tread carefully and try to rule out Sarah quickly and conclusively.

Chapter 16

The walk to Golden Square took no more than ten minutes. Daniel walked next to Jason in sullen silence, but Jason made no effort to bring the conversation back to Sarah or apologize for including her in the list of suspects. Daniel would have to make his own peace with whatever direction the investigation took. All Jason could do was follow the evidence and hope it didn't incriminate Sarah, and make sure that Daniel was with him every step of the way to hear the testimony of those they questioned for himself.

Number thirty-six Bridle Lane looked solid and respectable, the type of abode one might associate with a well-to-do merchant or civil servant. The sound of the brass knocker reverberated through the downstairs, announcing their presence. Jason thought he heard the barking of a dog, but then it subsided.

The door was opened by a neatly attired young woman whose eyebrows lifted in surprise. Jason introduced them and showed her his temporary warrant card.

"How can I help you, gentlemen?" she asked, but made no move to invite them inside.

"We are looking for a woman named Elise, who we believe resides at this address," Jason explained.

The servant shook her head. "This is the residence of Mr. John Driscoll."

"And what does Mr. Driscoll do?" Jason asked.

"He's a banker, sir."

"Have you ever heard of anyone called Elise who might have resided at this address?" Jason persisted.

"No, sir." The young woman looked thoughtful for a moment. "I think Mrs. Graham might be able to help. Wait here, please," she said, clearly reluctant to invite them inside.

A middle-aged woman in a dress of black bombazine opened the door a few moments later. She had iron-gray hair pulled into a severe bun and a face that could scare small children.

"Yes?" she asked.

"Mrs. Graham, do you know of anyone named Elise who might have lived at this address?" Jason asked. Daniel remained stubbornly silent.

Mrs. Graham looked like she was about to deny all knowledge but couldn't quite contain the need to vent her disapproval. "Yes. Mrs. Prentiss, her name was. And from what I heard, she was no better than she should be," she said nastily, lowering her voice to a conspiratorial whisper in case any passersby overheard what she had to say. "She passed herself off as a widow, but I highly doubt a woman like that had ever been respectable. She was kept by her benefactor for several years, but then the payments and the visits stopped, and she was forced to leave."

"When was this?" Jason asked.

"In June. Mr. Driscoll took possession of the house in early July."

"And do you know where Mrs. Prentiss went?" Daniel asked, his earlier pique forgotten.

"I don't, but I doubt it was anywhere nice," Mrs. Graham said, nodding self-righteously. "There's only one direction a woman of her character can go, and that's downward."

"Thank you, Mrs. Graham," Jason said. "You've been most helpful."

Daniel sighed deeply as they walked away, heading toward the corner, where they might have a better chance of finding a passing hansom or spotting a cab stand.

"A jilted lover would certainly have a motive for murder, especially if she had lost her home and the lifestyle the affair had afforded her," Daniel said.

"Yes, she would," Jason agreed. "Perhaps Mrs. Prentiss is connected to one of the people at the séance."

"Let's see if we can prove that theory," Daniel said as he lifted his hand to hail a passing cabby. He gave Roger Stillman's office address once they climbed in, and the cab set off, moving at a good clip toward the City.

Chapter 17

Stillman Imports was located in Eldon Street and consisted of one oblong room on the ground floor. The space had been partitioned to create a separate area for the clerk's desk, which faced the office door. There were several filing cabinets and two visitor chairs by the wall. The reception area was dim and unwelcoming, since the only window was located in the back room, where Mr. Stillman had made an office for himself.

Mr. Osbourne was at his desk when they arrived, his head bent over a ledger. He was in his mid-twenties, with neatly trimmed fair hair and a pencil moustache so thin it hovered over his upper lip like a third eyebrow. There was something vaguely ridiculous about him, but Daniel couldn't figure out precisely what.

"How can I help you?" Mr. Osbourne asked as he looked up from his work. His attitude was one of suppressed irritation. They clearly didn't have an appointment, or he would have been aware of their imminent arrival, so he wasn't inclined to waste his time.

"I am Lord Redmond, Special Advisor to the Essex Police, and this is Inspector Haze," Jason said, holding up his warrant card. He preferred not to rely on his title when involved in an investigation, but one look at Percival Osbourne's closed expression likely made him think that the man would be more forthcoming with a member of the nobility.

Mr. Osbourne looked abashed. "Mr. Stillman is not here today."

"We're here to speak to you, Mr. Osbourne. It is Mr. Percival Osbourne, isn't it?" Jason asked.

"Eh…yes. Has something happened?"

"Mr. Stillman was murdered last night. In Essex," Jason added.

Percival Osbourne paled, and his bottom lip began to tremble as if he were about to cry. "No," he whispered. "He couldn't have been. Who would do such a terrible thing?"

"That's what we're trying to figure out," Jason said, looking around. "Do you mind if we speak in the other office?"

"Mr. Stillman doesn't, I mean didn't like…" Mr. Osbourne's voice trailed off as though he suddenly realized it no longer mattered what Mr. Stillman liked or disliked. "Of course," he said. "Follow me."

They trooped into the larger office. Jason had no desire to sit behind Roger Stillman's desk, so he pulled out the chair and placed it near the two guest chairs that faced the desk. "Sit down, Mr. Osbourne," he invited.

The man perched on the edge of one of the chairs, his posture so erect, his back and shoulders had to be thrumming with tension.

"Mr. Osbourne, how long have you worked for Mr. Stillman?" Jason asked.

"Five years now."

"And what did you do for him, exactly?"

"Why, everything. I kept a diary of appointments, handled his correspondence, maintained the ledgers, inspected the warehouse. I suppose I'll have to find new employment now." He sounded despondent, probably because he wouldn't be able to get a reference from a dead man, and the past five years had been as good as wasted as far as he was concerned.

"What did Mr. Stillman import?" Daniel asked.

"Silk from China, tea and spices from India, rum from Barbados, and even ivory from East Africa."

Now that Mr. Osbourne had mentioned the exotic places Mr. Stillman had imported goods from, Daniel noticed the small ivory statue on the sideboard beneath a painting of what might have been a Caribbean beach. There was also an exquisite chess set, the ebony and ivory pieces prominently displayed, and a tribal mask, carved from teak or some other dark wood, positioned on a stand made exclusively for the purpose.

"Did any of Mr. Stillman's business partnerships sour recently?" Jason asked, his gaze also sweeping over the decor.

"Not as far as I know. Mr. Stillman was on amicable terms with all his suppliers," Mr. Osbourne said.

"Was Mr. Nathaniel Forbes one of them?" Daniel asked.

"Mr. Forbes?" The clerk made a show of thinking. "Yes, he was. Mr. Stillman bought rum from him."

"Has Mr. Forbes visited Mr. Stillman recently?"

"No, he hasn't. Is he in London?"

"Yes, he is, and staying not too far from Mr. Stillman's residence, as it happens," Daniel said.

Percival Osbourne looked nonplussed. "I've actually never met Mr. Forbes, and as far as I know, neither had Mr. Stillman. All business was handled via post and through Mr. Forbes' agent, Mr. Gilbert."

"Have you met Mr. Gilbert?" Jason asked.

"Yes, once, when I first started working for Mr. Stillman."

"Does he have an office in London?"

"No, I believe he resides permanently in Barbados," Percival Osbourne replied.

"Had Mr. Stillman had any dealings with Lord Julian Sumner?" Daniel asked, annoyed to have hit another dead end where a possible witness to dealings between Roger Stillman and Nathaniel Forbes was concerned.

"I don't believe so."

"What about someone named Lysander?" Jason asked.

"Sorry, no."

"Had Mr. Stillman ever corresponded with an S. Haze?" Jason asked, his gaze fixed on the clerk, probably to avoid looking at Daniel.

Daniel seethed with anger but said nothing. Jason was only doing what had been asked of him.

Mr. Osbourne looked confused. "Isn't that your name, Inspector Haze?"

"Yes," Daniel snapped.

"No, no one by that name," Mr. Osbourne replied, looking from Jason to Daniel as if he'd been asked a trick question.

"Had Mr. Stillman ever mentioned an Elise Prentiss?" Jason asked.

Percival Osbourne's lip curled in a derisive smile. "Mr. Stillman did not do business with women."

Daniel sighed, feeling utterly frustrated. "Can you recall anything at all that might have seemed odd or threatening to you, Mr. Osbourne?"

Mr. Osbourne looked like he was trying hard to recall any such occurrence, then brightened and looked to Jason, whom he rightly assumed was in charge. "He did receive an odd letter a few months ago," he said.

"What sort of letter?" Jason asked.

"This was at the beginning of October," Mr. Osbourne began. "I deal with all correspondence that comes to the office, so the letter was handed to me."

"Handed?" Daniel asked.

"Yes. A boy delivered it. A street child," Mr. Osbourne clarified. "It was addressed to Mr. Stillman, but there was no return address, postage stamp, or any other markings."

"What did the letter say?" Jason asked.

"It was just two sentences with no signature. It said, 'You will pay for what you've done. The reckoning will come when you least expect it.' I showed the letter to Mr. Stillman right away," Mr. Osbourne said.

"And how did he react?"

"He looked—I don't know—frightened, I suppose, but only for a moment. Then he became angry and ordered me to leave the room."

"What did he do with the letter?" Jason asked. "Burn it?"

"Well, yes, he did. Immediately."

"Mr. Osbourne, did you notice anything else about the missive?" Daniel asked.

"The only thing I noticed was that the letter was written on good-quality paper and the penmanship was beautiful. I thought at the time that it had been written by someone educated and wealthy."

"Was the handwriting masculine or feminine?" Jason asked.

"It was hard to tell from those two lines, but I would have said masculine," Mr. Osbourne replied. "And the ink was very dark, as if someone had pressed down hard when writing the lines."

"Was that the only threatening letter Mr. Stillman received?" Daniel asked.

"It was the only one I saw with my own eyes," the clerk replied.

"Mr. Osbourne, did Mr. Stillman ever speak to you of his personal life?" Jason asked.

"No, sir. Never. He was a very private man."

"Yes, so it would seem," Jason replied irritably. They seemed to be getting nowhere fast.

"What will happen now?" Percival Osbourne asked, looking from Jason to Daniel. "What will become of the goods and properties Mr. Stillman owned? What will become of me?" he asked, his anxiety palpable.

"Unless Mr. Stillman designated a successor in his will who intends to carry on with the business activities, you will need to find new employment," Daniel replied.

Mr. Osbourne nodded miserably. "Yes. I thought as much. Thank you, sir."

"Mr. Osbourne, news of Mr. Stillman's death will be in the papers," Jason said gently. "Any potential employer will know that you did not lose your position due to poor performance."

"Yes, that's something, I suppose," Mr. Osbourne said. "But not as good as a glowing character reference, is it? This was my first job, so I don't have any other recommendations to rely on."

Daniel glanced at Jason. He hoped Jason wasn't about to offer the man employment, as he was wont to do in these types of circumstances. The thought must have crossed Jason's mind because he looked pensive for a moment but resisted the urge to snap up Mr. Osbourne on the spot.

"I can't speak to your work, but if you require a letter to the effect that Mr. Stillman was murdered and you lost your position because of the tragedy, I will be happy to provide you with one," Jason offered instead.

"Oh, will you really?" Mr. Osbourne exclaimed, clearly buoyed by the prospect of a letter from a member of the nobility. "Would you mind writing one now?"

"I don't mind in the least," Jason replied magnanimously.

Mr. Osbourne exploded out of his chair and dashed around the desk, extracting a clean sheet of paper. Jason penned a quick note, which he signed with a flourish.

"There," he said, handing it to Mr. Osbourne. "I do hope this will help you secure a new position."

"Thank you, my lord. That's very kind. Very kind, indeed," Percival Osbourne gushed.

"I think you'd best lock up and be on your way now, Mr. Osbourne," Daniel said. "You no longer have a legal right to be here."

"Yes, of course. I see what you mean," Mr. Osbourne said as he walked them to the door. "I will collect my personal belongings and leave right away. Good day to you, gentlemen."

"Poor man," Jason said as soon as they were back out in the street. "When he woke this morning, he had no idea that his life was about to change so dramatically."

"No, I expect not," Daniel said bitterly, "but that's the nature of life, isn't it? When I woke on Wednesday, I had no idea my wife would be a suspect in a murder inquiry by the end of the day."

"Daniel, I don't suspect Sarah," Jason said, clearly striving for patience.

"Maybe you don't, but everyone else will. I would if I weren't her husband."

"The best thing we can do for Sarah is to find the real killer," Jason said. "We haven't learned much, but we now know that Mr. Stillman received a threatening letter several months back and that he'd scorned a woman he'd been with for a considerable period of time. It is possible the letter came from her."

"Yes, it is, but that's pure speculation at this stage."

"Every plausible theory begins with speculation," Jason said.

"How do you wish to proceed?" Daniel asked.

"I would like to speak to Mrs. Lysander. I don't think it's necessary for both of us to be present. Perhaps you should re-interview Mr. Forbes, since the two men now appear to have a connection."

"The letter was hand delivered in October. Mr. Forbes has only just arrived in London, so the letter can't be from him," Daniel pointed out.

"Just because he didn't deliver it himself doesn't mean he didn't send it. He may have mailed the letter to someone in London and asked them to see that Roger Stillman got it. Or the letter might be from someone else entirely; that doesn't mean Nathaniel Forbes can be ruled out as a suspect."

"Definitely not," Daniel agreed. "You know, I think Roger Stillman was scared."

"What makes you say that?" Jason asked as they walked down the street, the chill wind forcing them to huddle deeper into their coats.

"He kept nothing of a personal nature either at home or at his office. He disposed of all his correspondence and made sure not to write anything down in a diary. Perhaps he was afraid that whoever had threatened him would get access to his correspondence or social schedule and would gain the upper hand."

"That's certainly possible," Jason agreed. "I do wonder if that was the only threat he'd received."

"Perhaps whoever killed him had indulged in a little game of cat and mouse, frightening the man out of his wits first and making sure he was constantly looking over his shoulder. I wager he never thought to check his food."

"It's premature to imagine a campaign of terror based on one note, but we should keep that theory in mind. Now, I think it's time we went home."

"Do you not wish to call at Roger Stillman's club?" Daniel asked.

"Perhaps you can do that after you speak to Mr. Forbes," Jason said. "To be honest, I'm too tired to do anything more today. It's been a long day."

"Yes, of course," Daniel agreed, although he would have liked to continue. Jason did look worn out, so Daniel hailed a cab and they headed to the railway station.

Chapter 18

Daniel was relieved when Sarah and Harriet retired early. Charlotte had been fussing all day, her teething pain preventing her from taking her usual two-hour nap. The child was worn out, as were her mother and grandmother, who'd taken turns walking with her to ease her suffering. Daniel couldn't help noticing that Harriet had been keeping out of his way and wondered, not for the first time, if Harriet had been privy to Sarah's plans. He couldn't imagine that Sarah hadn't confided in her mother. Well, he supposed it was natural for Harriet to keep Sarah's secrets. After all, she wanted only to see her daughter happy.

Daniel retired to the drawing room, poured himself a very large brandy, and sat by the fire, his heart raw with emotion. Anxiety and fear for Sarah were uppermost in his mind, but he couldn't ignore the shame he felt for the way he'd treated Jason. It had been clear from the start that Jason hadn't wanted the responsibility of investigating this case. He'd only accepted because of Daniel, knowing Daniel would go mad with worry if a Scotland Yard detective took over or if DI Peterson had been assigned the case instead, which would be even worse

Peterson was the most dogged, tireless man Daniel knew, and would not only treat Sarah as a suspect but put so much pressure on her, she'd admit to worshipping the devil himself if only to get Peterson to back off. Jason would be gentle and kind when he spoke to Sarah, not only because he was a friend but because he knew Sarah had nothing to do with the murder of Roger Stillman. Speaking to Sarah would be a mere formality, just another sheet of paper to slip into the file before they arrested the killer and closed the case.

Daniel sighed miserably as he stared into the leaping flames. Jason had been considerate and respectful, treating Daniel as an equal, not a subordinate, which he was meant to be in this instance. He'd consulted Daniel on every decision, had given him free rein when it came to questioning suspects, and had not held back from disclosing his own theories, as DI Peterson surely would if he were in charge. Daniel, on the other hand, had been abrupt, impatient, and unkind, pushing his friend to do more when he was clearly not feeling his best. Jason was a strong, resilient man, but the year of imprisonment in a Georgia prison had taken a toll on his health, something he clearly tried to hide from both Daniel and Katherine.

Daniel took a gulp of brandy and felt the liquid burn its way down his gullet in a most satisfying way. What was wrong with him these days? Why couldn't he enjoy the blessings God had bestowed upon him? Why did he feel so worried, so restless? Perhaps tomorrow, after he'd interviewed Nathaniel Forbes and stopped by Roger Stillman's club, he'd do a bit of Christmas shopping. He'd get something nice for Sarah, and for his mother-in-law, her favorite lavender soap. Sarah's father used to buy her an ornament to hang on their holiday tree every year, and Daniel would continue the tradition and buy a lovely bauble for his own daughter. One day, he would point out the various ornaments to Charlotte and tell her about the time he'd bought them for her and how old she'd been.

The pleasant domestic fantasy calmed Daniel's worries somewhat, and he thought he might be able to rest. He finished the brandy, set the glass on the low table next to his chair, and heaved himself to his feet. Tomorrow was another day. Perhaps they'd have a breakthrough in the investigation and wrap this nasty business up before Christmas. And if not, he would not allow it to affect his holiday. And he would start this period of goodwill by apologizing to Jason.

Chapter 19

The house was quiet, only the ticking of the carriage clock on the mantel of the drawing room fireplace audible in the moonless darkness of the winter night. Jason crossed the foyer and walked through the green baize door that separated the rest of the house from the servants' quarters. It was past midnight, but he couldn't sleep and thought a glass of warm milk might help him settle down.

The warmth of the kitchen was a welcome respite from the chill of the ground floor, where the fires had been extinguished hours ago, but the flagstones were still icy against his bare feet, and he wished he'd worn the slippers that Fanny kept leaving for him by the bed.

Mrs. Dodson sat at the table, her round face illuminated by the glow of the oil lamp she used during her nocturnal forays into the kitchen. She was nursing a cup of tea, a split scone on a plate before her, each half liberally spread with jam. Jason slid onto the opposite bench, glad of the company.

"I couldn't sleep," he explained unnecessarily.

"Would you like some tea?" Mrs. Dodson asked.

"I was hoping for a glass of warm milk, but don't trouble yourself, Mrs. D. I can prepare it myself," Jason replied, but made no move to get up. He suddenly felt tired, his limbs as heavy as if they'd been weighted down with lead.

"Nonsense." Mrs. Dodson scoffed and pushed away from the table. "Really, Captain. I think I can make you a cup of warm milk," she said reproachfully. "And there are at least two scones left. I can warm them up for you."

"Thank you, Mrs. Dodson. You take such good care of me," Jason said as he rested his elbows on the table and propped up his cheeks.

"That's what I'm paid to do, isn't it?" she replied as she poured milk into a saucepan and set it on the still-warm cooker. Mrs. Dodson split the two remaining scones and laid them on a skillet, setting it on the stove as well.

A few minutes later, she presented Jason with a mug of milk and the scones and pushed the jar of jam and the dish of clotted cream toward him. He shook his head and crumbled up half a scone instead, popping the morsels in his mouth between sips of milk.

"You're not looking so good, if you don't mind me saying so," Mrs. Dodson observed. Few women in her position would speak so freely to the master of the house, but Jason encouraged the familiarity and thought of Mrs. Dodson as a surrogate mother. He missed his own mother desperately and relished the attention the older woman lavished on both him and Micah. She'd taken them under her wing when they first arrived and made them feel welcome and cared for. Micah hadn't said so in his letters, but Jason was sure he missed Mrs. Dodson and looked forward to being spoiled by her when he came home for the Christmas holiday.

"I'm all right," Jason replied, and reached for the second scone. "I didn't get much sleep last night, and it's been a grueling day."

"You should have come straight home after the autopsy and let Daniel Haze do the work he's paid to do," Mrs. Dodson admonished. "He relies on you too much, and you let him."

"I've been put in charge of the case," Jason said.

Mrs. Dodson stared at him, her surprise evident. "Have you now? Why's that, then?"

"Sarah Haze was present at the scene of the crime, so Daniel's judgment is understandably compromised. Had another inspector been assigned, Daniel wouldn't be allowed anywhere near the evidence, and he's desperate to remain on the case. I had no choice but to agree."

Mrs. Dodson waved her hand dismissively. "Surely the chief inspector knows Sarah Haze had nothing to do with it."

"He does, but procedure must be followed. Daniel has a personal stake in the case."

"Which will only make him try harder to solve it," Mrs. Dodson said.

"I wish it were that simple, Mrs. D.," Jason replied. "This case is complicated, to say the least."

"Every case is complicated until you figure it out, and you always do. You have a head for strategic thinking," Mrs. Dodson said, surprising Jason with her assessment of his abilities. "And you understand people."

"I'm not sure that I do. I think I have a firm grasp on the complexities of human nature until a new case comes along, and once again, I'm shocked and dismayed by the depravity human beings will resort to in their desire to harm someone. I've seen murder by gunshot, by poison, and by asphyxiation, but I have never yet seen killing by internal injury."

"I'm not sure I follow, Captain," Mrs. Dodson said, her brows knitting in concentration.

"The victim's stomach was coated with particles of glass. It glittered on the lining like diamonds on red velvet," Jason said, recalling the sight. He couldn't get the image out of his mind and instantly regretted his poetic description of something so grotesque.

"Well, bless my soul," Mrs. Dodson exclaimed, her hand flying to her ample bosom. "Who would even conceive of such a thing?"

"That's what I need to figure out," Jason replied. He pushed away the half-eaten scone, no longer hungry. "Whoever did this is cunning and levelheaded, but either their well of patience ran dry or we're dealing with two separate killers who'd targeted the same man. If that's the case, I can only ask myself why. What had this man done to elicit such visceral hatred?"

Mrs. Dodson tilted her head to the side as she considered his question. "Well, that's a question I'm sure I can't answer, and neither will you if you don't get some rest. Would you like a hot-water bottle?" she asked in that motherly tone that always made Jason feel like a little boy.

"Yes, please," he replied, already imagining the wonderful warmth as he climbed back into bed. His feet were ice cold.

"The kettle's still hot," Mrs. Dodson said as she bustled over to one of the cupboards and extracted the copper bottle. She filled it from the kettle and wrapped it in a towel before handing it to Jason. "Sleep well, Captain."

"You as well, Mrs. Dodson," Jason said. "And thank you for listening."

"Oh, you can always count on me for a bit of a chat," Mrs. Dodson replied with an indulgent smile. "And if you find my opinions helpful, then so much the better."

She picked up the oil lamp and headed for the door, Jason behind her. He returned to the bedroom and slid into bed, making sure not to disturb Katherine as he placed the water bottle at his feet. As warmth seeped into his chilled skin, he began to relax, his thoughts bobbing like a cork on rolling waves until he finally fell asleep.

Chapter 20

Friday, December 20

Jason set off for Bluebell Cottage immediately after breakfast, since he was due to collect Micah from school by midafternoon and didn't want to be late. He could have asked Joe to drive him in the brougham but decided to take the curricle instead. It was a frigid morning, but despite the cold, he enjoyed the drive through the wintry countryside. The frost-covered fields sparkled in the weak winter sunshine, and the bare tree branches formed a latticework against the nearly colorless sky. The scene was peaceful and lovely, and it gave Jason time to think and analyze what they had learned to date, which wasn't much. He hoped Mrs. Lysander would be more forthcoming this time but didn't hold out much hope. She was as sly as a fox, the type of woman who would hold her secrets close and pay any price to maintain her mystique.

Even in midwinter, with its roof dusted with snow, and holly bushes dotted with cherry-red berries adding a splash of color to an otherwise monotonous scene, the cottage was charming. It was probably doubly lovely in the summer, when roses clung to the white-painted arbor and the walls were green with climbing ivy. When Jason knocked, the door was opened by an older woman, who smiled at him in a motherly way.

"Oh, hello, my dear," she said. "Do come in. It's rather cold out there." She behaved as if he'd been expected. Perhaps she had mistaken him for someone else.

Inside, it was warm and welcoming, the smell of something delicious filling the small entryway.

"Can I offer you a cup of tea while you wait?" she asked, smiling at him as she held out her hands for his hat and gloves. "And there's cake."

"Wait for what?" Jason asked, now certain she had no idea who he was.

"For Alicia to return from her walk. She said you'd be calling by today, your lordship." She grinned. "It is Lord Redmond, isn't it?"

"Yes," Jason admitted with some reluctance.

"I'm Patty, by the way," the woman said in her companionable manner. "Patricia Barber."

"It's a pleasure to make your acquaintance, Mrs. Barber. And yes, tea would be lovely," Jason said, deciding to play along.

Mrs. Barber led Jason into a comfortable parlor and invited him to sit. "Perhaps you'd like to talk to Constantine," she suggested.

"And who is he?" Jason asked, fully expecting her to introduce him to her cat that was lounging on an armchair cushion.

"He's Alicia's assistant. He's not one for frigid country walks," Mrs. Barber explained. "He likes a lie-in on a cold winter's morning. But I know he's up. I heard him moving around."

"Yes, I would very much like to speak to Constantine," Jason replied, hoping the man was awake and ready to talk to him. He had been planning to ask Alicia Lysander about her assistant, so an opportunity to speak to him was rather fortuitous.

"I'll let him know you're here," Mrs. Barber said, and left the room.

A few minutes later, a man in his mid-thirties walked into the parlor. He was still in his shirtsleeves, a gross impropriety when receiving a visitor, but his black silver-embroidered silk waistcoat and puff tie saved him from looking underdressed. With his wavy chestnut hair falling over a high forehead, theatrically arched eyebrows, and wide blue eyes that sparkled with an almost childlike curiosity, he looked rather debonair.

"So, you're the American captain, surgeon, lord of the manor, and police attaché," he drawled, a slow smile spreading across his face. "Nice to meet you, your lordship. Constantine Moore," he said, holding out his hand.

Jason shook it and sat back down, not at all sure what to make of the man. He had the distinct impression that Constantine Moore found him amusing, but there was no derision in his gaze, only admiration. Constantine shooed off the cat and lowered himself into the armchair, crossing his legs.

"How long have you known Mrs. Lysander, Mr. Moore?" Jason asked, trying to take control of the interview.

"Oh, forever." Moore made a vague hand gesture. "Since before her husband died. And please, call me Constantine."

"And you act as her assistant? What do you do, exactly?"

"Not what you think," Constantine replied, his gaze never leaving Jason's face.

"And what is it that you think I think you do?" Jason asked, surprised by the man's reply.

"You think that I research Mrs. Lysander's clients and pass the information on to her so she can use it in her séances and trick those in attendance into believing she's truly making contact with their dearly departed," Constantine replied without missing a beat.

"Is that not what she does?" Jason asked, now really curious. He supposed he had thought that as soon as he'd discovered Mrs. Lysander used an assistant.

"No. Alicia is the genuine article, my lord," Constantine said. "And she'll prove it to you, if she's in the mood."

"And how can she prove it to me?" Jason asked. "There are plenty of people who are familiar with the details of my life. I'm not a secretive man. All you'd have to do is ask about me at the

Red Stag, and I'm sure Moll Brody would fill you in in short order. She's a chatty girl, Moll."

"I did not ask anyone about you. And Alicia will prove it to you in her own way," Constantine replied.

"So, if she's the genuine article, as you put it, what is it that you do for her?" Jason asked. He wasn't sure why, but he was goading the man and enjoying it just a bit.

Mrs. Barber bustled into the room with a tea tray before Constantine could reply. "Here we are, then, my dears," she said as she placed it on the low table before the settee. "Shall I pour out, or will you see to yourselves? The teacakes are still warm," she added. "Help yourselves."

"Thank you, Patty," Constantine said with a warm smile. "Don't you worry, I'll look after our guest."

"How do you like your tea, my lord? I bet you don't take milk," he said as soon as Mrs. Barber left the room.

"I don't," Jason agreed. "Just two sugars, please."

Constantine made the tea and handed the cup to Jason before pouring one for himself. "I can never say no to a cup of tea and cake." He reached for a teacake and bit into it delicately. Once he finished chewing, he washed the cake down with a sip of tea and turned his attention back to Jason, a knowing smile on his face.

"To get back to your very pertinent question, my lord. What I do for Alicia is offer her companionship and protection. It's not safe for a woman, especially one as beautiful and well known as Alicia Lysander, to travel on her own. I serve more as a chaperone-cum-bodyguard than an actual spiritual assistant."

"Are you lovers?" Jason asked. It was an extremely rude question, but one Jason thought he could guess the answer to. And given Constantine's playful attitude, Jason didn't think he'd mind overmuch.

"We are," Constantine replied. "Have been for years."

"And Mrs. Lysander is happy with this arrangement?"

"If she's not, she'll be sure to let me know. Alicia is not one for mincing words. I've asked her to marry me several times, but she prefers things as they are. The moment she changes her mind, I will be there, standing up in church with a ring in my pocket." Constantine reached for another cake. "Ah, there she is," he said, the cake suspended halfway to his mouth. "She loves her morning walks. Very invigorating, she says," he confided with a soft laugh. "I'm glad she enjoys them, but I'm not one for freezing my bollocks off."

He drained his teacup and set it on the table before rising to his feet. "Alicia, my dear, Lord Redmond is here to see you. Patty, be a dear and bring Alicia a clean cup," he called out to Mrs. Barber.

Patty appeared as if by magic, deposited a clean cup and saucer on the tray, and left without saying a word.

"It was a pleasure to meet you, my lord. Perhaps we'll see each other again someday," Constantine said, and bowed extravagantly before leaving Jason alone in the parlor.

He didn't have long to wait. Alicia Lysander walked in, or rather floated, her cheeks rosy with cold, her eyes sparkling with amusement.

"Good morning, my lord," she said as she took a seat across from him and reached for the teapot.

"Good morning, Mrs. Lysander," Jason said, unable to keep from smiling at her.

She really was lovely, and extremely independent, not something one saw in Englishwomen of her class often. They tended to get flustered easily and were too afraid to come off as overly educated or mannish. In fact, Alicia Lysander reminded Jason of his own wife when he'd first met her. Katherine had known her own mind and hadn't been afraid to offer an opinion or defend her beliefs.

"Mrs. Lysander, I'm afraid I'm in dire need of your help," Jason said, hoping he could appeal to her vanity if not her desire to see justice done. "It seems Mr. Stillman departed this earth without leaving behind anyone who'd known him well. I need to know everything you can tell me about the man, even if it's only your own impressions."

Alicia Lysander took a sip of her tea and studied Jason, a thoughtful expression in her eyes. "Why?" she asked. "You think me a fraud. Why would my impressions matter to you?"

"Because I believe you're a very observant woman. You would have to be in your line of work."

"Yes, I am observant," she replied. "For example, I can see that you're uncomfortable and would prefer to deal with someone you have a better handle on. You didn't think much of Constantine and have probably tried hard to discredit him, but despite your self-importance and typical American arrogance, he unnerved you and made you question your assumptions about my abilities. You believe me to be a charlatan, yet there's some small part of you that wonders if I do indeed commune with the spirits."

"Do you?" Jason asked, disregarding the verbal daggers she'd thrown at him and wondering what had brought on her impressive ire. Surely not everyone believed her to be a conduit between the realms of the living and the dead. "You have my word as a gentleman that nothing you tell me will ever leave this room. I can certainly understand people's desire for closure, but I can also see how someone who's clever enough to pull it off would cash in on that need. It's business, pure and simple. There's a demand, and you are happy to fill it."

Alicia Lysander tilted her head and looked at him as if she were trying to memorize his every feature. After a moment, her gaze clouded, a faraway look entering her eyes as she continued to stare. She seemed to have turned inward, no longer aware of him.

There was something ethereal about her presence, almost as if her corporeal form were there just for his benefit, and if she could, she'd shed her skin like a snake. Despite himself, Jason was mesmerized.

"The two trains collided at twenty past twelve, a terrible accident that could have been prevented, being the result of several unfortunate events that happened simultaneously and culminated in tragedy," she said, her voice soft and breathless. "The sun was bright that day, shining directly into the driver's face and preventing him from seeing clearly despite the visor of his cap shading his eyes. He'd chosen that particular time to eat the sandwich his wife had packed for his luncheon, taking his eyes off the track for the few moments it took him to take the sandwich out of his lunchbox and unwrap it. There was also a bottle of cold tea that he'd been looking forward to because he was thirsty."

Alicia Lysander's rosy cheeks paled as she recounted the disaster, her eyes widening as if she could see it happening before her. "The other train was not supposed to be there, least of all traveling on the same track in the opposite direction. Both trains were traveling at full speed. Had the drivers been paying attention, they might have had time to stop, or at the very least slow down to minimize the force of the impact, but the second driver was nursing a hangover and had barely been paying attention to the track before him, his headache exacerbated by the glare of the midday sun. Both drivers were killed instantly on impact, as were the firemen who'd been too busy feeding coal into the engines to notice anything was amiss."

Alicia Lysander's eyes misted with tears as she continued. "The passengers at the back of both trains fared better than those at the front. The cars were crushed, the people within broken like porcelain dolls. Your father died almost instantly, but your mother, though severely injured, lingered, calling for you in her agony. There was a doctor on board, and he got to her eventually, but it was too late. There was nothing he could do, so he moved on to those he could help. Your mother died of massive internal bleeding as she lay beside the tracks. She was all alone."

Alicia Lysander went quiet, her gaze clearing as she focused on Jason once again, the look of horror replaced by one of deep sympathy. Jason was trembling, silent tears sliding down his face. He hadn't realized the teacup was still in his hand and noticed it only when the porcelain cracked from the pressure of his fingers and bit into his hand. Blood was dripping onto his trouser leg and onto the carpet beneath.

"How... How did you know that?" he choked out.

Alicia Lysander reached for a napkin and gently wrapped his bleeding hand after removing the broken cup from his grasp and making sure there were no shards imbedded in Jason's skin.

"I saw it," she said simply. "It was awful."

"How can you be so calm?" Jason demanded, knowing what horror she must have witnessed.

"I'm used to it. I've been seeing people's worst nightmares since I was a child. Patty, dear, can Lord Redmond have a glass of water, please?" Alicia called out softly.

Patty appeared a moment later, as if she had been just outside, waiting for Jason's reaction to Alicia's words.

Jason drained the glass and set it down. His heart thudded against his ribs, and his head felt as if it were locked in a vise. Everything Alicia Lysander had said was true. He'd read all the reports from the accident, including the one made by the doctor who'd attended on his mother shortly before she died. Jason had never spoken to anyone of what he'd learned. He simply couldn't bring himself to utter the words, to paint the mental picture of what his mother had suffered in the final hour of her life. At least his father had been spared the pain and the knowledge that he was about to die. His head had been crushed, his brains spilling out like the insides of a melon.

"You are trying to figure out how I could have known that. Asking yourself if I had somehow been able to read the reports, had prepared for my encounter with you," Alicia said calmly. "I haven't. I saw it all when I looked into your eyes. You are still grieving, but I want you to know that your parents loved you more than life itself, and they were so proud of you. They want you to move on and be happy. And they heartily approve of Katie," she added, the side of her mouth lifting into a smile.

"Tell me what you saw in Roger Stillman's eyes," Jason rasped. He couldn't bear to talk about his parents anymore, not if he wished to retain some grasp on his self-control.

"I saw a man who was heartbroken and frightened."

"What did he fear?" Jason asked.

"He thought someone was trying to kill him."

"Who?" Jason demanded.

"I can't answer that because he didn't know. He only knew someone wished to see him suffer."

"Why was he heartbroken?" Jason asked.

"He had lost someone he loved. A woman. He'd lost her twice," Alicia amended.

"What does that mean?"

She shrugged. "I had only just begun the séance when Mr. Stillman took ill. Had I had more time…"

"What about the others?" Jason asked.

"They all had their secrets, but I won't share them with you. You have no right to them."

"Just tell me one thing. Did any of them have a connection to the victim?"

"They all did," Alicia Lysander said. "Does that surprise you?"

"Yes," Jason admitted.

"The universe has its own plan, Lord Redmond. It brings people together when the time is right."

Before he'd arrived at Bluebell Cottage, Jason would have thought that was some spiritual mumbo-jumbo, but now he wasn't so sure. All he knew was that he needed to leave, to get out into the fresh air and be alone for a while. He wouldn't tell anyone what Alicia had shared with him, not even Katie. He didn't want his pregnant wife picturing the horror of the train wreck or envisioning his parents' final moments. By the time he returned to Redmond Hall, he would be his old self, his private pain locked away deep inside him.

"Thank you, Mrs. Lysander," Jason said as he stood to leave. "I appreciate your assistance."

"I'm sorry to have caused you pain, but I thought it necessary," Alicia Lysander replied. Her gaze was soft and sympathetic.

Jason nodded, unsure how to reply. Alicia Lysander had proved her point. Or had she? He couldn't be sure, but he was willing to approach what she'd shared with him with an open mind, particularly the revelation that all the guests had some connection to Roger Stillman. That he could easily believe.

But what possible connection could there have been between Sarah Haze and Roger Stillman? Walking down the stone path toward the curricle, Jason wondered if the two could have met while Daniel and Sarah lived in London all those years ago. Was it possible that Sarah and Roger Stillman had been romantically involved? Roger Stillman was a good-looking man, and Sarah had been left on her own quite a bit in those days, since Daniel had worked the night shift several times a week. Had Sarah known that Roger Stillman would be at the séance? Was that why she had decided to attend? Had there been some unfinished business between Sarah and the victim, or was their meeting a mere coincidence that had nothing to do with his death?

Jason climbed into the curricle and took up the reins. He still had several hours until he had to collect Micah from school, and with Daniel in London, this was the perfect time to get Sarah on her own and conduct the interview without his interference. Forcibly putting his parents' suffering from his mind, Jason headed back to Birch Hill.

Chapter 21

"Jason, what a pleasant surprise," Sarah exclaimed when Tilda showed him into the drawing room. She was alone, a book she'd been reading in her lap. Sarah smiled, but the smile was overly bright, as was her gaze, which radiated anxiety. She knew why he was there and was bracing herself for the inevitable.

"Sarah, this is just a formality," Jason reassured her as he sat down across from her, although he was no longer sure that was strictly true. Still, there was no sense in alarming her when all he had to go on was the word of a psychic. "I need to ask you a couple of questions and then I'll be on my way. I'm collecting Micah from school this afternoon."

Sarah nodded. Normally, she would have inquired how Micah was getting on and asked after Katherine's health, but small talk seemed beyond her just then. "Daniel is not here," she said, her gaze darting toward the door as if she hoped Daniel would suddenly materialize.

"I know," Jason replied softly. "It's you I've come to see."

Sarah looked down at her hands, her head drooping like a flower after the rain.

"How did you come to be at that séance, Sarah?"

"I already told Daniel all this," Sarah replied somewhat defensively as she lifted her head to face Jason. "I know Amelia Tarrant from our time in London. When the Tarrants moved into Ardith Manor, she wrote to me, hoping to renew our acquaintance. She'd recently lost her son," Sarah said, her voice catching with emotion.

"Is that why she invited you to the séance? Because she knew about Felix?"

Sarah nodded. "Only a woman who's lost a child can understand that kind of pain," she whispered, her voice urgent. "I know Daniel thinks I've moved on, but I can't, Jason. Felix is always in my thoughts. I love Charlotte to bits, but there's a hole in my heart where Felix was that no one can fill."

She pulled a handkerchief from her sleeve and dabbed at her eyes. "Amelia Tarrant is not a gullible woman," Sarah went on in a rush. "She's shrewd and pragmatic and would never allow herself to be duped. When she told me she believed Mrs. Lysander to possess genuine ability, I believed her. I would have never agreed otherwise."

"Yes, I heard good things about her," Jason said as neutrally as he could manage. "Sarah, I'm not questioning your decision to connect with your boy or passing judgement," he said gently, "but I do want to talk to you about the murder."

"I don't know anything," Sarah exclaimed. "I was so nervous, I barely noticed the others. I only accepted a drink to calm my nerves."

"Were you introduced to the other guests, or was there an element of anonymity?" Jason asked.

"Yes, we were introduced, but that's as far as our interaction went. We never spoke to each other. There was an atmosphere of mute expectation in the room. It was palpable. We were all preparing ourselves for what was to come."

"Who poured the drinks?" Jason asked.

"Amelia served everyone herself. She didn't want anyone present in the room aside from the participants."

"Did anyone else take Scotch?" Jason asked.

Sarah looked blank. "I didn't notice. I had sherry."

"Did you see anyone besides Amelia Tarrant near the decanter of Scotch?"

"No, but I wasn't really paying attention."

"Try to remember, Sarah. Did Mr. Stillman seem more nervous than the rest?"

Sarah tilted her head to the side as she considered the question. "He was nervous to start with but seemed to grow more agitated once it was time to begin. He squeezed my hand tight when we sat around the table, and his fingers were icy."

"Had you met Mr. Stillman before?" Jason asked, slipping in the question just when Sarah might have thought they were almost finished.

Sarah looked surprised. "No. The only person I knew was Amelia."

"Are you sure? Perhaps when you lived in London?" Jason persisted.

Sarah shook her head. "I would have remembered." She colored slightly as she met his gaze. "He was rather good looking. I think I would recall meeting him."

Jason nodded. "May I speak to Mrs. Elderman now?"

"You wish to question Mother?" Sarah asked, clearly surprised.

"Yes. I'd like to ask her a few questions, if you don't mind."

"No, of course not. I'll go fetch her. She's in the nursery with Charlotte."

Harriet Elderman entered the room a few minutes later and took the seat Sarah had vacated. She smiled at Jason warmly. "How are you, Jason? Are you here in your professional capacity? Daniel tells us you've been asked to take the lead on this case."

"I'd much rather pay a social call on you all," Jason replied diplomatically. "But I'm afraid I do need to ask you some questions."

"You're helping Daniel, and for that, I'm grateful, and so is Sarah, even if she hasn't said so. I honestly don't know how you do what you do," she said, shaking her head in wonder. "I've seen a few corpses in my day, but to cut them up and examine their insides does seem a bit ghoulish to me. You must have a stronger stomach and a stiffer spine than most men."

"I prefer to operate on the living, Mrs. Elderman. To know that I helped someone or saved their life is the only validation I need as a surgeon, but since I'm unable to practice medicine in my current situation, I'm glad to know that I can help bring about justice for those who can no longer speak for themselves."

"You're an idealistic man," Harriet said. "And an ambitious one."

"How do you mean?"

"Well, here you are, leading the investigation in lieu of Daniel. Next thing you know, you'll be an inspector in your own right." Jason sensed a hint of resentment in her words and decided it was time to bring Harriet's speculations to a close.

"I have no desire to become an inspector, Mrs. Elderman. Had I not taken the case, it would have been turned over to a man from Scotland Yard, and their handling of the suspects might not have been as gentle," Jason reminded her. "Now, if you don't mind, I'd like to talk about the murder."

"I don't see how I can help. I wasn't there," Harriet said, visibly embarrassed by Jason's rebuke.

"I know, but you're a student of human nature," Jason said, hoping to flatter her into cooperation.

Harriet inclined her head in acknowledgement.

"How well do you know Amelia Tarrant?"

"Not well at all. I met her at the fete, and then when Sarah invited her to tea. I thought her good company," Harriet added.

"Did Sarah tell you she was going to attend a séance?" Jason asked.

Harriet glanced toward the window, her shoulders drooping with guilt. "Yes," she said at last. "I lied to Daniel and told him she'd been invited to an evening of cards."

"Had you heard of Mrs. Lysander before Sarah mentioned the séance?"

"Yes, I'd heard of her, which was why I didn't discourage Sarah from attending. I thought Mrs. Lysander might be able to help."

"What could Mrs. Lysander have said that would bring Sarah peace?" Jason asked. The question had nothing to do with the investigation, but he was curious what people hoped to hear when attending a séance.

"If she had passed on the message that Felix was well and happy, Sarah would have felt better."

Or perhaps, Jason thought, Sarah needed to know that Felix didn't blame her for his death. Had she held on to his hand more firmly, he might not have run under the wheels of the carriage and been crushed. But would a three-year-old child know to blame someone or be able to offer words of comfort to a grieving mother? Jason didn't believe so, but grief wasn't a rational emotion, and neither was forgiveness. Sarah needed to forgive herself in order to finally let Felix go and get on with her life. He supposed she resented Roger Stillman's untimely death and lamented her failed attempt to connect with Felix one last time. Jason wondered if she might try again, but now that Daniel was on to her, he didn't think it would be as easy.

"Mrs. Elderman, had you ever met Mr. Stillman?" Jason asked. "Perhaps while your husband was still with us."

Harriet made a show of thinking. "Roger Stillman was considerably younger than my husband, so I don't see how they might have met. It would be more likely that Mr. Elderman may have known Roger Stillman's father, but I don't recall the name ever being mentioned."

Jason watched Harriet intently as she answered but saw no signs of subterfuge. He thought that perhaps Roger Stillman had tried to court Sarah before she became engaged to Daniel, but that didn't appear to be the case. Perhaps Alicia Lysander was wrong about Sarah's connection to Roger Stillman. He was sure she was far from infallible.

"Thank you for speaking to me," Jason said as he stood to leave.

He hadn't expected to learn much from either Sarah or Harriet, but he was still somewhat disappointed. There had been a killer at the séance. Surely they must have done something to betray themselves, even something as minute as watching their victim or passing close to the drink Roger Stillman had been about to consume. The killer had managed to get the arsenic into the glass somehow, unless it had already been mixed into the Scotch, which would mean that the person had managed to gain access to the drawing room before the others had arrived. That would point to Mrs. Tarrant, but what reason did she have to kill Roger Stillman? Jason would have to speak to her again, he decided, and there was no time like the present.

Chapter 22

Ardith Hall looked like a slumbering beast, its bulk resting on frost-covered ground amid the sprawling park that looked gloomy beneath an overcast sky. Despite its sizeable staff, there were no signs of activity, no sense of life passing behind the numerous windows. Jason pulled up before the entrance, jumped down, tossed the reins to the groom who'd materialized at his side, and knocked on the door.

When it finally opened, a startled Innes stared back at him, his surprise at seeing Jason again evident.

"I'd like to speak to Mrs. Tarrant," Jason said.

"Ah, yes. Of course, sir. If you'll just wait here a moment."

Innes disappeared and returned a few moments later. "Mrs. Tarrant will see you in the drawing room, sir."

Jason surrendered his greatcoat, hat, and gloves and followed the butler to the drawing room.

Mrs. Tarrant sat by the window, an embroidery hoop in her lap. Today she wore a simple gown of mauve wool trimmed with black velvet, and her hair was gathered into a hairnet held in place by matching black velvet ribbon. She clearly hadn't been expecting any visitors and wore a put-upon expression. Mrs. Tarrant set the hoop aside and came forward to greet him, belatedly rearranging her features into an expression of welcome.

"How nice to see you again, my lord," she said, holding out her hand as if this were nothing more than a routine social call.

"The pleasure is all mine, Mrs. Tarrant," Jason replied, taking her hand and bowing over it politely. He had no wish to put the woman on her guard, if she wasn't already.

"Do sit down. Can I offer you some refreshment?" Mrs. Tarrant asked as she settled on the butter-yellow settee.

Jason sat on a matching settee across from her. "Thank you, no," he said.

Mrs. Tarrant looked at him quizzically, as if she couldn't fathom why he was there.

"Mrs. Tarrant, I have a few more questions to put to you," Jason said.

"Of course. How can I help?" she asked, sounding resigned to her fate.

"You told us on the night of the séance that Mr. Stillman, Mr. Forbes, and Lord Sumner were all business associates of your husband. Is that correct?"

"Yes, it is," Mrs. Tarrant replied.

"Yet you also said that the men had never met before that night. I find that somewhat puzzling," Jason said, watching the woman to see if she would become flustered. She didn't.

"Yes, I see how you would find that odd, but it's easily enough explained," Mrs. Tarrant said. She looked perfectly calm, like a woman who had nothing to hide. "John never speaks to me of the business side of things. He doesn't think I'll understand, and frankly, I am not all that interested. I am, however, interested in any of his associates who might be unmarried, on account of Flora. That's our daughter," she hastened to remind him. "Flora is twenty-four and still unspoken for. She's a source of great worry to us, Lord Redmond. It's not that she lacks the necessary qualities to attract a man, but she holds some rather radical ideas that tend to put potential suitors off."

"Such as?" Jason asked, genuinely curious.

Mrs. Tarrant sighed heavily. "Flora believes that women should have more rights. She sees no reason women shouldn't be allowed to vote, for instance, or why they should legally surrender their property to their husbands once they marry. She's rather vocal about her beliefs, which, as you might imagine, is very off-putting to potential suitors."

Jason smiled, wishing he could meet this firebrand. "I don't think her ideas are radical at all, Mrs. Tarrant. I've met many a woman who's vastly more intelligent than her male counterpart. I don't believe the powers that be will ever allow women to vote, but I see nothing wrong with a woman owning property and managing it the way she sees fit."

"You're kind to say so, my lord, but I doubt you would ever consider marrying such a harridan," Mrs. Tarrant said, smiling at him sadly.

"You wouldn't say that if you were better acquainted with my wife," Jason replied, a grin tugging at his lips. He had no doubt Katherine would support the idea of a women's vote if such a thing were a possibility. "Lady Redmond is intelligent and independent, traits that I find admirable and have no wish to suppress."

"At any rate," Mrs. Tarrant went on, "John invited the gentlemen to dine with us, one by one, in the hope that they might take an interest in Flora. Sadly, his efforts were in vain. Mr. Forbes was married already, something John wasn't aware of. Lord Sumner was newly betrothed to Lady Anne Weathers, and Mr. Stillman's affections appeared to be engaged elsewhere."

"Did Flora come downstairs at any point before the séance?" Jason asked.

"No. Flora is of the opinion that psychics are parasites who feed on the grief and desperation of the bereaved and use parlor tricks to fool their gullible followers while lining their pocket with their marks' hard-earned coin. She went up after tea and remained in her room until morning."

"Nevertheless, I'd like to speak to her," Jason said.

"What? Why?" Mrs. Tarrant cried, losing her composure for the first time.

"She sounds like an observant young lady, and since she'd previously met the gentlemen who attended the séance, she might be able to help me paint a clearer picture of their character."

"I see," Mrs. Tarrant said, sounding somewhat mollified.

"Mrs. Tarrant," Jason said, finally getting to the real reason he was there, "who besides Innes had access to the decanter and the bottle of Scotch he opened on the night of the murder?"

Mrs. Tarrant looked bewildered. "Why, no one. Except me," she admitted grudgingly. "My John has no taste for whisky, so we stock it strictly for guests. I knew Mr. Stillman preferred Scotch from his previous visits, so I asked Innes to bring up a new bottle. He keeps all spirits under lock and key," she said, reminding Jason that it was the butler's duty to safeguard the alcohol. "Innes was suddenly called away, so I opened the bottle myself and poured the contents into the empty decanter just before Mr. Stillman arrived. As I said on the night of the séance, none of the servants had entered the room nor had any of the guests come near it."

"Which would mean that you were the only person who had the opportunity to poison the man," Jason pointed out.

Mrs. Tarrant stared at him, her cheeks turning a mottled red with indignation. "But why would I wish to poison Roger Stillman? I scarcely knew the man."

"So, why did you invite him, then?"

"I only wanted to make contact with my Hector," Mrs. Tarrant whined pitifully. "I would have been glad to do so in private, but Mrs. Lysander said the séances work best when there are a number of people present. She said the spirits are drawn to their grief and are more likely to appear. Six is the perfect number, she said," Mrs. Tarrant explained, her gaze pleading with Jason to understand. "So I wrote to several ladies of my acquaintance, but they refused the invitation."

"Which forced you to widen your net," Jason concluded.

"Precisely. I knew that Mr. Forbes had recently lost his wife, and Lord Sumner was grieving the death of his fiancée. And Mr. Stillman had recently lost someone close to him as well. John had mentioned it. So I wrote to them, asking if they might wish to participate. And, of course, I knew that Mrs. Haze had lost her dear little boy. I invited her in person when I called on her last week," she added. "Sarah seemed reluctant at first. She didn't think her husband would approve, but when I promised her that no one she knows would be present, she finally agreed."

"Did Mrs. Haze ask who would be present?" Jason inquired.

"No, but I told her anyway. I thought the information would put her mind to rest. She did not know any of the gentlemen, so her presence would go unremarked."

"I see," Jason said. "May I speak to Flora now?"

"Yes, if you wish it," Mrs. Tarrant said, an edge creeping into her voice. She seemed to have hoped he'd change his mind about speaking to her daughter.

"I wish it," Jason replied. "And I would like to speak to her in private," he added.

Chapter 23

Mrs. Tarrant bustled from the room and returned a few minutes later with a dark-haired young woman. Mrs. Tarrant made the introductions and left the room, as requested, leaving Jason alone with her daughter.

Flora perched on the settee and folded her hands in her lap demurely, studying Jason as if he were a curiosity. He supposed to someone like her, he was. He was quite intrigued by her himself. Unlike her mother, Flora wasn't observing half-mourning and wore a tartan gown of blue and green, a matching ribbon wound through her hair. A delicate emerald pendant and matching earrings completed the ensemble.

"How can I help you, my lord?" Her dark gaze was direct and seemed to be challenging him, a small smile playing about her full lips. Jason felt an instant kinship with her.

"I'd like to ask you a few questions about the gentlemen who were your mother's guests on the night of the séance. She said you'd met them before. I'd be interested to hear your impressions of them."

"And will you take what I tell you seriously or disregard the bits you don't care for because I'm a woman?"

"I will hang on every word and take it as gospel," Jason replied, unable to keep from grinning.

She grinned back, amused by his response. "All right. I suppose you'll want to hear about the victim first?"

"No, I'd like to hear about the other two men before you get to Mr. Stillman," Jason said, curious to hear if her opinion of them aligned with his.

"All right. My father invited Mr. Forbes to dine with us when he last visited London. It was at the end of May. Despite the fact that Mr. Forbes was never really a matrimonial prospect, given that he was already married, I found him to be intelligent, well-mannered, and charming. Having been born to a slave, he could relate to my views on women's rights, which are nonexistent in this country, in case you were wondering," she added acidly. "Had he been single and interested, I would have enjoyed seeing him again," she added, a bit wistfully. "And I think the feeling was mutual."

"And Lord Sumner?"

"Lord Sumner is a typical representative of his class. Spoiled, pompous, and entitled, but not so elitist as to ignore a promising business opportunity. From what I gather, unlike most noblemen, who rely on their estates for income, he is quite proactive in improving his financial situation—which has been undermined by his father's lifelong love of cards—through trade. He made for an amusing dinner companion, but he was clearly besotted with Lady Anne Weathers, to whom he became engaged shortly after we met. In either case, he's not the type of person who would ever marry beneath him."

"Did you ever meet Lady Anne?"

"No, I'm afraid we didn't move in the same circles," Flora Tarrant replied with a defiant thrust of her chin.

"Now tell me about Roger Stillman," Jason invited.

"I met Roger Stillman at the end of October. I must admit that he was something of an enigma."

"In what way?"

"He was scrupulously polite, well mannered, and attentive, but I sensed a sadness in him, a deep grief that he couldn't share with anyone."

"Was he in mourning?" Jason asked.

"No. Not even an armband, which led me to believe that the person he grieved for had not been someone he could openly acknowledge."

"A woman, do you think?"

"Most likely. Or a child. Perhaps a son or a daughter who'd been born out of wedlock."

Jason nodded. That wasn't a prospect he'd considered. Was it possible that Roger Stillman had a family no one knew about? "Did he mention his loss?" he asked.

"No, but my father said someone close to him had died quite recently," Flora replied.

"How did your father know? Did Mr. Stillman confide in him?"

"I don't think Mr. Stillman was the type of person to confide in anyone, but it's not difficult to figure out, is it? Some people wear their grief like a suit of armor."

Yes, they do, Jason thought. And some simply moved on, as his fiancée Cecilia had done when she'd heard he'd been imprisoned and might already be dead. She'd simply married his best friend and got on with her life.

"I think we as a society spend too much time grieving," Flora said. "My brother died nearly three years ago, but my mother has yet to accept his death. Death is part of life and must be accepted as such. We should live while we can, not spend years observing silly rituals that make our grief that much more difficult to bear. Of course, some people prefer to shut themselves away until they're ready to face the world again, but there are others who need to get out, to be around other people, and to enjoy what life has to offer in order to make peace with their loss. Grief should be private," Flora added.

"I couldn't agree more," Jason said. He liked Flora more and more and hoped she'd find a man who would appreciate her passion and candor.

"I'm sorry, Lord Redmond, I tend to go off topic when something upsets me. Please, go on. Do you have any more questions for me?"

"Only a few more. Have you ever met Mrs. Haze?" Jason asked.

"You mean Sarah? Yes, I have met her several times, in London, when the Hazes lived there, and then more recently here in Essex. I like her very much," Flora said. "She's the sort of woman I find easiest to talk to."

"Why is that?"

"Because she's not a blank slate, like most of the unmarried women I'm forced to spend time with, nor is she like the married women, who seem to think only of their husbands' needs and their children's future prospects. She has thoughts, ideas. She has courage."

"Yes, Sarah Haze is a remarkable woman," Jason agreed.

"Partly because she is married to a man who doesn't stifle her," Flora said wistfully. "I would rather enjoy being married to a police inspector. I think it would be wonderfully stimulating to discuss the various cases he's working on and speculate as to the motive and opportunity and such."

Jason smiled, thinking that Katherine would wholeheartedly agree with Flora. They would form a fast friendship if they ever met. "Thank you, Miss Tarrant, for sharing your thoughts and observations with me."

"I hope you found them helpful."

"I did," Jason said as he got to his feet. "And now I will wish you a good day."

"Good day, my lord." Flora Tarrant held out her hand to him. "Perhaps in a different world, we might have made a connection," she said, her eyes reflecting the sadness in her soul. Life was very lonely when one wasn't understood.

Jason smiled and kissed her hand. "You are a delight, Miss Tarrant. Don't ever change," he said, and absolutely meant it.

Retrieving his things, Jason put on his greatcoat, hat, and gloves, and allowed the butler to see him out. While he had been inside, the clouds had parted, and a weak sun shone in a pale blue sky, the park beyond no longer forbidding but a winter wonderland sparkling playfully in the gentle light. Jason consulted his pocket watch. It was nearly time to pick up Micah, and his heart lifted at the thought. He missed the boy and couldn't wait to hear all about his first term at Westbridge Academy.

Chapter 24

Daniel arrived in Charing Cross Station at a quarter past eleven and proceeded directly to Brown's Hotel, where Mr. Forbes was staying. Daniel had never been inside a London hotel and inspected his surroundings discreetly, impressed with the hotel's quiet comfort and unpretentious luxury. The wood paneling glowed in the soft light of the gas lamps. There were urns of fresh flowers and several groupings of armchairs and low tables in an area just off the reception area, where the guests could read a newspaper, smoke a cigar, or enjoy a cup of coffee or tea.

Approaching the reception desk, Daniel identified himself and asked for Mr. Forbes. The smiling clerk behind the desk instantly turned frosty, either because he didn't relish having a policeman on the premises or because Mr. Forbes was not the type of guest the hotel normally welcomed, and Daniel's presence confirmed his worst suspicions. Most people were deeply mistrustful of foreigners, especially those of color, and many an establishment would not rent them a room or serve them in their dining room, no matter how wealthy and influential the patron happened to be.

"I think it's best if you go directly to Mr. Forbes' room, Inspector," the clerk suggested. "The setting is more conducive to private discourse," he explained. "I assume this is a conversation you wouldn't wish to be overheard."

Daniel concluded that this was a conversation the hotel staff wouldn't wish to be overheard by other guests, but that was fine with him. He hoped Mr. Forbes would be more forthcoming in a private setting than when surrounded by other guests and hotel staff.

The room was on the second floor, facing the rear of the building. Unlike the reception area downstairs, there were no bells or whistles here, just a plain, serviceable room with a bed and a small seating area.

"Ah, Inspector Haze," Mr. Forbes said. "I must admit, I didn't expect to see you again so soon. Do come in and make yourself comfortable."

Daniel and Nathaniel Forbes settled in the provided chairs and faced each other across the small space.

"How can I help?" Mr. Forbes asked when Daniel failed to explain the purpose of his visit quickly enough for his satisfaction.

"It has come to my attention that you and Mr. Stillman were in business together," Daniel said. "Which would mean that you lied to us about having known the man."

Mr. Forbes leaned back in his chair. He didn't seem surprised by Daniel's accusation, nor did he appear worried. In fact, he seemed annoyingly relaxed.

"I told you the truth, Inspector. Roger Stillman and I had never met in person. Yes, we had been doing business together for several years, but all his dealings were with Mr. Gilbert, my man of business. You see, Inspector, when cultivating new business relationships, I leave it to Mr. Gilbert to go in my stead."

"Why?" Daniel asked, although he could guess at the answer easily enough.

"Because he's white," Mr. Forbes replied. "People like Roger Stillman don't much care where their goods come from, but they have no wish to be seen in the company of a black man, particularly here in London. I did have an appointment to see Mr. Stillman in his office the following week. Wednesday, to be precise. I'm sure his clerk, Mr. Osbourne, will confirm that."

"Why were you coming to see him face to face now, after all this time?" Daniel asked.

"Because the man was cheating me, Inspector Haze. I realize you'll now think this gives me a motive for murder, but I assure you, I had no reason to kill him. There are many dishonest businessmen, and murder is not the way to bring them to heel."

"I see. And how was he cheating you, Mr. Forbes?"

"Mr. Stillman was buying an agreed-upon number of cases of rum and was shipping them on to the United States. He kept our labels on the bottles."

"I don't see how that's—" Daniel began, but Mr. Forbes held up his hand to indicate he hadn't finished.

"Mr. Stillman had a forger duplicate the labels and create additional bottles. He then diluted my rum and sold it at a lower price to dockside taverns and brothels. Not only did he knowingly decrease the value and reputation of my product, he kept the additional profits, which were considerable, for himself."

"And how did you plan to address this situation?" Daniel asked.

"I was hoping we could come to an agreement regarding the quality of the product and the distribution of profit."

"How?" Daniel asked. "Did you think Mr. Stillman would simply apologize and compensate you for the funds he'd appropriated?"

"No, I didn't, but I'm on good terms with the other plantation owners on the island and could easily make life very difficult for Mr. Stillman should he refuse to come to an agreement. He would have to buy his rum elsewhere if the others found out what he was up to."

"So, you would offer to keep his secret as long as you were recompensed?" Daniel asked. *Some would call that blackmail*, Daniel thought, but kept that opinion to himself for the moment.

"In essence, yes. It's not my responsibility to apprise the other planters of what Mr. Stillman was doing once he took possession of the product. It's up to them to protect their own interests."

"And you would permit him to continue to dilute the rum?" Daniel asked. He didn't know much about business, but it seemed to him that Mr. Forbes would be letting Mr. Stillman get off easy when the man was undermining the reputation of his product.

"I thought perhaps we could agree on distributing two separate products: a low-quality rum for the taverns and a higher-quality rum for the finer establishments, which would be shipped under a new label."

"And did you think Mr. Stillman would be open to your proposal, given that you had never met in person and he didn't care to deal with someone he thought inferior?" Daniel asked.

Mr. Forbes winced slightly at Daniel's brutal words but didn't take the bait. "Inspector, business is business. If we could agree on mutually beneficial terms, I don't think Roger Stillman would care much about the color of my skin, especially if the meeting took place in the privacy of his office."

"But he was cheating you, Mr. Forbes," Daniel reminded him. "People have killed for less."

"I'm sure they have, but I had no idea Mr. Stillman would be at the séance at Ardith Hall. Mrs. Tarrant's husband and I have known each other for many years, and Mrs. Tarrant invited me based on the strength of that friendship."

"How do you know Mr. Tarrant?" Daniel asked.

"He comes to Barbados quite frequently. He is a shipping agent."

"I see," Daniel said. "What happens to your product now that Mr. Stillman is dead?"

"Nothing," Nathaniel Forbes answered with a shrug. "I find a new distributor. There's no shortage of men looking to make a profit."

"And will you be sending Mr. Gilbert forth to make those connections for you, Mr. Forbes?" Daniel asked, trying once again to get under the man's skin.

"That depends on their reputation, Inspector, and the depth of their prejudice. It's not against the law to send a representative in one's stead, is it?"

"No, it isn't," Daniel conceded. "How much longer will you be in London?"

"I sail back on January fifteenth," Mr. Forbes answered. "And I seriously doubt you'll find a reason to detain me. Now, if you're finished with your questions, I have an appointment to get to."

"Thank you for your time, Mr. Forbes. I'll see myself out," Daniel said, and left.

Chapter 25

Stepping outside, Daniel decided to walk to the East India Club. The air was brisk, but he could use the exercise and the time to think. In this affluent part of town, the streets weren't too crowded, and weak sunshine shone from a pale blue sky, giving a false impression of warmth. This was the type of winter day Daniel liked best. He slowed his steps so as not to get to his destination too quickly, and made the most of this opportunity.

Nathaniel Forbes had clearly had the motive and the opportunity to administer the arsenic on the night of the séance, but it seemed to Daniel that he didn't have much to gain by poisoning Roger Stillman. If it were a matter of satisfying his honor, using rat poison surely wasn't the way to accomplish that, and he would not recoup his losses by killing the man. The shipping line had confirmed that Mr. Forbes had indeed arrived in England on December fifteenth, so he would not have had the time to dispense the amount of ground glass Jason had found in Roger Stillman's stomach, at least not in person.

It's an awfully impractical way to kill a man, Daniel thought as he walked on. It smacked of visceral hatred, the type that ate at one's soul and stole one's peace of mind, and Daniel hadn't seen any signs of such strong feeling in Nathaniel Forbes. Unless he was a consummate actor—and Daniel didn't think he was, based on the bitterness and anger he'd allowed himself to show on the night of the séance—the method of murder just didn't fit with his personality. Daniel mentally moved Nathaniel Forbes to the bottom of the list of suspects and hoped he'd learn something useful at the club.

The East India Club was housed in an elegant building in St. James's Square, the imposing façade and the location a silent reminder of the prestigious nature of its membership. Daniel was in no doubt that the powers-that-be wouldn't welcome a police investigation and would do their best to steer it away from their stately doors. He entered and was immediately approached by the secretary, who manned the door like some mythical gatekeeper.

"Good afternoon, sir. How can I help you?" the man asked, looking like the only thing he wanted to help with was Daniel's swift exit from the premises.

Daniel held up his warrant card. "I'm Inspector Haze of the Essex Police. I'm here regarding the murder of one of your members, Mr. Roger Stillman. I need to ask you a few questions and speak to anyone who might have known him."

"I'm sorry, Inspector, but I cannot permit you to enter," the secretary said in an annoying nasal tone.

"This is police business," Daniel snapped, trying to keep his irritation in check. He hated these types of establishments that cared only for their own reputation.

"I didn't say I wouldn't help," the secretary replied, affecting a tone of false patience. "I only said I can't allow you to come inside. Club rules, I'm afraid." He motioned to a member of staff. "Jones, watch the door a while. There's a good man. Please, follow me, Inspector."

The secretary led Daniel into a small parlor that must have been reserved for private meetings or discreet conversations best kept away from the public rooms of the club. There were four comfortable wingchairs grouped around a low table where refreshments might be served. A thick rug in shades of blue and cream picked up the neutral tones of the damask drapes held back with thick tasseled cords. A fire burned in the grate, and the room smelled pleasantly of polish and affluence.

"Do sit, Inspector Haze," the man invited.

"What is your name?" Daniel asked as he settled in one of the wingchairs and withdrew his notepad.

"Dustin Wentworth. I'm a senior member of staff," he added, seemingly eager to underline his own importance. "Now, tell me about this murder."

Daniel filled him in on the details and watched the man's eyes grow wide with amazement. "Ground glass, you say? Well, that would never have occurred here. We uphold the highest standards in our kitchen. Our chef has been with us for nigh on twenty years."

Daniel nodded. He wasn't really interested in the club's kitchen. He didn't for a moment think that someone would have been so bold as to try to feed the man ground glass in an establishment of this caliber. It'd be too risky and impractical. He was more interested in the individuals Stillman had come in contact with.

"Mr. Wentworth, how long has Mr. Stillman been a member of the club?"

"Even since he returned from India, so about ten years now."

"And whom did he spend time with when he was here?" Daniel asked.

"Mr. Stillman was a solitary man, Inspector. Despite his longstanding membership, he didn't associate with too many people. There are two members with whom he dined regularly, though, Mr. Charles Hornsby and Mr. Hamish Dunbar."

"I'd like to speak to them," Daniel said. He didn't expect the men to be at the club at present, but he hoped Wentworth would furnish him with their addresses.

"As it happens, Mr. Hornsby is here now. He often takes luncheon in the dining room. Mr. Dunbar is away, I'm told," Wentworth added.

"I see. Well, I'd like to speak to Mr. Hornsby right away."

"If you'll wait here, I will see if he's available," Mr. Wentworth said.

"Please impress on him the urgency of my request," Daniel said. The words stuck in his throat, but he needed to play the game to gain results. Demanding that the man speak with him would get him nowhere, and he'd have to discover his address and call on him at home in hopes of more fruitful results.

Thankfully, Mr. Hornsby was eager to speak to Daniel. He burst into the parlor, his gaze anxious, his face ashen. He was a slight man with brown hair and brown eyes and the tanned skin of someone who'd spent a considerable part of their life in warmer climes.

"Roger has been murdered?" he cried. "Please tell me there's been a mistake, Inspector. It is Roger Stillman of Stillman Imports you're speaking of?"

"Yes, Mr. Hornsby. I'm afraid it is."

Charles Hornsby plopped into a chair and seemed to slide downward, as if his spine had turned to putty. He hunched over, his shoulders slumped as he covered his face with his hands. Daniel thought he might be crying and looked away to give the man a moment to compose himself. When Hornsby finally looked up, his eyes were red-rimmed and his cheeks damp. He extracted a handkerchief, dabbed at his eyes, wiped his cheeks, and folded it neatly before replacing it in his pocket. He then sat up straighter, squaring his shoulders as if expecting an interrogation rather than just a friendly chat. The transformation in his manner was remarkable, almost theatrical, Daniel thought.

"How? How did it happen?" Mr. Hornsby demanded.

Daniel explained once again what had happened and waited for Mr. Hornsby to process the information before asking him any questions.

"I don't understand," the man said, staring at Daniel in some confusion. "You are telling me that there were two attempts on his life, and the second was successful because of the first?"

"Yes, that's correct," Daniel replied.

"But who would want to do such a thing?"

"That's what I'm trying to find out," Daniel replied patiently. "Please, tell me about your relationship with Mr. Stillman."

"Roger and I were the best of friends. True confidants," Charles Hornsby said. "We met in India and became inseparable. You know how it goes, two young men, away from home for the first time in an exotic and unfamiliar land. We were overcome with the sights and sounds of the East, intoxicated by its beauty."

Once again, Daniel got the impression that the man was overly affected. It was almost as if he were delivering a monologue on stage rather than talking to a police inspector, which made it difficult to imagine him as the confidant of someone who was as private and selective as Roger Stillman appeared to have been.

"Did Mr. Stillman have any enemies?" Daniel asked, watching the man for any telltale signs of surprise or subversion.

"There were people he didn't see eye to eye with, certainly, but I wouldn't call them enemies. Men of business always have those who would be glad to see them fail."

"Mr. Hornsby, Mr. Stillman received a threatening letter at his office in October. Can you think of anyone who might have sent such a thing?"

Hornsby shook his head. "I really can't. If there was any unpleasantness, especially of a business nature, it generally happened face to face, not by anonymous letter."

"Whom do you think Mr. Stillman wished to contact at the séance?" Daniel asked. He was despairing of learning anything useful from Charles Hornsby.

Charles Hornsby hung his head again, as if preparing for a tragic scene. "Her," he said.

"Her?"

Mr. Hornsby sighed dramatically. "Roger never divulged her name to me."

"Why? I thought you were true confidants."

Charles Hornsby colored slightly. "Despite my best efforts, I've been indiscreet on more than one occasion."

"I see," Daniel said. That he could believe. "Can you tell me something about this woman?" he invited calmly, but he was fuming inside. Finally, he had a clue, but without a name, it was worthless.

"Roger met her in June, at a house party he had been invited to. I don't know if you're familiar with such gatherings, Inspector, but they generally last a few weeks during the summer, an opportunity for people to get away from the heat and pollution of the city without dying of boredom in some remote village, with only themselves for company."

Daniel nodded. What would he know of house parties? The only opportunities he'd had to get away from heat and pollution were brief trips to the seaside, once when he was a boy, and once after he and Sarah were married and spent a few days in Brighton.

"She was there with her cousin. Roger was not given to romantic notions, but I believe it was love at first sight. He was smitten."

"And did the woman in question return his feelings?" Daniel asked, surprised to hear about this side of Roger Stillman, who up to this point had seemed like someone who wouldn't allow himself to be ruled by his emotions. But he had come to the séance, so perhaps he hadn't been as controlled as he'd liked people to believe.

"Yes. It seems she felt the same. They spent a few idyllic weeks together in Suffolk, but things didn't quite work out as Roger had hoped once they returned to London."

"In what way, Mr. Hornsby?" Daniel asked.

"Her father refused Roger's offer of marriage and encouraged his daughter to accept someone else. She did."

"So, Mr. Stillman was spurned by this woman?"

"Indeed, he was. He was heartbroken. And so was she, according to the letters she sent him, but she wasn't brave enough to stand up to her father. Or maybe she only told him so to soften the blow. Or maybe it hadn't been love at all, just a pleasant diversion to make her stay in the country more enjoyable. She had toyed with him, Inspector; that's my belief. Then she simply got on with her life."

"If Mr. Stillman was trying to contact her through Mrs. Lysander, that would mean the lady had died," Daniel observed, watching Charles Hornsby. He seemed to have forgotten that small fact.

"Ah, yes," Mr. Hornsby said, rearranging his face into an expression of sorrow. "She did. She passed in October.."

"Had Mr. Stillman seen her after she rejected his proposal?" Daniel asked.

"I don't believe so. He never said. Perhaps they met by accident. Perhaps not."

"Were you aware that Roger Stillman kept a mistress?"

"Yes, Elise Prentiss," Charles Hornsby said, coloring again. Daniel would wager it had been Mrs. Prentiss whom Hornsby had been indiscreet about, probably assuming a mistress didn't deserve the same respect as a wife.

"It seems Mr. Stillman had ended the relationship and withdrawn his patronage sometime in June," Daniel said.

"Yes. Roger ended things with Elise as soon as he returned from Suffolk."

"And how did Mrs. Prentiss take the rejection?" Daniel asked.

Charles Hornsby looked at Daniel wistfully and shook his head. "Inspector, I'm most impressed with your investigative powers, but Elise Prentiss did not kill Roger."

"How can you be so certain?" Daniel asked, disappointment rising like bile within him.

"I met Elise before Roger did. In fact, I was the one who introduced them. I maintained a friendship with her throughout her relationship with Roger and knew all the particulars of their ill-fated romance. Elise is an astute woman, Inspector. She realized that Roger had cooled toward her long before he met the other woman. She made arrangements."

"What sort of arrangements?" Daniel asked, intrigued.

"She found another lover, as women like her are wont to do," Charles Hornsby said, looking at Daniel as if he were a simpleton who knew nothing of life. "Her new man is American, and he took her to San Francisco with him. She left London in early July, so she can't be your culprit."

"I see," Daniel said, sounding more resigned than he liked to let on. "Mr. Hornsby, is there anything else you can tell me? Anything you can think of that might have led to Mr. Stillman's death?"

The man shook his head. "Sorry, I really can't. That's all I know."

"What about Mr. Dunbar? Was he a close friend?"

"Yes, he was. I was a little jealous of Hamish, I must admit," Charles Hornsby said, with a guilty little smile. "I was never invited to dine with Roger and Hamish, nor was I asked to visit him at his home in Scotland. I'm not one for grouse shooting or stalking stag, but I would have enjoyed the scenery. It's quite dramatic, I'm told. But," Mr. Hornsby said with an exaggerated sigh, "Roger liked to keep Hamish to himself, even though we'd all known each other since our company days. Thick as thieves, they were, especially of late."

"And where can I find Mr. Dunbar?" Daniel asked, even though Wentworth had told him the man was away.

"Hamish always goes home for Christmas. His family owns a drafty old castle in the Highlands. It's quite medieval, a perfect setting for a gothic story. He should be back after the New Year, or Hogmanay, as he calls it," Mr. Hornsby said with a chortle. "Even the name sounds heathen."

"Can you provide me with the address?"

"Sure." Charles Hornsby chuckled. "Only there are no addresses in places like that, just names. This one is aptly named Dunbar Castle. It's near Edinburgh." Charles Hornsby seemed to have lost interest in the interview, his mind probably already on luncheon or the gossip he would enjoy with the other members, discussing his friend's death. "Well, I wish you luck, Inspector. You have your work cut out for you, it seems. When's the funeral to be, do you know?"

"The body will be released to Mrs. Stillman on Monday," Daniel replied.

"Right. After Christmas, then. Well, I suppose that's best for everyone involved. To ruin Christmas is not the done thing, after all, is it?"

Daniel had no idea what the done thing was when it came to burying someone at Christmas and really didn't care. It seemed odd that Roger Stillman would count someone as superficial as Mr. Hornsby among his closest friends, but then sometimes people had the oddest of reasons for pairing up. He supposed there were some who questioned Daniel's bond with Jason, but it was one of the most satisfying friendships of his life and he hoped never to lose it.

Having finished with Charles Hornsby, Daniel thanked Mr. Wentworth for his assistance and took his leave. He walked over to Oxford Street, where he purchased three bars of lavender soap for his mother-in-law, a pretty pink bauble and a rattle for Charlotte, and a gorgeous maroon and gold silk shawl for Sarah. He smiled as he imagined her wearing it on a chilly evening as they sat in the garden, stars twinkling in the sky above and a soft breeze moving through the trees that whispered their secrets to the romantic couple below.

Finished with his Christmas shopping, he headed to Charing Cross, where he purchased a hot pie from a street vendor and a penny dreadful to read on the train. He would go home, hide the gifts, then call on Jason later tonight to discuss his findings and formulate a plan for tomorrow.

Once aboard the train, Daniel tried to read but found it impossible to concentrate. He was alone in the compartment, so he divested himself of his coat and hat, leaned back against the seat, and closed his eyes, lulled into sleep by the gentle swaying of the railcar.

Chapter 26

Jason smiled happily when Micah emerged from the grand entrance of the Westbridge Academy and hurried down the steps. Micah wore a coat over his school uniform and carried his case in his left hand, and he waved to Jason enthusiastically as he made his way toward the curricle. Given the weather, it would have made more sense to use the brougham, but Jason knew how much Micah enjoyed driving the curricle and thought he wouldn't mind the cold as long as Jason relinquished the reins during the drive home.

Micah climbed into the vehicle and grinned. "Can I drive?"

"Of course," Jason replied.

He was thrilled to see the boy but made no move to hug him in front of his peers. Micah might not like that. He'd still seemed like a boy when Jason had dropped him off at the school at the start of term, but there was a pronounced difference in him, a maturity that hadn't been there before. Gone was the coltish boy, replaced by a self-assured young man. Jason congratulated himself on deciding to send Micah away to school. Perhaps he'd been wrong to coddle him for so long, fearing the separation would traumatize him after the losses he'd suffered during his incarceration at Andersonville Prison at the end of the American Civil War. Micah had clung to him, depending on Jason not only for financial support but for emotional stability, but now it seemed Micah no longer needed him as much.

Micah guided the horses toward the massive wrought-iron gates and into the lane, urging the beautiful animals to go faster once they were in the open countryside.

"How's school?" Jason asked.

Micah shrugged. "Boring, but I did make new friends," he added happily. "I've been invited to spend Easter with Will Hanes' family. Can I go?"

"If you want to, sure," Jason said, and felt a pang of hurt that was followed by a strange hollow feeling in his chest. Was this how parents felt when their children didn't need them anymore? He was glad for Micah. He was doing precisely what a boy his age ought to be doing, but somehow, it still felt like a betrayal.

"How's Liam?" Micah asked.

"He's well. He likes his nursemaid." Jason wanted to tell Micah that Liam missed his mother and if he had the words to express his grief would probably tell Micah so himself, but he wasn't yet two and could only cry when he felt the ache of loneliness. Both Jason and Katherine visited Liam often, playing with him and reading to him so that he wouldn't feel abandoned, but they were a poor substitute for his mother, who'd decided to return to the States unencumbered by a small child. Jason didn't blame her. Mary had been through hell since the outbreak of the Civil War, but he couldn't imagine leaving his own child behind, no matter how good a guardian he'd appointed.

"I miss him," Micah said, his exhilaration at driving the curricle replaced by bitterness. "I still can't believe Mary ran out on us."

"She's doing well, Micah. She's happy," Jason said, quoting Mary's latest missive.

"Yeah?" Micah challenged him. "What about Liam? And what about my happiness? I never thought she'd be so selfish."

Clearly, Mary's desertion still rankled. "I've been assigned my own case," Jason said in an effort to distract Micah from his anger.

"You're in charge?" Micah asked, turning his head just enough to look at Jason, his astonishment apparent. "Are you official now?"

"Well, not official in the true sense of the word, but Daniel can't be the lead on this case. His wife is involved."

Micah let out a low whistle. "Do tell."

Jason filled Micah in on the details of the case, glad to see the bitterness dissipate as he became absorbed in the story.

"Jesus, Mary, and Joseph," Micah exclaimed. "Sarah Haze was there when the cove was snuffed?"

Jason was a little taken aback at the turn of phrase, but he supposed it was normal for Micah to pick up some of the expressions the other boys used.

"Yes, Sarah had gone to the séance to contact her little boy."

Micah nodded, his expression growing morose once more. "It's hard to let go," he said. "The dead are always with you, aren't they?"

Jason almost told Micah about Mrs. Lysander's description of his parents' deaths but stopped himself. He didn't think he could bear to speak of it, but his silence wouldn't make the images go away. Ever since he'd spoken to the psychic, they kept replaying in his brain, the desperate cries of the injured, the terrible smells of coal soot, blood, charred flesh, and impending death. He could almost hear his mother's voice in his head, calling for him, hoping against hope that somehow, he would hear her across the miles and know that she was thinking of him in her final moments. Jason closed his eyes for a moment, wishing he could block out the image of his father, lying on the upturned side of the train carriage, his body twisted, his head smashed, his eyes staring.

"You all right, Captain?" Micah asked, reverting to his usual form of address.

"Of course. Just tired," Jason lied. "Haven't been sleeping well."

"Nervous about the coming baby?" Micah asked wisely.

"I suppose."

"It'll be all right. You'll be a good father to it," Micah said, but his mind was clearly elsewhere. "How's Inspector Haze handling his wife's involvement?"

"Not well. He's terrified she'll be branded a suspect."

"Is she?"

"She didn't know any of the guests at the séance. She'd only met them that night, so no, she's not a suspect. Only a witness at this stage."

"Did she see anything?" Micah asked.

"Doesn't seem so. I think she was too preoccupied with the upcoming séance to notice what anyone else was doing."

"Some women can't let go of their dead children, and others just leave theirs behind, like a bit of rubbish," Micah said angrily, reverting to his earlier train of thought.

"Micah, you will see Mary again someday," Jason said. "You can visit."

Micah shook his head stubbornly. "I'm not going to visit her. If she wants to see us, she can just come here."

"You might feel differently in time," Jason suggested.

"I won't. Mary has made her choice, and I've made mine. Liam and I will be all right without her. And we'll enjoy Christmas."

"Of course we will," Jason said, hoping this Christmas would be less dramatic than the one before.

Micah turned the curricle through the gates of Redmond Hall, and a sweet smile spread across his tense face. "It's good to be home. I hope Mrs. Dodson remembered I was coming today."

Jason chuckled. Mrs. Dodson had been baking for the past two days in anticipation of Micah's return. He was her darling boy, and she'd feed him cakes and pies baked with love until he was fit to burst.

"Can I invite Tom?" Micah asked as they pulled up before the house and Joe came striding from the stable to greet them and see to the carriage and horses. "I have a lot to tell him."

"You don't need to ask permission, Micah. This is your home and always will be."

"Thanks, Captain," Micah threw over his shoulder before he greeted Joe, jumped down from the bench, and ran inside, probably straight to the kitchen and into the ample arms of Mrs. Dodson.

"He's grown," Joe said gruffly as he took hold of the reins. "A proper young gentleman he is now."

"Yes, he is," Jason agreed as he descended from the carriage, the hollow feeling he'd experienced earlier returning in full force.

Chapter 27

When Daniel arrived at Redmond Hall later that afternoon, Jason was pleased to see him. Katherine and Micah had gone up to the nursery to spend some time with Liam before dinner, but Jason was itching to find out what Daniel had discovered in London. He hadn't been pleased to find himself in charge of the case, but now that he was, he found that he couldn't stop thinking about it and needed to feel connected to the investigation at all times.

Dusk had fallen, and the sky beyond the window was already sprinkled with a multitude of stars. The park was nothing more than a dark outline of bare-limbed trees, and a crescent moon hung above the massive gates, its ends as sharp as the points of a sickle. A fire blazed in the hearth, and the drawing room was pleasantly warm and cozy, the perfect setting for their discussion. Daniel took his customary place, accepted a drink, and related the details of his interviews with Mr. Forbes and Mr. Hornsby. He was disappointed by his lack of progress, but Jason rushed to reassure him.

"I think what you've learned is significant, Daniel. Not only had Nathaniel Forbes known Roger Stillman, possibly better than he let on, but he'd been cheated by the man. That's a solid motive for murder."

"I agree. Forbes might have been the one to administer the arsenic, but he couldn't have been responsible for the glass unless he found someone to do it for him. Everyone has their price, and if Forbes paid enough, I'm sure he could have found someone to carry out his plan, though killing Roger Stillman would not recompense him for the money he'd lost," Daniel mused. "But it would appease his wounded pride. A man of his background must be used to being regarded with suspicion and treated with disrespect. Perhaps Roger Stillman's treatment of him was the last straw and Forbes convinced himself that Stillman wouldn't have dared to cheat a white man."

"I highly doubt that," Jason said. "Once a cheat, always a cheat. All the money in the world can't buy honor." Jason took a sip of his drink. "I do wish we could discover the identity of this woman he was in love with. Perhaps the murder had something to do with her untimely death," Jason speculated.

"Charles Hornsby appeared to be jealous of Dunbar's relationship with Roger Stillman. Perhaps the two men were close and Dunbar will know more about Stillman's private life."

"There's something that puzzles me about this case," Jason said.

"What's that, then?" Daniel asked.

"The method. It defies all logic."

Daniel tilted his head to the side, considering Jason's point of view. "I'm not sure I agree. The killer had settled on an unusual murder weapon, but one he could deploy from a distance, ensuring he'd never be connected to the victim's death. When Stillman failed to die, the killer grew frustrated."

"And threw caution to the wind?" Jason asked.

"Perhaps he saw an opportunity to speed matters along and took it," Daniel suggested.

"But how?" Jason asked. "In order to mix ground glass into Stillman's food or drink, the killer would have to gain access to the household, either on his own or through someone else. Supposing he or she had managed to access the kitchen at Stillman's house, that still doesn't explain how on earth they mixed the arsenic into the Scotch. Mrs. Tarrant readily admitted that she was the only person to have handled the decanter. Unless she was the one to administer the arsenic, which would be a foolhardy thing to do in her own home, someone managed to add the poison without being seen. Either that person knew for certain that only Roger Stillman would drink the Scotch or didn't care if someone else ingested the arsenic by accident. Perhaps they realized it wasn't a lethal dose and assumed the other victim would recover. The whole thing just seems sloppy, which is inconsistent with someone who'd managed to feed his victim ground glass. That's not something you could do on the spur of the moment. That part had been carefully planned and executed."

"Yes, I see what you mean," Daniel agreed. "What's your theory?"

"I am convinced there are two separate killers," Jason said. "One who is meticulous and controlled, the other opportunistic."

"In which case, this murder will be that much harder to solve," Daniel pointed out.

"That's what I was thinking. Given that the arsenic was administered at Ardith Hall, we can narrow down our list of suspects, but the arsenic was not the actual cause of death. Our killer is the person who'd been biding his time, feeding Stillman spoonfuls of death."

"Wait, hold on," Daniel said. "You said yourself that whoever had done that would have had to gain access to the house. I highly doubt that a stranger could simply walk into Mrs. Murray's kitchen and casually add some ground glass to the dishes she'd prepared. Besides, that would also mean that Mrs. Stillman and the staff might fall victim to this method of murder. Whoever added the glass had to be a member of staff and managed to target only Roger Stillman."

"There is no way for us to tell if Mrs. Stillman or any of the staff have ingested the glass," Jason pointed out. "However, you're right in thinking it must have been someone no one would suspect, someone who could come and go freely."

"But how would that someone target Roger Stillman?" Daniel mused.

"We don't know that he did," Jason reminded him. "However, if he had managed to single out Stillman, it would have been through something only Roger Stillman would consume."

"Like Scotch," Daniel said.

Jason shook his head. "I don't think so. The particles of glass would settle on the bottom of the decanter unless someone gave the contents a good swirl before pouring the Scotch into a glass. It would have to be something dense."

"Soup, perhaps," Daniel suggested.

"Yes, a cream-based soup or something thick like mashed potatoes."

"Which only Mrs. Murray would have access to," Daniel said.

"Had I not met Mrs. Murray, I would probably agree with you, but I simply don't see it," Jason said. "She seemed genuinely taken aback when we spoke to her. Besides, unless someone paid her a considerable sum to act as their accomplice, she would be risking not only her future but her very life."

"What about the maidservant and the valet?" Daniel asked.

Jason considered this theory, eager to reason it out. "Mrs. Murray would hand the dishes to Martha, who would then deliver them to the dining room. She would have to stop along the way to add the glass and mix it in and take the chance of killing both Roger Stillman and his mother, which would leave her unemployed and without a reference. Unless she was paid enough to keep her in comfort for the rest of her days, which could be decades, she is not the one," Jason said, shaking his head. "Besides, the leftover food was eaten by the staff. Unless Martha scrupulously avoided eating the dish that had been tampered with, she would have been risking her own life."

"And Burns would have no access to the food," Jason said, thinking of his own valet as an example. Henley went down to the kitchen to have a cup of tea or pilfer a scone, but he did not come into contact with the food that was sent up to the dining room. Having met Burns, Jason didn't think the man would acquiesce to doubling as a footman. He took too much pride in his skills as a

162

gentleman's valet. "In either case, they would be the accomplice, not the actual murderer."

"Not so," Daniel said. "Whether it was the accomplice's own initiative to kill Stillman or not, that person is the one who carried out the physical killing, as was the individual who administered the arsenic. Had they not attempted to poison him, Stillman might have lived for weeks, possibly even months. So, for all intents and purposes, the poisoner is as guilty as the original perpetrator."

"Which is why this case is making my head spin," Jason said with a weary smile.

"How did you make out with Mrs. Lysander?" Daniel asked.

Jason sighed. "She told me about the deaths of my parents," he said quietly. "In great detail."

"I'm sorry, Jason. That must have been horrible. So, you think she's the real thing, then?"

Jason thought about that for a moment. Alicia Lysander had shocked him with the description of the train wreck and left him feeling shaken and helpless, but now, faced with the question, he suddenly realized that he'd probably been taken in.

"I won't categorically discount the possibility of her seeing or feeling some form of connection, but there are other ways she might have come by the information. Her assistant strenuously denied carrying out any background research, but that would be one way to prepare. Peppering the narrative with minor truths is probably enough to convince her subjects that she's communing with the dead. It's no secret that my parents died in a train collision, and it doesn't take a great leap of the imagination to conceive of what such a tragedy might entail. Alicia Lysander might have used my own personal tragedy to destabilize me emotionally and make me incapable of focusing on the investigation."

"Which would make her look very guilty, indeed," Daniel said.

"But not necessarily of the murder. Her popularity depends on her reputation, and any opportunity to prove that she's a gifted psychic only helps to pave the way for her engagements. Perhaps duping me is her attempt at damage control," Jason mused.

"Yes, I suppose that could be true," Daniel agreed. "She's a clever woman, to be sure."

"Clever enough to keep an assistant who's free to go everywhere she's not. A pint in a local tavern, a friendly chat, and he's armed with all kinds of information," Jason speculated. "And just to prove that my theory is correct, I will speak to Moll Brody at the first opportunity and see if anyone has been asking questions about me."

Daniel nodded. "Will it put your mind to rest if she confirms your suspicions?" he asked gently.

Jason sighed deeply. "I know my parents died in horrible circumstances. My mother would have suffered, possibly for hours, before succumbing to her injuries. Whether or not Alicia Lysander could actually sense my mother's agony doesn't alter the facts, but proving she's a fraud might help me put the situation in perspective."

"I agree," Daniel said. "So, what's our plan?"

"We can't afford to wait for Hamish Dunbar to return," Jason said, having made up his mind. "At this stage, we don't have much to go on, and he might be able to shed some light not only on Roger Stillman's character but also on his private life. How long does it take to get to Edinburgh?" he asked. Daniel and Sarah had taken a trip to the Highlands the previous summer and had enjoyed the trip immensely.

"The Special Scotch Express departs from King's Cross at ten and arrives in Edinburgh around eight thirty. There's a half-hour stop in York," Daniel said. "We'll need to find accommodation and a carriage to take us to Dunbar Castle."

"I'm sure that won't be a problem. If we leave tomorrow, we'll be back in time for Christmas."

"We'd better be, or Sarah will have my head," Daniel muttered.

Jason chuckled. "Katie won't be overly pleased with me skipping out just before the holiday either, but she'll see why I have to go. I'll come for you at seven tomorrow. Joe will take us to the station in Brentwood. That should give us plenty of time to make the train."

He had expected Daniel to take his leave, but Daniel remained where he was, his cheeks turning a deep pink and his fingers tightening around his empty glass. He clearly had something to say, so Jason leaned back in his chair, took a sip of his drink, and waited patiently until Daniel was ready to say his piece.

"Jason," Daniel began, his gaze sliding away from Jason's face and fixing on the flames in the hearth instead. I want to apologize—"

Jason didn't allow him to finish the sentence. "You've nothing to apologize for, Daniel. You're worried about Sarah, and you want to do everything in your power to protect her, not only from being treated as a suspect, but from the damage such an accusation could do to her already fragile state of mind." Daniel nodded miserably.

"I completely understand and would do the same in your position. Please, think nothing of it."

"Thank you," Daniel said and set down his glass. "I appreciate your understanding."

"You don't need to thank me either," Jason said, smiling at Daniel, who looked like a changed man now that he got that off his chest.

"I'll see you tomorrow, then," Daniel said, rising to his feet. "I'll go and break the news to Sarah that we are off to Scotland."

"Till tomorrow," Jason said and walked Daniel to the door.

Chapter 28

Jason glanced at the clock on the mantel. It was only half past five, but the world outside was as dark and still as if it were the middle of the night. He still had an hour until he had to change for dinner, so he decided to go see Moll at the Red Stag. It was a short walk to the village, and he hoped Moll would be able to speak to him without too many interruptions, since most of the heavy drinkers tended to drift in after supper.

Jason informed Dodson he was going out and waited for the butler to fetch his things. Stepping outside, Jason took a deep breath of the frigid air. It was fresh and fragrant, and suddenly he looked forward to his solitary walk.

The Red Stag was overly warm and smelled of hops, roasting meat, and men who could use a wash. Several tables were already occupied, and a few regulars stood at the bar, chatting to Davy Brody, who was filling tankards with a practiced hand. Moll, who'd just emerged from the back with two bowls of stew, smiled broadly at Jason and thrust her chin toward one of the empty tables, inviting him to sit down. He wasn't planning to stay, but to stand in the middle of the room seemed pointless, so he took a seat and waited for Moll to come over.

"What can I do ye for, yer lordship?" Moll asked when she sauntered over. "If it weren't for church, we'd hardly see ye at all."

"Thanks, Moll, but I'm not here to drink. I just wanted a word," Jason said, smiling back at her. It was impossible not to smile at Moll, since she was so good-natured.

"Come, order something," she urged him. "Uncle Davy gets cross when I talk to customers who are just passing the time of day."

"All right. I'll have a half pint of ale," Jason replied.

"Be back in a tic."

Moll returned with his drink and set it on the table. "Now, what is it ye'd like to talk about?"

Now that he'd taken a good look at her, Jason noticed that she looked pale, there were dark shadows beneath her eyes, and the smile that always came naturally seemed a bit forced.

"Are you all right, Moll?" he asked. "Have you been ill?"

"Look that poorly, do I?" she asked, clearly stung by his questions.

"No, but as a doctor, I can't help noticing you're not quite yourself."

"I'm fine, my lord, but thank ye for asking. Nothing ails me that time won't heal."

Jason nodded in understanding. If Moll didn't want to confide in him, he had no right to press her, but he hoped she wasn't with child. Her young man, Tristan Carmichael, had given her a promise ring last summer, but the relationship seemed to have stalled, probably on account of Tristan's father, a local thug who didn't approve of his son's choice of bride.

"Now, what was it ye wanted?"

"Moll, has anyone come asking about me these past few days?" Jason asked, putting Moll's love life from his mind.

"No," Moll replied immediately.

"Are you sure?"

"I'll check with Uncle Davy, but no one's asked me nothing. Why? Who'd be after ye?"

Jason described Constantine Moore, but Moll looked nonplussed. "No, haven't seen no one like the bloke ye're describing. 'Ave ye got yerself into trouble, my lord?" Moll whispered, smiling knowingly. "Is 'e some lady's well-meaning brother come to avenge 'er 'onor?"

Moll chuckled when Jason's eyebrows lifted in surprise at the suggestion. "Nah, ye're not the type, are ye?" she asked, suddenly melancholy. Tears welled in her eyes, and she angrily wiped them with the back of her hand. "Sorry, yer lordship, but I 'ave work to be gettin' on with. If someone comes asking after ye, I'll be sure to let ye know."

"Is it Tristan?" Jason asked, unable to simply walk away from Moll's obvious grief.

She nodded, his concern breaking through her reluctance to confide in him. "Tristan is to wed. Or 'aven't ye 'eard? Got a face like a potato, 'is bride, but what's it matter when there's money to be got and profitable connections to be made?"

"Is that why he's marrying her?" Jason asked.

Moll shrugged. "What do I know? 'E says 'e's doin' it to protect me. Protect me from what? 'Is old man? 'Is Da would come round if Tristan really wanted to be with me. But I've got nothin' to offer, do I? Other than the obvious, that is. And 'ere I was. Silly old me, thinking 'e loved me."

"Moll, Tristan Carmichael can bring you nothing but grief."

"Don't I know it!" Moll exclaimed. "'E already 'as."

"I mean the sort of grief that can ruin your life, not just leave you with wounded pride and a sore heart," Jason clarified.

"I know," Moll replied miserably. "I'll get over it. I always do. Good old Moll. Skin like a rhinoceros."

"You can always come to me if you need help, Moll," Jason said, hoping she took his meaning.

"Oh, I'm not with child, if that's what ye're thinkin'," Moll whispered. "But thank ye. It means a lot to me, knowin' ye'd 'elp a girl like me. Ye were so kind to Mary. She were a fool to leave. If I 'ad me a benefactor like ye, I'd stay forever, I would," Moll said dreamily. "But who'd want a trollop like me darkenin' their doorstep?" The bitterness had returned, especially once Moll espied Davy's dark look, willing her to stop yapping and see to the other customers.

Jason reached out and covered Moll's hand with his own. "You have a heart of gold, Moll, and don't let any man tell you different. If you ask me, Tristan did you a favor. Find yourself a good, decent man and don't look back."

"Thank ye, yer lordship," Moll replied, a watery smile tugging at her lips. "I'll look for a bloke like ye, only one not so grand," she joked.

"And stay away from Henley," Jason added.

Henley had been smitten with Moll for a time, but Henley was an even worse bet than Tristan Carmichael, who at least had the means to support a wife, even if they didn't come from legitimate sources.

"'Ave no worries on that account. I 'ave no time for the likes of 'im."

"I'm happy to hear it," Jason said. He pushed away his untouched drink, placed a few coins on the table, and stood. "You know where to find me if you're ever in need of help," he said under his breath.

"Oh, go on with ye," Moll said, grinning again.

Jason stepped back into the street and headed for home. A part of him was disappointed that Moll hadn't seen anyone who answered to the description of Constantine Moore, but another part of him was relieved. He would hate to think that someone was out there gathering information on him. As he briskly walked along, he allowed the tension to flow out of his body until he felt lighter of spirit. Alicia Lysander might have managed to take him by surprise, but deep down, he didn't believe in her self-professed ability. He didn't completely discount the notion of an afterlife but didn't think people like Mrs. Lysander could pierce the veil any more than he could. She was simply a gifted actress and a student of human nature who interjected a few relevant phrases into the narrative to dupe her clients.

Jason stopped walking and looked up at the sky, where countless stars were strewn across the heavens like diamonds carelessly tossed onto black velvet. His mother had adored this kind of night and often talked him into going for a moonlit walk along the streets of New York, forcing him to take a break from his studies, since his father refused to leave the warmth of the firelit parlor. Jason missed them both so much, it hurt. He closed his eyes and allowed the silence of the night to settle on him, until all he heard was the sound of his own breathing.

"Mom, Dad, if you're out there somewhere, know that I love and miss you," Jason said softly.

He didn't expect any sort of reply but felt a pleasant warmth in this chest just the same. He had been loved. Alicia Lysander had been right in that, and he would do his damndest to be a good father to his child.

Feeling more at peace, Jason quickened his steps, suddenly eager to get home.

Chapter 29

"Where are you going, Jason?" Katherine asked, a brush suspended in her hand as she met Jason's gaze in the mirror. She had already undressed for bed and was brushing out her hair, as was her nightly custom.

"I thought I'd read for a while," Jason said. "I'm not ready for bed."

"Is it the investigation? You haven't been yourself these last two days."

Katherine's look of concern made Jason feel guilty. He'd thought he'd done a fine job of hiding his disquiet from his wife, but clearly, he was more transparent than he'd imagined. She hadn't taken the news that he was going to Scotland too badly, all things considered, but he didn't want her to worry about him.

"This case troubles me, Katie," Jason said. "I can't put my finger on it, but there's something there, just out of my reach, that's the key to it all."

Katherine set down the brush and turned around to face him. The silk of her dressing gown hugged her rounded belly, making him feel like a cad for giving her cause for concern. He should be worrying about her, not the other way around.

"Jason, what do you want from this?" Katherine asked, her dark gaze caressing him tenderly.

"How do you mean?"

"I mean, what do you hope to accomplish beyond solving this case?"

"I want to help Daniel," Jason replied, hoping she'd believe his answer.

Katherine shook her head reproachfully, as if he were a child who'd disappointed her. "That's not what I mean, and you know it. Do you see this case as an opportunity to prove your worth to Chief Inspector Coleridge in the hope that he will offer you a permanent position? I don't mind, you know. Not if becoming a full-fledged detective would make you happy, but I'm not so sure that's what you're after."

"What do you think I'm after?" Jason asked, intrigued by her assessment of the situation.

"I think it's a burden," Katherine said. "You enjoy participating in the investigations in an unofficial capacity. You like the mental challenge, the intrigue, the thrill of the chase. But you don't relish the responsibility that's been forced on you. When you solve this case, and you will," she added with a small nod, "you will be sending someone to the gallows. It will be on your head, even though the person knowingly committed a crime and deserves the punishment that goes with such a decision. You don't want this, sweetheart," she added softly.

Jason smiled sadly. "No, I don't think I do," he admitted. "I'm not courting a permanent position with the police." He sat down on the bed and looked at his hands, studying his fingers as if seeing them for the first time. "I miss surgery, Katie. I chose medicine because I wanted to help people, not send them to their deaths, even if they deserve it, which I'm not sure I agree with. The death penalty is so final, so cruel. I'm not suggesting that a murderer should go free, but perhaps repaying murder with murder is not the way to bring about order. Surely there are other ways."

Katherine stood and came toward Jason, positioning herself between his legs and wrapping her arms about his neck. "Jason, I will support you in whatever endeavor you choose to pursue. And if that means moving to London so that you can open your own clinic or find a position teaching a new generation of surgeons, I will gladly follow."

"Don't you want to remain here in Birch Hill?" Jason asked, taken aback by the suggestion. It was as if she'd peeled away the layers of self-denial and exposed his innermost thoughts, making his desires known to him before he'd had a chance to acknowledge the ideas to himself.

"Darling, I've lived in Birch Hill my whole life. It's a pleasant enough village, but there's a whole world out there, and a life that doesn't revolve around the never-changing routines of this tiny community."

Jason wrapped his arms around Katherine and pulled her close, lifting his face up to kiss her. "You are an extraordinary woman, Lady Redmond."

"And you're an intelligent, highly skilled man whose talents are utterly wasted in this backwater."

"I love you," Jason whispered as he smiled into her eyes. "I love you so much."

"Still feel like reading?" Katherine asked huskily.

"No, I'm fine right here," he replied, and reached for the belt of her dressing gown.

Chapter 30

Sunday, December 22

The carriage Jason had hired from a livery in Edinburgh when they arrived on Saturday evening swayed soothingly as it rolled down a dirt road that ran through a frost-covered valley flanked by rolling hills. Jason hadn't seen a dwelling for miles and was beginning to wonder if the coachman had taken a wrong turn somewhere, but the man had assured them he knew the way. Jason resisted the urge to knock on the roof to get the coachman's attention and ask him to confirm that they were getting closer to Hamish Dunbar's Highland estate. Daniel, who'd nodded off about an hour ago, sat hunched in the corner, his spectacles perched on the end of his nose, his arms crossed over his chest.

Jason pulled his greatcoat closer about him, grateful the livery had provided some blankets to keep them warm on their journey. It had been considerably colder than at home when he'd briefly got off the train at the stopover in York, but by the time they'd arrived in Edinburgh last night, the air had been frosty, and a biting wind had nipped at the exposed skin of his face and neck. Jason wasn't sure what he'd expected, but Scotland had a vastly different feel. What he'd seen of the English countryside was green and lush, the land divided into neat plots that had been farmed, often by the same family, for generations. Man controlled the land, nature at his beck and call.

On this land, deep gorges and windswept mountains were the masters, the men mere tenants who were permitted to stay as long as they didn't leave too large a footprint on the wild terrain. Even on an overcast day like today, there was a stark beauty, a silent majesty to the landscape, and Jason felt awed by it.

Katie would love it here, he though drowsily as they finally left the valley behind and rolled into a wooded area, the trees standing close and tall, their branches casting a deep shadow over the narrow road. The carriage passed through the stretch of wood and emerged on the other side, offering Jason his first glimpse of the castle. It looked so much a part of its surroundings, it was almost as if it had arisen from the earth, the gray towers like stony fingers pointing toward an equally gray sky. If the castle had ever been surrounded by a curtain wall or a moat, there was no sign of them now, but there was a massive stone gateway, complete with a barbican, through which the carriage passed in order to enter the courtyard.

"Are we here, then?" Daniel asked as he stared drowsily out the window.

"Dunbar Castle," the coachman announced as Jason and Daniel stepped out. He seemed amused by their reaction to the place but said nothing, simply waiting for them to stand away from the carriage before walking the horses toward what had to be the stables.

A young red-headed manservant in traditional Scottish dress opened the door, his astonishment obvious. "How can I help ye, gentlemen?" he asked. "Are ye lost?"

"We're here to see Mr. Dunbar," Jason replied.

"All the way from America?" he asked, his eyes round with surprise at hearing Jason's accent.

"No, we've come from the south," Daniel explained. "We are with the Essex Police. It's regarding a case we're working on."

"Aye. Right," the man said, nodding as if everything made sense now. "Well, ye'd best come in, then. I'll inform the master ye're here. He's just back from kirk, ye ken."

He disappeared through a low oak door at the far end of the foyer and returned a few moments later, beckoning for them to follow him. Jason was actually glad the servant hadn't taken their coats and hats. The castle was as cold and drafty as the valley they'd just crossed, and just as silent.

The manservant led them into a wood-paneled parlor, the walls decorated with paintings of pastoral scenes and mounted stag heads, whose eyes seemed to stare directly at the men, reflecting the light of the lamps. Swaths of tartan covered the windows, blocking out the thin winter light almost entirely and picking up the reds, browns, and muted greens of the thick rug. Two deep armchairs stood before the hearth, one of them occupied by the master.

He stood when they approached and took a moment to study them before offering a word of greeting. Hamish Dunbar was a bear of a man—tall and broad with a mane of coppery hair and wide blue eyes. He was at least forty, but the strength and virility he radiated made him appear younger. He wore a tweed jacket in a rich, earthy shade of green, paired with matching knickerbockers and yellow argyle socks. On any other man, Jason would have found the short, voluminous trousers ridiculous, but they did little to dispel the impression of a man who was as imposing as he was commanding.

"What have I done to earn a visit from the Essex Police?" he boomed, his face breaking into an amused grin.

"Mr. Dunbar, we're here in regard to the murder of your friend, Roger Stillman," Jason explained.

Hamish Dunbar's smile slid off his face, his eyes widening in disbelief. "Roger is deid?" he asked softly, his brogue coming through in his distress.

"I'm afraid so. We have some questions to put to you, and we've come a long way to do so," Jason said, hoping the man wouldn't send them on their way.

"Of course. Anything I can do to help," Hamish said. "Come, sit by the fire. You must be chilled to the bone. Alastair," he called to the young man. "Take their things, tell Cook there'll be two more for dinner, and bring us refreshments."

The servant nodded, held out his hands for their coats, hats, mufflers, and gloves, and left.

"You'll join me in a wee dram?" Hamish asked. "In memory of Roger."

"Of course, Mr. Dunbar." Jason had no idea what he was agreeing to, but if it was in memory of Dunbar's dead friend, it likely involved alcohol, and he would drink liquid fire right now just to regain feeling in his cold-numbed feet.

"Ach, call me Hamish. No need to stand on ceremony."

He dragged over another chair, and the three men settled as close to the fire as they could without setting themselves aflame. Jason held out his hands, his stiff fingers finally regaining the ability to bend.

"I gather you've never come this far north before," Hamish said. "Too bad it took the death of a dear friend to bring you to my beautiful Scotland."

"It is beautiful," Jason agreed. "I'd like to bring my wife, but perhaps I'll wait till summer."

Hamish smiled. "It's lovely in the summer, it is. You should come when the heather's in bloom. It's a sight to behold. A carpet of purple as far as the eye can see, offset by the vivid green of the mountains and the clear blue sky. Balm to a troubled soul," he added dreamily.

He was prevented from waxing poetic any further when Alastair appeared with a tray bearing a teapot, cups, sugar, and milk, and a plate of sandwiches. He set the tray on the low table and looked to Hamish for instructions.

"Pour us a dram, lad," Hamish said.

Alastair walked over to a cabinet and extracted a decanter and cut crystal glasses, then brought them over and filled each glass halfway before setting the bottle on the table and seeing himself out.

Hamish picked up a glass and raised it in a toast. "Roger," was all he said before tossing back the drink.

Jason and Daniel followed suit. It was whisky—damn good whisky too, Jason noted as the fiery liquid slid down his gullet and settled as a warm glow in his belly. Hamish refilled their glasses, and they drank again before helping themselves to tea and sandwiches. Half were with ham, the other half with smoked salmon. Daniel avoided the salmon, but Jason helped himself, then took another one, seeing as no one else was eating them. They were delicious.

"This will tide you over till dinner," Hamish said, and reached for a sandwich.

"It's a long way back to Edinburgh," Daniel began, his gaze sliding toward the window. "We can't stay long." It had taken them nearly four hours to reach the castle. If they didn't leave in an hour or two, they'd have to travel over dark, desolate roads as the temperature dropped even further.

"Nonsense," Hamish boomed. "You'll spend the night. There's plenty of room, and I could use the company. My mother has been unwell, and my brother and his brood are not due to arrive until tomorrow. And don't worry about your coachman. Alastair will see to him."

"Thank you, Mr. Dunbar," Daniel said. "That's very generous of you." He was visibly relieved not to have to travel by night.

"Selfish, more like," Hamish Dunbar replied. "Can't stand my own company," he said with a shake of his head. "Bore myself silly. Now, please, tell me what happened to Roger," he invited, his gaze misty with either drink or his loss.

"Roger Stillman died during a séance at Ardith Hall," Jason began. "Are you acquainted with the Tarrants?"

"Yes, I've had the pleasure," Hamish replied. "How did Roger die?"

"He was poisoned with arsenic, but had he not been, he would have died within the coming weeks anyway. Someone had been feeding him ground glass," Jason said, watching Hamish Dunbar for a reaction.

"What?" the man cried as his hands slammed against the armrests of the chair, then gripped them tightly. "Are you certain?"

"I am. I performed the postmortem myself," Jason explained.

"Jesus bloody Christ!" Hamish Dunbar exclaimed. "Who would do such an evil thing? Why, that's diabolical, that is."

"It is, rather," Daniel agreed, and nodded vigorously. "And darn clever. No one would have ever suspected, leaving the murderer to walk free." The whisky had mellowed him, making him seem almost relaxed.

"Not if the culprit decided to finish him off with the arsenic," Hamish pointed out.

"We think there might have been two separate attempts on Mr. Stillman's life, by two different people," Jason said.

"Who worked in tandem?" Hamish asked.

"That's something we have yet to determine," Daniel said. "How long had you known Roger Stillman?"

"About fifteen years now," Hamish said. "We met aboard a ship bound for England. *Adelaide,* she was called. Roger had been on his way to visit his mother. He'd been employed by the East India Company then but had managed to get some paid leave. It was a shipboard romance, so to speak," Hamish said with a sad smile. "We made a connection one seldom makes with another human being, and it being a long voyage, we had plenty of time to solidify our bond. We have been the closest of friends since."

"Did Mr. Stillman have any other close friends?" Daniel asked, watching Hamish closely from behind his spectacles.

"He had maintained a close relationship with Charles Hornsby, whom he'd met when he first arrived in India, but their friendship was different."

"In what way?" Jason asked.

"They had both been employed by the East India Company and knew a number of the same people. Charles Hornsby was also a valuable resource when it came to new business ventures, since he's something of a social climber and makes it his business to get invited to as many suppers and balls as he can possibly attend without falling over with lack of sleep."

"Was there anyone else?" Daniel asked.

Hamish shook his leonine head. "Roger wasn't the type of man who sought social connections for their own sake."

"Hamish, did Mr. Stillman have any enemies that you know of? Are you familiar with any of the other guests who attended the séance?" Jason asked after naming the other attendees.

"I never met Mr. Forbes but have heard Roger mention him," Hamish replied. "I am familiar with Lord Sumner, but not with the woman."

"Can you think of a reason anyone who attended the séance might wish to poison Mr. Stillman?" Jason asked.

"No."

"Mr. Forbes has disclosed to Inspector Haze that Mr. Stillman had cheated him of profit by diluting his rum and selling it on at a cheaper price but in much greater quantity," Daniel said. "That's certainly a motive for murder."

"I don't see how it would be," Hamish replied. "I'm a man of business myself. I export whisky to America and Canada, and several European countries. Once Roger bought the rum, it belonged to him, to do with as he pleased. If he chose to dilute it, that had nothing to do with Forbes, who'd collected the agreed-upon sum on delivery," Hamish said matter-of-factly.

"The rum still bore the Forbes name, therefore undermining the reputation of his product," Jason pointed out.

"Perhaps, but if that was a source of concern for Mr. Forbes, he should have found his own means of distribution or shipped the rum without labels," Hamish said with a shrug. "My guess is that he wished to take advantage of the free advertising of his product. The scheme backfired. Now, I'm not suggesting Nathaniel Forbes killed Roger, but from what I heard, he has a quick temper and takes offense easily, but as a man of business, he has to follow the profit, not his pride."

"Speaking of strong spirits, was it common knowledge that Roger Stillman preferred Scotch?" Jason asked.

"It was for those who knew him, I suppose," Hamish replied. "Roger wasn't a big drinker, though. One dram was his norm. Two if he was really anxious."

"Was he concerned with losing control, do you think?" Jason asked. He always monitored his own intake, knowing from experience how easy it would be to keep refilling the glass, particularly when one was in low spirits.

"Yes, I believe he was," Hamish replied. "There was an incident a few years ago that left a mark on him."

"What sort of incident?" Daniel asked.

"He witnessed an accident. Someone was run over by a carriage. The driver of the vehicle was drunk and unable to stop in time. The victim was crushed beneath the wheels."

Daniel paled at the description but made no mention of his own tragedy.

"Hamish, who would Roger have been trying to contact at the séance?" Jason asked, hoping the change of topic would distract Daniel from thoughts of the accident that had claimed Felix's life.

"Anne," Dunbar replied without missing a beat.

Neither Jason nor Daniel said a word, waiting for Hamish to fill the silence that had descended on the hall, the only sounds the crackling of the fire and the moaning of the wind outside.

Hamish sighed. "Roger was a bit persnickety. He'd never stoop to visiting whores; he found the prospect repellent, but he had his needs and was happy to pay to satisfy them. He tended to remain faithful to one woman as long as she didn't make unreasonable demands."

"What sort of demands?" Jason asked.

"Marriage," Hamish replied, as if that should be obvious. "He set them up, gave them an allowance, and treated them with kindness and respect, but he'd never make the arrangement legal."

"And was Anne one of his mistresses?" Daniel asked.

"No," Hamish said with a shake of his head. "Anne was the one woman he'd truly loved, but she got away."

"You mean by dying?" Jason asked.

"No, by accepting a proposal from someone else."

"How did they meet?" Jason inquired, wondering if this was the woman Charles Hornsby had alluded to.

"As I said before, Roger wasn't the type of person who sought out social situations, but he had accepted an invitation from Lance Mayhew to spend a fortnight at his country estate. Mayhew owns several merchant vessels, and Roger was hoping to leave his house with a signed contract in his pocket that would guarantee him excellent shipping rates for five years, at the very least. It was there that he met Anne."

"Tell us about the relationship," Jason invited, hoping that Roger Stillman had been forthcoming enough to share some of the details with his friend.

"Anne was witty and vivacious, the complete opposite of the marriageable young ladies he was normally introduced to, who were timid and unworldly and held no interest for him. I suppose she managed to break through his reserve and draw him out," Hamish speculated. "They spent much of their time together during those two weeks, walking and talking, and participating in the entertainments the Mayhews had devised for the guests. Anne won an archery competition. That really impressed Roger since he is…was," Hamish amended, "fond of archery."

"What went wrong?" Jason asked.

"Roger asked Anne to marry him on the last night of the visit, and she said yes, but when he asked her father for her hand, he was refused. Despite his wealth, a match with Roger would have been a step down for her."

"Why?" Jason asked. Roger Stillman had been handsome, wealthy, and well respected. Any man would see him as a good prospect for his daughter.

"Roger could have offered Anne a comfortable life, have no doubt on that score, but she would have gone from being Lady Anne to becoming plain old Mrs. Stillman. Her father accepted an offer of marriage from Lord Sumner instead, and in the end, she chose status over love."

Jason and Daniel exchanged shocked glances. "Lord Sumner and Roger Stillman were in love with the same woman?" Jason asked.

"Yes. Lady Anne Weathers."

"Cor," Daniel exclaimed, resorting to the slang of the London streets he'd picked up while walking the beat as a Peeler. "That's a fine kettle of fish."

"What happened to Lady Anne?" Jason asked.

"She became ill and died sometime in early October. Roger was heartbroken. I think he still believed there might be hope for them. So much so that he ended things with his then-mistress."

"Did he continued to pursue the lady after she'd agreed to an engagement to Lord Sumner?" Jason asked.

"He never said, but I believe he tried to change her mind," Hamish Dunbar said. "He wasn't a man to give up easily on something he wanted."

"How did he take news of her death?" Daniel asked.

"Not well. He was convinced there was something unnatural about it. He even went to see the doctor who had attended on her in her final moments."

"And was he able to confirm his suspicions?" Daniel asked.

"The doctor wouldn't speak to him," Hamish said. "Turned him away at the door."

"Would you happen to recall the name of the doctor?" Jason said.

"I do, as it happens," Hamish said. "A rather unfortunate name for a man in his profession. Dr. Earnest Graves. Has consulting rooms in Harley Street."

"Did Mr. Stillman blame Lord Sumner for Lady Anne's death?" Daniel asked.

"I don't believe so, but perhaps Lord Sumner blamed Roger," Hamish suggested.

"On what grounds?" Jason asked.

"Perhaps he feared Anne had still been in love with him," Dunbar said.

"And died of a broken heart?" Jason asked, a tad sarcastically.

"It's been known to happen," Hamish replied archly. "The loss of love is a devastating thing, Lord Redmond. It can kill as surely as a bout of influenza."

Jason didn't reply. He was a man of science, and as much as he believed a broken heart could lead to depression and other psychological and physiological conditions, he didn't believe it could kill.

"Could Lord Sumner have wished to revenge himself on Roger Stillman for courting his fiancée?" Daniel asked, looking from one man to the other.

"Why would he?" Hamish asked. "Anne had agreed to marry him and would have gone through with the nuptials. She was a dutiful daughter, and a marriage with Sumner would have benefitted her family. And what would Sumner accomplish by poisoning Roger months after Anne's death?" Hamish asked. "Besides, unless he knew for certain that Roger would be at the séance, I can't see him carrying around a vial of arsenic on the off chance that he might have to murder someone."

Daniel nodded. It was a good point, one he could hardly argue with.

"Perhaps Lord Sumner blamed Roger Stillman for Lady Anne's death," Jason suggested.

"How could Roger possibly be responsible for her getting ill?" Hamish asked.

"They might have met in secret just before she became ill," Daniel suggested, clearly intrigued by the idea. "Perhaps she'd caught a chill."

"That's hardly grounds for murder," Hamish scoffed. "Lady Anne had the best care. Whatever illness she'd contracted, it wasn't just an autumn chill."

"Had Roger Stillman been ill at about the same time?" Jason asked.

"Not that I know of. Besides, do you honestly believe that Lord Sumner would devise a plan to kill Roger in order to revenge himself on the man for his fiancée falling ill? The very idea is laughable."

"Is it, indeed," Daniel agreed. "There's something much darker at play here."

"Well, whatever it is, you two will have to figure it out and let me know once I'm back in London," Hamish Dunbar said when Alastair entered the room to inform them that dinner was about to be served. "I don't know about you, lads, but I'm ready to eat. Come through to the dining room. You won't be disappointed," he boomed, rubbing his hands together in childlike glee.

The man clearly liked his food, Jason reflected as he followed his host into the spacious dining room, which was adorned with as many stag heads as the parlor. Jason wondered if the head of whatever animal they were about to consume would soon end up on the wall, joining its predecessors as they watched the master of the house consume its flesh.

Dinner was an unexpectedly pleasant affair. The venison was exquisitely prepared, the wine never seemed to run out, and Hamish Dunbar did his best to entertain them with stories of life in the Highlands, never touching on the more painful subjects, such as the crushing defeat of the Scots in the Jacobite rising of 1745 and the decades of extreme physical and mental suffering that had followed, inflicted on the Highlanders by their vengeful king.

It was nearly midnight by the time Jason and Daniel were finally shown to their rooms and fell into bed, tired after hours of traveling in a carriage that was hardly more than a wooden box and then hours of drinking Mr. Dunbar's fine wine. Jason was glad of the fire that had been laid in the room; otherwise, he might have woken with frostbite, he decided. As he undressed and climbed into the tester bed that was hung with thick velvet curtains, probably to keep out the arctic chill of the Highland winter, Jason thought he'd fall asleep the moment his head hit the pillow. But he lay awake for some time, his thoughts going in circles until he finally wore himself out.

Chapter 31

Daniel climbed into bed and pulled the heavy eiderdown up to his chin. He was freezing, but not just because of the biting cold. He'd done his best to enjoy their host's fine meal and amusing conversation, but deep down he'd wanted to howl. When Hamish Dunbar had so casually described the carriage accident that Roger Stillman had witnessed, he'd had no idea that he was invoking Daniel's worst nightmare. Daniel hadn't been there when Felix was crushed beneath the wheels of a wealthy man's curricle, and Sarah had never been able to share the more painful details of the accident, but his mind had supplied all the necessary images, and they had haunted him for the past four years.

The wind outside the casement window sounded like the keening of a woman, or the anguished screams of a child that lay broken in the road, his lifeblood seeping out into the dirt. Felix's face hovered at the edge of Daniel's vision, the child's dark eyes pleading for help, his hands reaching out to a father who wasn't there. Daniel had been angry with Sarah for lying to him and attending the séance, but now, as he lay shivering and alone in a bedroom high in the tower of a Highland castle, he suddenly understood her desperate need for forgiveness. She had blamed herself when the accident happened, and she blamed herself still.

Daniel had foolishly thought that having another child would finally allow Sarah to forget, to move forward and find joy in her life. But he'd been wrong, as he had been about so many things. Sarah adored Charlotte and doted on her in a way few mothers did. She had refused to hire a nursemaid and took care of the baby herself, seeing to her every need and guarding her as if some tragedy were imminent. It had taken one unguarded moment for Sarah to lose her son. Felix had seen something that caught his attention and tore his hand out of his mother's as they were walking home from the park. He'd run into the street, oblivious to the curricle that came barreling down the street at full speed, the driver unaware of the little boy who didn't have the sense to stop in time.

Now that he had allowed himself to feel the pain of his loss once again, Daniel almost wished Mrs. Lysander had been able to get on with the séance. He didn't for a moment believe that she would have been able to summon Felix's spirit, but whatever parlor tricks she used to dupe her trusting clients, he wished Sarah had been able to witness them. Perhaps believing that Felix forgave her, that he was in heaven, would finally allow Sarah to, if not forgive herself, at least make peace with her part in Felix's death.

After all, everything in life was God's will, or so the Church wanted them to believe. If that were the case, then it had been God's will that Felix die a horrible, excruciating death. Why? They'd never know. But his suffering had been over a lot quicker than his parents' would be. Sarah never spoke of it now, but Daniel was sure she relived those awful moments every day of her life. No subsequent children would ever replace Felix, and no amount of reassurance that it wasn't her fault would ever assuage her guilt.

Daniel curled into a ball, making himself as small as possible in the massive bed. He wasn't a believer in taking tonics or potions to help one sleep, but he'd give anything for a few drops of laudanum that would offer him the oblivion he craved to get through this long, cold night.

Chapter 32

Monday, December 23

Daniel gazed out the window as the carriage rolled down the same valley they'd crossed yesterday. The day had dawned sunny and bright, and the wind had died down during the night, making this journey more pleasant. Hamish had made sure they ate a hearty breakfast before setting off, complete with porridge, fried eggs, and thick slices of bacon. After breakfast, he'd walked them to the waiting carriage and clapped Jason on the shoulder in the universal gesture of male bonding. Daniel thought Jason and Hamish Dunbar would make the best of friends if they ever found themselves moving in the same social sphere. They were cut from the same cloth, both men charming, self-assured, and utterly comfortable in their own skin.

At the moment, Jason looked well rested and alert, while Daniel wished he could huddle into the corner of the carriage and allow its gentle swaying to rock him to sleep. He had finally fallen into a fitful sleep in the small hours, but his slumber had consisted of vivid, awful dreams produced by his troubled thoughts.

"So, what do you reckon?" Daniel asked, suddenly uncomfortable with the lengthy silence.

Tearing his attention away from the stark beauty of the Highland morning, Jason turned to face Daniel, his gaze thoughtful. "We now have a tangible link between Roger Stillman and Julian Sumner. They both loved the same woman, and both lost her. That they attended the séance to contact the same spirit is too great a coincidence to ignore."

"The only person who might have had a hand in bringing them together is Mrs. Tarrant," Daniel said. "She'd organized the séance and sent the invitations."

Jason shook his head. "Having interviewed Mrs. Tarrant twice, I find it hard to imagine that she had knowingly facilitated the meeting between Roger Stillman and Julian Sumner. Besides, who's to say she knew of the connection between the two men? Roger Stillman kept the relationship private, even from those close to him. No, whoever orchestrated this performance is much more subtle and cunning that Amelia Tarrant."

"Which rules out nearly everyone," Daniel pointed out.

"Yes," Jason agreed. "Sarah has no previous relationship to anyone except Mrs. Tarrant. Mr. Forbes resides in Barbados and visits England twice a year. He had a motive for wishing to hurt Roger Stillman, but I can't see how he would benefit by killing the man. He could simply have cut ties with Stillman and sold his rum to a different buyer. But wounded pride is never to be discounted, so I will not take his name off the table."

"And, as far as we know, Roger Stillman and Julian Sumner had never met before the séance, but their connection was the most personal in nature," Daniel said.

"Sumner was the last to arrive. Had he been planning to kill Roger Stillman, he'd have needed more time to put his plan into action," Jason mused.

"So, where does this leave us?"

"Exactly where we started," Jason said, grimacing with distaste. He pulled out his pocket watch to consult the time. "I do hope we make the London-bound train," he said. "I'd like to get home tonight."

"How do you wish to proceed once we return?" Daniel asked.

"I'd like to speak to Lord Sumner, but first, I think we should call on Dr. Graves," Jason replied.

"Why?" Daniel asked. "How do you think he can help?"

"If we subtract the ladies, who had no motive to kill Roger Stillman that we know of, then we are down to the two men. Nathaniel Forbes had a motive, but honestly, I don't see him resorting to grinding glass or relying on the possibility of slipping arsenic into the man's drink. He's too proud and practical a man to resort to such histrionics. Had he wished to kill the man who'd cheated him, I believe he would have chosen a more direct method. Which leaves us with Lord Sumner," Jason theorized.

"The man claimed never to have met Roger Stillman before the night of the séance, yet Stillman had been in love with Sumner's fiancée and had believed himself engaged to her until her father put an end to their affair. Two men and one woman is rarely a recipe for a peaceful resolution. Had Anne not died, perhaps there would have been a showdown of a different nature."

"So, you think her death is the key to this mystery?" Daniel asked.

"I think her death has a bearing on the case," Jason said. "I happen to agree with Hamish Dunbar. Something about the way she died doesn't ring true. There was no outbreak of influenza in London this October, and even if there had been, an otherwise healthy young woman wouldn't die so suddenly. She would have been ill for a few days, at least."

"Perhaps Hamish got it wrong and it wasn't influenza. People die all the time, Jason, even young ones. I know as a doctor you need tangible proof, but it is quite possible that there was nothing suspicious about her death."

"That's what I intend to find out, Daniel. If only to rule out the possibility of foul play."

"That sounds like a reasonable plan," Daniel said.

What a relief it would be to solve this murder before Christmas, Daniel thought as he leaned his head against the jolting side of the carriage. This was their first Christmas with Charlotte. Given what he'd come to understand about Sarah's frame of mind, he no longer expected it to be either merry or festive, but was it too much to hope that it would be peaceful?

Daniel must have dozed off because before he knew it, they were at the railway station, Jason paying the driver, who was inordinately pleased to receive an additional fiver on top of the livery fee for having to spend the night. He pocketed the note and tipped his hat.

"Thank ye, guv. Pleasure doing business with ye. If ever ye come this way again, do ask for me. Arch McDonald is the name," he reminded Jason.

"Thank you, Mr. McDonald. I do hope we didn't put you out too much," Jason said as he retrieved his case from the back of the carriage.

"Not at all, guv. Not at all. My missus likely 'ad a fair peaceful night without me snoring in 'er ear," he said with a grin. "And she'll be pleased as punch 'bout the extra dosh." Arch McDonald handed Daniel his case and tipped his hat again. "Happy Christmas, gentlemen, and a pleasant journey."

Daniel and Jason boarded the train and settled in for the long ride. Thankfully, no one joined them, so they had the compartment to themselves and were able to spread out a bit. As the train pulled out of the station, Jason closed his eyes and relaxed into his seat, leaving Daniel alone with his turbulent thoughts once again.

Chapter 33

Tuesday, December 24

The following morning found Jason and Daniel in Harley Street. Dr. Graves' office wasn't difficult to locate. It was housed in a red-brick building with a white portico and a brightly polished brass plate that announced the good doctor's name. The reception area was expensively and elegantly furnished with several comfortable leather chairs arranged around a thick carpet and flanked by potted plants. A neat desk occupied the space near the door, where a middle-aged woman, possibly the doctor's wife, greeted the patients and took down their information. Her sparse eyebrows lifted in surprise when they stated their business, and Daniel produced his warrant card to reassure her their visit was no ruse.

"The doctor is with a patient right now," the woman said. "You really should have made an appointment." She consulted her book. "I can fit you in around four."

"We're happy to wait," Jason said. "You don't seem all that busy."

There was no one in the reception area besides them, so Jason settled into one of the chairs and Daniel followed suit. Sometimes he envied Jason's self-assurance. He simply did what he felt was right and expected everyone else to fall in line.

The woman's face puckered with disapproval, but she didn't make any further comments and fixed her attention on a leather-bound ledger instead. It took more than half an hour, but the patient within departed at last, and the gatekeeper disappeared into the consulting room, presumably to express her outrage and seek instructions.

"This way, please," she said when she emerged a few moments later. "Dr. Graves can spare you ten minutes before his next patient arrives."

"That's very generous of him," Jason said, bestowing his most charming smile on her and leaving her looking bemused as they entered the office.

Dr. Graves was clearly not her husband. He was no older than thirty, with neatly pomaded hair and a pencil moustache that made him look rather debonair. His dark eyes showed neither surprise nor curiosity, but simply watched them as they settled across from him in the chairs reserved for the patients and presented their warrant cards.

"How can I help you, gentlemen?" The inquiry was polite, but the doctor's tone was businesslike and brisk, that of a man who valued his time and wouldn't like to see it squandered.

"We would like to ask you a few questions about Lady Anne Weathers, as part of our investigation into the death of Mr. Roger Stillman," Jason stated.

"I'm afraid I'm not at liberty to divulge anything of a confidential nature," he replied a little too smugly.

"What was the cause of death, Dr. Graves?" Jason asked, undeterred.

Dr. Graves looked distinctly uncomfortable but held his ground. "What relevance does this information have to your investigation?"

"The man who was murdered had been close to Lady Anne, and we believe the feeling was mutual. How she died might have a bearing on the outcome of the investigation," Jason explained.

Dr. Graves looked away, his gaze straying to the street beyond the window. He still looked uncertain.

"Dr. Graves, a man is dead, and the life of another in imminent danger. It is your sworn duty to uphold life. What you share with us will be held in strict confidence," Jason assured him.

"If Lord Weathers discovers that I spoke to you, he could very well ruin my reputation," Dr. Graves replied. "He's a man of considerable influence."

"Lord Weathers will never know what was said here today," Jason assured him.

Dr. Graves nodded. "I was called to the Weathers' residence on the evening of October ninth. I normally don't make house calls, but the summons was urgent. When I arrived, I found Lady Anne, who'd been my patient for several years, in her bed, her hair dripping wet and her wrists thickly bandaged."

"She tried to take her own life?" Daniel exclaimed.

"She slashed her wrists with a shard of broken mirror while in the bath. Her maid found her and raised the alarm."

"Was she alive when you got to her?" Jason inquired.

"Yes, but only just. I performed an examination and concluded that there wasn't much I could do. She'd lost a lot of blood. Either she would pull through on her own, or she would succumb. She passed less than an hour later."

"Dr. Graves, at the time, had you formed any theories on why Lady Anne would wish to commit suicide?" Jason asked.

The doctor nodded gravely. "During my examination, I discovered that Anne's womb was enlarged. She was about three months gone with child. I had no way of knowing what was in Lady Anne's heart, but from a practical standpoint, I could see how the pregnancy might be an issue if the child hadn't been fathered by her fiancé."

"Was Lord Sumner present at the time of Lady Anne's death?" Daniel asked.

"No. Only her parents and the servants were aware of what had happened."

"What did you put as the cause of death on the death certificate?" Jason asked.

All color drained out of Dr. Graves' face. "Influenza."

"So, you lied?" Jason said, fixing the man with an accusing stare.

"Lord Weathers threatened to ruin me if I didn't do as he asked. I didn't think I was harming anyone. Lady Anne was buried with all the respect due to her, and her memory has been preserved, as well as the emotional well-being of her parents. What purpose would it have served to let the world know that she had killed herself because she was carrying an illegitimate child?"

"Thank you, Dr. Graves," Jason said, and pushed to his feet.

"Do I have your word that this conversation will go no further than this room?" Dr. Graves demanded. He looked panicked. If it got out that he had knowingly lied and falsified the information on the death certificate, his reputation would be tarnished, and his medical career might be over for good.

"You have my word," Jason replied coldly. "Good day to you, Dr. Graves."

"Good day," the man muttered as they left his office.

"Whose life is in danger?" Daniel asked once they were back in the street. "Do you believe the killer will strike again?"

"No," Jason replied. "I only said that to force his hand. It is a doctor's sworn duty to uphold life, so if he believed someone might die because of his refusal to answer our questions, he would be liable."

Daniel smiled. "It's like you were born to do this," he said, gazing at Jason with admiration.

"I hate to admit it, but I do enjoy detective work," Jason replied. "And I believe Dr. Graves has just handed us the missing piece of the puzzle."

"You believe Lord Sumner tried to revenge himself on Roger Stillman for the death of Lady Anne?" Daniel said.

"The theory does fit the facts, at least some of them," Jason replied. "Lady Anne had fallen in love with Roger Stillman and believed they were to be married, a certainty she had relied on when she had relations with him. Never having met her, it's hard to guess what went through her mind when her father refused Roger Stillman's offer of marriage, but she was either too timid to stand up to him or was persuaded to recognize the advantages of accepting Lord Sumner instead, since, from her father's point of view, he was a much more suitable match for someone of Lady Anne's social standing.

"The engagement went ahead, and she would have gone through with the marriage had she not discovered she was with child. A young lady of her position would not know how to rid herself of an unwanted pregnancy and likely couldn't think of anyone to turn to for help. Feeling trapped in a situation she couldn't cope with on her own, she took her own life, setting her doting fiancé on the path to revenge.

"According to Percival Osbourne, the letter Roger Stillman received was written on expensive paper, the penmanship that of an educated person. It could have been penned by Lord Sumner, particularly if he was already in the process of carrying out his threat. I believe Lord Sumner is responsible for the ground glass in Roger Stillman's stomach," Jason said.

"Yes, that does make perfect sense," Daniel agreed, "but I can't imagine Sumner would have administered the ground glass himself."

"He wouldn't. He would pay someone to do it, and if I'm correct, I know who."

"Mrs. Murray?" Daniel asked. "She had access to everything Roger Stillman consumed."

"No, Roger Stillman's valet," Jason replied. "I expect Lord Sumner paid the man handsomely to tamper with his employer's food and promised him a position in his own household. For someone like Burns, serving a man of Lord Sumner's social standing would be a dream come true, especially since it seems Roger Stillman didn't have much use for him, being the near-recluse he was. Burns must have found a way to administer the glass without arousing anyone's suspicion."

"Shall we go speak to Lord Sumner?" Daniel asked.

"That's the plan."

"Jason, I think we should stop in at the nearest police station, explain the situation, and ask for assistance. We don't have the jurisdiction to make an arrest in London, and if we show our hand and then seek reinforcements after the fact, we might lose the chance to cuff the culprit."

"That's a very valid point. I hadn't considered that," Jason admitted ruefully. "You are absolutely correct, Daniel. Reinforcements will be needed."

Chapter 34

Lord Sumner's residence in Grosvenor Square attested to his wealth and influence. It was on the north side of the park and appeared to have been recently refaced, the white brick façade gleaming in the pale sunshine, the front entrance reminiscent of the great Italianate palaces so admired by the rich they tried to replicate them in London. The Palladian structure boasted four floors as well as an attic level with a row of dormer windows, where no doubt numerous servants spent their nights either freezing or sweltering, depending on the season. The park at the center of the square was dusted with freshly fallen snow, bare tree branches stark against the pale blue of the winter sky. It was a peaceful scene, all the more so because most of the residents, at least those abovestairs, had yet to stir.

Jason used the brass knocker to announce their presence, his breath coming out in white puffs as he exhaled the chill air. The day was cold, despite the bright sunshine that shone from a cloudless sky. A man of about sixty with rheumy blue eyes and a balding pate opened the door, his eyebrows rising comically as he beheld the two men.

"The tradesmen's entrance is around back," he said sharply, although he probably realized they weren't tradesmen.

Jason held up his warrant card, bringing it dangerously close to the man's prominent nose. "I am Lord Redmond, Special Advisor to the Essex Police, and this is Inspector Haze," he said rather loudly, making the old man cringe as he quickly looked around to see if anyone might have overheard. "We'd like to speak to Lord Sumner. Now," Jason added, realizing the man would probably try to fob them off.

"His lordship is not at home to visitors," the butler said, standing his ground.

"We're not visitors, we're police," Jason reminded him.

"The tradesmen's entrance—" the man tried again, but Jason's patience was at an end.

"Step aside, or be made to step aside," he drawled.

The butler hesitated but finally saw the wisdom of complying. He moved aside and permitted Jason and Daniel to enter the foyer. It was grand, with a black-and-white tiled floor, pale yellow walls, and an urn of fresh flowers on a round table at the center. A curious maidservant peeked out from one of the rooms, but the butler gave her a vicious look, and she promptly shut the door before he could reprimand her.

"We'll be happy to wait in the drawing room," Jason informed the man.

"This way," the butler said, and directed them to a room on the other side of the grand foyer. "His lordship will be down presently."

The drawing room gleamed with gold accents and pale-green marble that matched the lavish sea-green settees and armchairs and the gold-tasseled curtains at the tall windows. The walls were painted cream, the light color and high ceiling making the room seem airy and light. Two beautiful still lifes hung on the walls, and delicate antique vases were carefully positioned on the mantel. Daniel couldn't help wondering what the rest of the house looked like, but he was sure it was magnificent. No wonder Anne Weathers had had second thoughts about defying her father. Roger Stillman would never be able to offer her the decadent luxury Lord Sumner could provide.

It took nearly a half hour for Lord Sumner to finally appear, and when he did, he looked like a man who'd been roused from his bed and hadn't had sufficient time to see to his toilet. His hair was tousled and his jaw unshaven, but he was impeccably dressed in a dark-gray suit paired with a paisley waistcoat of silver on a mauve background. He slumped onto one of the settees and stared at the two men through sleep-clouded eyes, his mouth twitching with wry amusement.

"Have you never heard of calling hours?" he complained. "But then again, what can one expect of a backwater copper and an American upstart who likes to play at being a peer of the realm while carving up the dead like a common butcher?"

"This is not a social call," Jason replied sharply, ignoring the insults.

"No, I don't suppose it would be," Lord Sumner retorted. "Well, whatever the reason for your unwelcome visit, let's get it over with, shall we? I have to leave in a few hours. Going to my sister's for Christmas," he divulged sulkily.

"This won't take long," Daniel said. "I'm arresting you for the murder of Roger Stillman." He showed Sumner a temporary warrant card issued by Division C.

"I didn't know the man," Lord Sumner replied smoothly.

"Maybe not in person, but you knew of him," Daniel replied.

"So? I know of many people. Doesn't mean I intend to kill them."

"But you had a strong motive to want Roger Stillman dead," Daniel said.

Lord Sumner actually laughed at this. "Really? Did I? I've never had much faith in the police, but you are thicker than most, Inspector. Do tell, on what grounds are you arresting me?"

"You blamed Roger Stillman for the death of the woman you loved and wanted to revenge yourself on him," Daniel snapped.

"Wishing someone dead doesn't quite stand up in a court of law, does it, Inspector?" Daniel noted that Sumner didn't deny knowing that Roger Stillman had been indirectly responsible for the death of Lady Anne.

"No, but a confession from one's valet does," Jason replied, his smug look clearly infuriating Lord Sumner.

"My valet has nothing to confess," Lord Sumner scoffed, but he did look more alert now, his eyes darting toward the door as if he expected Burns to come in and deny all.

"On the contrary. We picked up your new valet not twenty minutes before we arrived at your door when he ventured out to the chemist to buy you tooth powder and lavender soap. He had quite a lot to say once he realized he'd be charged with murder."

"That lying bastard," Sumner hissed from between clenched teeth.

"I think he was surprisingly truthful," Daniel said, enjoying the moment. He would have liked to continue but felt he should defer to Jason, since he was the lead on this case.

"Burns confessed to adding ground glass to Roger Stillman's hot chocolate every morning. He had cleverly decided on chocolate because of its rich consistency and the fact that it was prepared specifically for his master. His mother and the household staff prefer tea. He mixed in half a teaspoon a day, ensuring that his master never noticed the fine powder floating in his drink. Over the course of several weeks, he hoped to have fed him enough to cause internal bleeding that would lead to death," Jason said.

"And if Mr. Stillman complained of abdominal pain or had blood in his stool, his doctor would simply assume he was suffering from an ulcer or perhaps even cancer of the stomach and attribute his death to that," Jason continued. "A very neat solution. I congratulate you on your ingenuity, my lord."

Sumner remained silent, staring at the two men balefully. "It's his word against mine," he snarled at last. "No one will believe a servant over a peer."

"You must have really loved her," Jason mused, ignoring Sumner's outburst. "And to think that all along she was carrying Stillman's child."

"I would have married her anyway," Lord Sumner said softly, again not bothering to deny that he had known of Anne's pregnancy. "All she had to do was trust me. I would have claimed the child as my own."

"And then made sure it never lived to see its first birthday," Jason countered.

"I would never harm an innocent child," Lord Sumner said. Coupled with the horror in his gaze, his statement rang true.

"But you had no trouble slowly killing a grown man?" Daniel demanded.

"A grown man who was completely devoid of decency or honor," Sumner said.

"So, you did kill him," Jason stated flatly.

Sumner allowed himself a small smile. "I didn't say that."

"You didn't have to. Burns said it all for you," Daniel replied.

Lord Sumner looked from Daniel to Jason and back again. "You two have nothing. The word of a disgruntled employee is not proof of guilt. Even if the judge could be persuaded that I convinced Burns to murder Roger Stillman, I never lifted a finger to harm the man myself."

"You paid Burns to carry out your plan," Daniel retorted. "And I suspect you sent Roger Stillman a threatening letter. A handwriting expert would no doubt prove the letter came from you."

Sumner shrugged. "Even if an expert can prove that the letter was penned by me, which he won't, since it wasn't, that's hardly enough evidence to convict me of murder. People make threats all the time; it doesn't mean they carry them out. If they did, the slabs in morgues would be piled ten deep."

Daniel felt frustration simmering in his gut. Sumner was right. They had nothing on him. Burns had confessed quickly enough when he was brought to the police station by the local coppers, thinking his employer would get the blame, but Lord Sumner was untouchable within the law. There was no proof of him having paid Burns. It wasn't against the law to hire a man who'd lost his position due to his employer's death. Lord Sumner's counsel could claim he'd had no knowledge of the plot and propose that Burns had his own reasons for wanting his employer dead. Burns would swing, while the orchestrator of this elaborate drama would walk away unscathed, his reputation as intact as his neck.

"Do you not care that a man will be hanged in your stead?" Daniel asked, but he already knew the answer.

"Every man decides what's important to him, Inspector," Lord Sumner replied. "For Burns, it was clearly money. He took a risk, and he lost."

"Burns wasn't at Ardith Hall on the night of the séance," Daniel said, watching Lord Sumner intently. "You were the one who administered the arsenic."

Lord Sumner looked genuinely surprised. "I was the last one to arrive. Once I was there, Mrs. Tarrant offered me a drink, then invited us to follow her into the parlor when I refused her offer. Roger Stillman tossed back his drink and followed her from the room. I never came near him, nor did I go anywhere near the decanter, as anyone who was present will attest. Now, if we're finished here, I have preparations to make. Give my regards to Burns," he added flippantly. "I'm sure he'll be expecting to hear from me. Good day, gentlemen."

Lord Sumner stood and gestured toward the door, inviting them to leave. As much as Daniel wanted to drag the blackguard to the police station and see him locked up in the cells, he had no choice but to comply. He followed Jason outside, ignoring the butler's triumphant stare.

Once back in the street, Daniel couldn't help but fume. "What an unrepentant scoundrel Sumner turned out to be. The villain had been setting up Burns to take the fall all along. We can't touch him, and he knows it."

"He is clever; I'll give him that," Jason agreed. "Even if witnesses can be found to attest that Lord Sumner met with Burns and money changed hands, their testimony would not be enough to convict him of murder. It's all circumstantial. Burns had means, opportunity, and motive. Sumner had a strong motive, but not the means or the opportunity, nor could his motive be proved in a court of law, since the death certificate states that Anne Weathers died of influenza, not suicide."

"How had he known that Lady Anne died by her own hand?" Daniel asked. "Surely Lord Weathers didn't tell him as much, and I doubt Dr. Graves would have risked his professional standing by violating the doctor/patient privilege. Do you think she might have confided in him?"

"I doubt it. Had she done so, she'd probably still be alive. He clearly loved her enough to forgive her any transgression. I strongly suspect that Burns was not the only servant Lord Sumner had in his pay. Perhaps he wished to keep tabs on Lady Anne, in case she was meeting with Roger Stillman, or maybe he'd approached a member of staff after Lady Anne's death. For the right price, it wouldn't have been too difficult to discover the truth," Jason said matter-of-factly.

"I also think that he had someone write the threatening letter for him. Perhaps there were several, designed to let Roger Stillman know that someone was coming for him. Stillman might have guessed who the letters were from, or he might not have, but the knowledge that someone out there meant him harm and could carry out their threat in myriad ways anytime they chose to would have been enough to make him look over his shoulder every day of his life."

"Would Sumner not want his rival to know that he was the one who was going to mete out justice?" Daniel speculated.

"I think it was enough for him to know that he'd punished Stillman for his crime against Lady Anne. And he had."

"And yet, we won't be able to prove any of this in a court of law, even if we were to obtain a statement from the other servant in Sumner's pay or a confession from the individual who wrote the letter," Daniel said with disgust.

Jason kicked at a clump of snow, clearly exasperated. "It would be easy enough for his lawyer to prove that Sumner never came anywhere near Stillman. As far as we know, the two men had never met face to face before the séance, and Lord Sumner never set foot inside Stillman's home. Paying someone for information is not a crime, nor is sending vaguely threatening letters."

"Do you believe him about the arsenic?" Daniel asked. He felt angry and deflated, a sense of failure souring his stomach.

"I do," Jason replied. "I'm afraid we'll never know who mixed the arsenic into his whisky. Perhaps it had been there all along, a bottle meant for someone other than Roger Stillman."

"You think it was all a mistake? A tragic accident?" Daniel sputtered.

"It's a possibility, although a slim one," Jason admitted. "Come, Daniel. I think it's time we went home. It's Christmas Eve, and I would like to spend it with my family."

"As would I," Daniel replied. "We have our man. Even without the arsenic, the glass would have killed Roger Stillman in its own time. As you said, it wasn't a fatal dose of arsenic, so Burns is the culprit."

"Yes, he is," Jason agreed, but there was a faraway look in his eyes and a downturn to his mouth.

Chapter 35

The journey home was a nearly silent one, both men lost in their own thoughts as they stared at the wintry landscape beyond the grimy window. CI Coleridge would be satisfied with the result, since not only had they arrested the culprit, they had a signed confession to prove his guilt, but neither Daniel nor Jason could accept that Julian Sumner would not face any sort of justice. In the eyes of the law, he was squeaky clean, just as he had always known he would be.

It had been arranged that Joe would meet them at the Brentwood railway station at three o'clock, a plan that ensured they'd both get home as quickly as possible. Daniel was about to wish Jason a happy Christmas as they pulled up before his house when Jason asked if he might come in.

"I'd like to wish Sarah and Harriet a happy holiday," he said.

"Of course. And please pass the season's greetings to Katherine and Micah," Daniel said.

Tilda let them in the house and held out her arms for their coats and hats.

"Please inform Mrs. Haze and Mrs. Elderman that Lord Redmond wishes to see them," Daniel said.

"Mrs. Elderman is upstairs, resting, and Mrs. Haze is in the greenhouse," Tilda said. "Perhaps ye'd care to wait, my lord."

"I'll just pop out to speak to her," Jason said before he had a chance to take off his coat.

"Shall I come with you?" Daniel asked.

"Don't trouble yourself. I'll only be a moment."

Jason stepped outside and walked around the building toward the back of the garden, where Sarah's tiny greenhouse was tucked away. She was inside, humming softly to herself as she watered the plants. Despite the chill outside, the inside of the greenhouse was pleasantly sunny and warm, and Sarah wore only a woolen shawl over her gown.

"Jason," Sarah exclaimed when she saw him. "Is something wrong?"

"No. I only wanted to speak to you for a moment."

Sarah set down the can, her hand trembling slightly as she raised her face to look at him. "Oh?"

"Why did you do it?" Jason asked. "Why did you try to kill Roger Stillman?"

The metal can crashed to the floor as Sarah accidently knocked it over with her hand. She looked terrified, but then her expression slowly changed to one of resignation. "Because he killed my son," she said at last. "How did you know it was me?" Her voice was utterly flat, as if she didn't really care but was mildly curious.

"I didn't," Jason replied. "Not for certain, but I had a feeling you'd met Roger Stillman before, and I've been able to rule out the others to my satisfaction. What did Roger Stillman have to do with Felix's death?" Jason asked softly, his innards writhing with apprehension. He'd so wanted to be wrong, but he'd learned to trust his instincts, and once again they'd pointed him in the right direction.

"Roger Stillman was the one driving the curricle that struck Felix. Had he been sober, he might have noticed a little boy running into the road, might have tried to stop, but he was drunk, his senses dulled by strong spirits."

"How do you know that?" Jason asked. Daniel had never mentioned the name of the person driving the curricle, only that he had been drunk.

210

"A young man, his groom perhaps, screamed for him to stop. He called him Mr. Stillman. It was too late, of course. By the time he reacted, Felix was already under the horse's hooves, mere inches from the wheels that rolled over him as if he were nothing more than a dead cat."

Sarah's eyes clouded with the memory of that day, and Jason thought she wouldn't be able to go on, but she took a shuddering breath and continued. "The horse tripped over Felix and went down on its front legs, breaking them in the process. I suppose there must have been some damage to the curricle as well. Roger Stillman jumped down and went to examine the damage. He cursed furiously and struck the animal with the crop again and again when he realized the horse wouldn't be able to get up and would have to be shot. He was so angry. And then he turned his fury on me," Sarah said, her voice barely audible.

"Tell me," Jason said, wishing he could do something to comfort her but keeping his distance.

"I was on the ground, holding Felix as he lay bleeding and mad with pain, crying for me to help him, when Roger Stillman approached. He hadn't spared a glance for Felix but cursed me for letting my brat run into the street and destroy his property. 'Do you have any idea how much I paid for that horse?' he screamed in my face. As if I cared," Sarah snarled, a look of pure disgust on her face. "He reeked of spirits, and his speech was slurred. And it was barely eleven in the morning."

"Did Daniel know the name of the man who was driving the carriage?" Jason asked, wondering if Daniel had intentionally omitted that little detail in order not to draw attention to Sarah's relationship with the victim.

"No, he didn't. I never told him. I couldn't bring myself to utter the man's name, and I was afraid Daniel would decide to take justice into his own hands. You see, the law was on Stillman's side. No one would hold him accountable for the accident, since Felix had run into the road. It was his fault. My fault," she cried. "My fault for not holding on to him tight enough, for becoming momentarily distracted." Silent tears slid down Sarah's cheeks as she spoke, her gaze begging Jason to understand.

"After Felix died, I made it my business to find Roger Stillman. I never approached him, but I needed to know who he was and what his life was like. I couldn't bear the thought of him going about his business, rising every day and going to bed, healthy and safe, and happy. I suppose it became an obsession, so I told Daniel I wanted to come back to Essex. Remaining in London would have driven me mad."

"Did you know Roger Stillman would be at the séance?" Jason asked.

"Yes. When Amelia invited me, I was reluctant to accept. I knew Daniel wouldn't approve, and frankly, I was afraid of what would happen. If Felix didn't show, I'd be devastated. But if he did, I wasn't sure I could handle it, especially since I'd be there on my own, with no one to comfort me. But then Amelia mentioned the other people who'd be there, to assure me that no one I know would be present and Daniel need never know. When I heard the name, I knew I had to go."

"How did you manage to administer the arsenic?" Jason asked, not really wanting to know. He had hoped Sarah would deny the whole thing, accuse him of being stark raving mad, and walk out in a huff, but she'd admitted to the crime so easily, so completely. What was he to do now? Was it his duty to tear apart this family he'd come to care so much for? Could he bear to be responsible for Sarah's death?

"It was easier than I had expected," Sarah said, her tone now flat and matter-of-fact. "Daniel had purchased a quantity of arsenic during the investigation into the death of Elizabeth Barrett. He left it in the potting shed, where no one would accidentally ingest it, and forgot all about it. On the night of the séance, I mixed the contents of one packet into a medicine bottle and put it in my reticule. I wasn't sure how I would slip it to Stillman, but I'd be damned if I wasn't going to try. In the end, it was almost too easy. Amelia offered us a drink when we got there and mentioned that she had prepared Scotch for Mr. Stillman, who preferred it. There were only two decanters on the sideboard, and it was easy to tell the contents apart. Mr. Forbes and Amelia took sherry, and Lord Sumner was said to be a teetotaler. I thought it was safe to try."

"How did you do it?"

"I took the bottle out of my reticule when no one was looking and kept it in my hand as I walked up to the sideboard, pretending to examine the painting that hung above it. It was of Venice, a city I've always longed to visit," she said with a mirthless chuckle. "While I pretended to study the scene, I poured the contents of the vial into the decanter of whisky. No one saw me do it, since my body blocked it from view. I returned to my seat and waited."

"Were you not afraid someone would drink the whisky after Roger Stillman? Surely he wasn't going to consume the entire contents of the decanter himself."

"To be honest, I never considered that possibility," Sarah replied, shrugging. "I figured the last thing he drank would be considered suspect and not offered to anyone else."

Sarah took another quivering breath and looked up at Jason, her eyes swimming with tears. She looked so achingly vulnerable, he wished he could simply pretend they'd never had this conversation, leave the greenhouse, and go home to Katie and Micah, but as the Brits liked to say, in for a penny, in for a pound. He needed to know the whole truth, hear Sarah's confession to the bitter end, and make one of the hardest decisions of his life.

Sarah reached out and grabbed his wrist, staring earnestly into his face, her gaze pleading with him to listen to her, to try to understand.

"I never meant to kill him, Jason. Daniel told me how much arsenic it would take to poison someone when he brought it home, so I knew the dose wasn't lethal. I only wanted to make him suffer, to make him feel a fraction of the agony Felix must have felt as he lay dying, and to punish him for his cruelty. He hadn't had any pity to spare for the child he had maimed or the woman who'd wished only to have been the one lying beneath the wheels of that curricle, her life flowing out of her into the dirt. And even for the poor horse that had been completely innocent of any wrongdoing. It must have been in terrible pain and he just beat it with that crop, needing to take his anger out on anyone other than himself."

Tears spilled down Sarah's pale cheeks. "I only wanted to make him ill," she cried desperately. "How was I to know that his health was compromised and that small bit of arsenic would tip the scales? I spent that whole night agonizing about it. I wanted to tell you and Daniel the truth, I really did, but I couldn't bring myself to do it. Not because I feared for myself, but because of Charlotte. And Daniel," she added miserably.

"I'd be putting him in an impossible situation. Daniel is an honest man, Jason, a just man. He'd feel it his duty to arrest me, and then he'd blame himself for the rest of his days for taking Charlotte's mother away from her, and for punishing me for something he probably would have done in a heartbeat had he known the truth."

Sarah wiped her eyes with the back of her hand. Her nose was running freely now, so Jason silently offered her his handkerchief, which she accepted.

"I was stupid and selfish," she said once she regained control of her emotions. "I'd been thinking only of my own pain, my own inability to move on with my life. You never get over the death of a child, Jason. Never. No matter how many other children you have. I stupidly thought that hurting Roger Stillman might bring me some peace, but it hasn't. I've been in hell these past few days, torn between coming clean and praying this murder would go unsolved and I would get away with my crime. I never meant to kill him, but I did," she said, her voice vibrating with tension. "Am I to be arrested for murder?"

"No," Jason replied softly. "Your secret is safe with me."

"You are willing to compromise your conscience to save me from the noose?" Sarah said, gripping his wrist with all her might.

"Sarah, you are right in thinking that the dose you gave Roger Stillman would have made him seriously ill, but it wouldn't have been fatal, not by a long shot. I don't know if the courts would see it that way, but I won't give them the chance to make that decision, not when your life is at stake. My guess is that you would be found guilty of attempted murder," he said softly.

"And you don't think I am guilty?" Sarah asked, her brow knitting in confusion as she tried to understand his reasoning.

You are, Jason thought, but couldn't bring himself to utter the words. "I don't condone what you did, but I can understand it. Had someone mowed down my child in the street, I'd be tempted to do the same, more so if they hadn't shown any sympathy or contrition. Since one person is already going to be tried for the murder of Roger Stillman, I see no added benefit to sacrificing you to the cause of justice."

"Please, don't tell Daniel," Sarah whispered. "The knowledge will kill him."

"I won't tell him," Jason promised. "But I think you should. The weight of this secret will crush you and ultimately destroy any chance of happiness you might have as a family. Daniel will feel angry and betrayed, but he will forgive you. And I know he will understand."

"Do you really think so?" Sarah asked, her voice small and frightened.

"Yes, I do. You two have suffered enough. It's time you put Felix's and Roger Stillman's deaths behind you and faced the future. Otherwise, the past will haunt you forever."

Sarah nodded. "I don't know how to thank you, Jason. Your coming here truly changed our lives."

"Thank me by being happy, Sarah, and by allowing Felix to rest. There's nothing more you can do for him."

"I know. I suppose I was afraid to let go. It felt like a betrayal."

"He would want you to be happy. And perhaps, by letting go, you will set his spirit free."

"I thought you didn't believe in spirits," Sarah said, allowing herself a wan smile.

"There are more things in Heaven and Earth, Horatio, than are dreamt of in your philosophy," Jason replied, quoting one of his favorite passages from Hamlet.

"Does this mean you now believe?" Sarah asked.

"It means I don't actively disbelieve," Jason replied with a smile. "Happy Christmas, Sarah. May the coming year bring you peace."

"And you as well," Sarah said.

Jason felt her gaze upon him as he walked out of the greenhouse and toward the waiting carriage.

Chapter 36

January 2, 1868

Daniel approached Redmond Hall on foot. He could have taken the dogcart, but he'd needed time to organize his thoughts and achieve some semblance of calm before speaking to Jason. He had been a mass of contradictions the past few days, his mental state more volatile than that of a lunatic in Bedlam. He went from weeping openly to railing against the blind injustice of the legal system to questioning everything from his own perception of events and judgment to the future of his marriage.

Some part of him resented Sarah for telling him the truth, while another admired her for her daring. He hated her for not telling him about Roger Stillman's part in Felix's death but was secretly grateful that she'd spared him the knowledge and the need to act. Sarah had done what she had out of love—for Felix, for Daniel, and even for Charlotte—but the knowledge that she hadn't trusted him enough to confide in him had stung, his anger burning bright enough to consider leaving her, at least for a time. And then he imagined what might have happened had Jason not been in charge of the case. Had someone like DI Peterson or an inspector from Scotland Yard been assigned, Sarah might have been in prison at this very moment, awaiting the farce of a trial that would bring in a guilty verdict and a sentence of death by hanging. Sarah had risked that to bring about her own justice, an outcome she hadn't trusted Daniel to secure.

Well, Stillman was dead now, and not only by Lord Sumner's hand. Sarah had played her part and had brought about a climax that had been a long time coming, at least for her. Burns would hang, Lord Sumner would get on with his life, and Daniel and Sarah would be forever bound by secrets and lies. Not the marriage he had hoped for when he'd stood before Reverend Talbot next to the girl he'd loved since adolescence. But life went on, and he had the future to think of, a future that suddenly seemed just a little bit brighter than it had yesterday afternoon.

Daniel raised his hand and knocked on the door, bracing himself for the conversation to follow. Dodson, haughty as ever, invited Daniel into the drawing room, where Jason sat by the fire, Katherine by his side. She looked radiant in a pale green gown, her cheeks rosy from the heat of the flames. Liam was in her lap, his chubby hands gripping a wooden horse, his eyes appraising Daniel with all the seriousness of a suspicious toddler. He seemed to grasp the horse tighter, for fear that Daniel would covet his toy.

"Happy New Year, Daniel!" Katherine greeted him. "Please, come warm yourself by the fire."

"Happy New Year!" Daniel replied, and sank into his favorite chair.

Katherine looked from him to her husband, then rose to her feet, setting Liam down and taking him by the hand. "It's time for Liam's nap," she said diplomatically, astutely realizing that Daniel wished to speak to Jason alone.

Daniel waited until the door closed behind Katherine, then turned to Jason, all the emotions he'd been trying to wrestle into some semblance of order spilling from his overwrought mind. "I know, Jason. Sarah told me everything. How could you keep the truth from me?" Daniel hadn't realized he was shouting until he stopped to draw in a shaky breath, his words hanging in the air like noxious fumes.

"I didn't think it was my place to tell you," Jason replied calmly.

"You are my friend, my colleague," Daniel retorted hotly.

"And Sarah is your wife. I thought you needed to hear the truth from her."

Daniel opened his mouth to argue but went silent when he felt the sting of tears and the shortness of breath that came upon him every time he imagined what might have happened had Jason chosen a different path. He huddled into the chair, deeply ashamed of his outburst and desperate to gain control of his emotions.

"She could have died," Daniel finally choked out.

"But she didn't. The case is closed, Daniel. There's no need for anyone to know what Sarah tried to do."

"Did," Daniel corrected him. "For all intents and purposes, she was the one that killed Roger Stillman."

"Not according to my report," Jason argued. "Stillman was a dead man walking when he arrived at Ardith Hall."

"Thank you," Daniel whispered hoarsely. "Thank you. We owe you our very lives."

"You owe me nothing. I did what I believed to be right. Roger Stillman was drunk when he caused the accident that killed your son. He should have been held liable, but he wasn't. He walked away without any repercussions while you lost a child. Sarah would have been charged with attempted murder had I told the truth."

"Attempted murder is still a crime," Daniel said softly.

"Yes, it is, but her attempt failed, and Lord Sumner's succeeded. No good would be come of Sarah serving a life sentence or being hanged for avenging her son. Yes, I know that's preferential treatment, but I wouldn't be able to live with myself had I deprived Charlotte of her mother and you of your wife. As it is, you will have to live with the knowledge of what Sarah has done for the rest of your lives, and that's punishment enough."

Jason was right in that, Daniel decided. The knowledge of what Sarah had done would stand between them forever, no matter how much they tried to ignore the truth.

"There's something I have to tell you," Daniel said, feeling marginally calmer now. Jason looked at him expectantly. "Superintendent Ransome came to see me yesterday."

"I'm afraid I don't know him," Jason replied.

"He's from Scotland Yard."

"Was it about the case?" Jason asked, his calm expression faltering.

"No. He offered me a job. His brother lives in Brentwood and has been reading about me in the papers. He told the superintendent that I've managed to solve every murder I've been tasked with investigating. Superintendent Ransome has offered me the position of Detective Inspector."

"Congratulations," Jason said. "But would that not mean moving to London?"

Daniel nodded. "A few months ago, I would have turned him down flat, but in view of what's happened, I feel some distance would help me put things in perspective. I've discussed it with Sarah, and she's in agreement. If, after a few months, I wish to remain in London, Sarah and Charlotte will join me. If not, then I will return to Birch Hill and to the Brentwood Constabulary."

"I see," Jason said. "Well, I suppose I'll be seeing you there."

"Will you?" Daniel asked, his spirits suddenly lifting. "Are you moving to London, then?"

"I have been considering ways in which I can return to practicing medicine. I might volunteer at one of the London hospitals, or organize a course for aspiring surgeons. It was Katie's idea, truth be told, but it has taken hold. If I go ahead with this plan, Katie and I will take a house in London after the baby is born."

"Jason, that's brilliant," Daniel said. "You're too skilled a surgeon to hide yourself away in the country, dissecting cadavers for the Brentwood Police."

"I will continue to dissect cadavers," Jason replied with a half-smile. "That's the most practical way to teach incoming students without inflicting pain and harm on living patients, at least at first. And should you want my help, I will be happy to assist you in your cases, in an unofficial capacity, of course."

"Unless you happen to offer your services to Scotland Yard," Daniel said, smiling for the first time since Sarah had said she had something important to tell him. "In fact, I will go one step further and say that you can use victims of crime to teach your students about what to look for during a postmortem."

"That's an idea," Jason replied, his smile widening. "When will you be making the move to London?"

"By the end of the month," Daniel replied. "I need time to find lodgings, and I'd like to give CI Coleridge at least a few weeks' notice. I hope he'll give Constable Pullman a chance now that I will be leaving. The Brentwood Constabulary can't function with only Inspector Peterson, and Constable Pullman is a clever young man. I think he'll do well for himself."

"I'd be happy to put in a good word for him," Jason said.

"Will you stay on as an advisor until the baby is born?" Daniel asked.

"I don't think so. I can use a break, and Katie needs me here now that she's getting closer to her due date. I wouldn't want Dr. Parsons to deliver our child. I don't trust the man."

"I won't come to say goodbye," Daniel said, thinking he'd find it too difficult.

"Then don't. I'll see you in London, Inspector," Jason said, smiling at him.

"See you," Daniel replied.

It wasn't until he left Redmond Hall that he realized he no longer felt as emotionally raw as he had when he'd arrived. He supposed that under the circumstances, this was the best outcome he could have hoped for, and knowing that Jason would be there to assist him soothed some of his anxiety about joining Scotland Yard. Perhaps, in time, things between him and Sarah would return to normal, or some form of new normal, and maybe this would be good for them in the long run. But in the meantime, London was full of opportunities.

As he turned his face up to the glow of the winter sun, he felt hopeful for the first time in days. Daniel took a deep breath, filling his lungs with the frosty air, and began to walk. Anyone who might have seen him would remark that he had a spring in his step.

Epilogue

March 1868

Milky light filtered through the leaded panes of the drawing room window, slowly dispelling the shadows of the night. Jason carefully settled in the chair by the window, so as not to disturb the sleeping child in his arms. The baby was swaddled in a warm blanket, her silky dark hair covered with a frilly bonnet. Jason smiled down at his daughter. A week old today. He could hardly believe it.

It had been a difficult birth. Katie had been in labor for almost three days, and Jason had thought he might have to perform a cesarean section to save both mother and child. But then, miraculously, things had begun to progress, and when it came time to push, the baby had slid out like a greased pig, filling the room with the sounds of her displeasure as soon as Jason cleaned her airways.

She lay quietly now, her mouth slightly open, her dark lashes fanned across rosy cheeks, angelic in sleep. He hoped she'd stay that way for a while and give her mother a chance to rest. Katie hadn't let the baby out of her sight for more than a few minutes since she was born, allowing only Jason to pick her up. He could understand her overprotectiveness. He felt the same way. There'd be time for nurses and governesses later.

Jason was surprised when Dodson stealthily entered the room, his gaze softening at the sight of the sleeping child. "I'm sorry to disturb you, sir," he whispered, "but this came for you last night. You had already retired," he explained.

Holding out his hand, Jason took the letter and nodded his thanks.

"Do you require anything, sir?" Dodson whispered.

"Thank you, Dodson. We're just fine."

Dodson turned and tiptoed from the room. Jason carefully tore open the cable and read the brief contents.

Dear Jason,

I urgently require your assistance. Please come as soon as you're able.

Warm regards,

Daniel

Jason felt a glow of pleasure at Daniel's words. He missed his friend, and he missed working a case. He wished Daniel had elaborated, but perhaps he simply wished to speak to Jason in person.

Looking down, Jason was surprised to find his daughter awake. She stared at him solemnly, her gray eyes studying him as if she could see right through him.

"What do you think, Lily?" Jason asked the infant softly, still ridiculously emotional at the sound of her name, even after a full week. Lily had been his mother's name, and he hoped some small part of her lived on in her granddaughter. "Will you behave for your mother for a day or two while I help out an old friend?"

"She will," Katherine replied from the doorway. She was wrapped in her favorite dressing gown, her hair loose and cascading halfway down her back. She came into the room, sat across from Jason, and reached for the baby, who instantly smacked her lips. "Go on, Jason," Katherine said, smiling at him. "We'll be just fine, Lily and I. Aren't we, sweetheart?" she cooed.

"Are you sure?"

"Of course I am. We'll be right here waiting when you get back."

Jason sprang to his feet, suddenly full of energy. He'd wash and dress, have some breakfast, then ask Joe to drive him to the railway station. He kissed first Katie, then Lily on the forehead, and left the room, eager to see what the day would bring.

The End

Turn the page for an excerpt from Murder on the Sea Witch

A Redmond and Haze Mystery Book 7

Notes

I hope you've enjoyed this installment of the Redmond and Haze mysteries and will check out future books. Reviews on Amazon and Goodreads are much appreciated.

I'd love to hear your thoughts and suggestions. I can be found at

irina.shapiro@yahoo.com, www.irinashapiroauthor.com,

or https://www.facebook.com/IrinaShapiro2/.

If you would like to join my Victorian mysteries mailing list, please use this link.

https://landing.mailerlite.com/webforms/landing/u9d9o2

Excerpt from Murder on the Sea Witch

Prologue

The museum had finally closed, the lofty halls echoing with Mason Platt's footsteps as he hurried through the silent rooms toward the rear of the building, where the storerooms were located. Mason was giddy with excitement as he pushed open the door marked 'Private' and trotted into the vast space beyond. It had been empty this morning, but now the area was full of crates, the shipment from the *Sea Witch* having finally arrived a few hours ago, the caravan of wagons delayed by heavy traffic from Southampton. Mason had to admit that he liked the name of the vessel and found it appropriate to the cargo it had carried. A sea witch was a mythical creature, someone found in legends and spooky stories told by sailors, as were some of the artefacts that had been stored in its spacious hold.

Up until a few years ago, mummies and hieroglyphs had been the stuff of legend, but now the museum had its very own Egyptian Hall filled with breathtaking artefacts, the display open to the public, rich and poor alike able to see the glorious finds for the price of an admission ticket. Maybe one day archeologists would find a sea witch, Mason mused as he gazed around the room, his heart thumping with anticipation. A mermaid skeleton would be nearly as exciting as the unique find he was about to behold.

Mason Platt had been a curator at the British Museum for nearly twenty years, but it was only recently that he had finally been promoted to director of the Egyptian section, a position he'd coveted for years. Mason was the in-house expert on anything pertaining to Egypt and one of the few people in London who could be called a true Egyptologist. Although he had never set foot in Egypt, he'd read everything he could get his hands on and always personally catalogued and arranged the displays, complete with a detailed description and background of each item.

He'd been waiting for this hoard for more than a fortnight now, the ship's departure having been delayed by Egyptian authorities, who'd demanded to come on board and personally examine the artefacts that were being taken out of their country. As a historian, Mason could certainly understand their reluctance to part with such important bits of their history, but, on the upside, the treasures would be displayed in one of the greatest museums in the world, something the Egyptians should be grateful for, in his opinion.

But, at last, the *Sea Witch* had docked this morning, and now Mason could spend a few happy hours examining the newly arrived treasures before getting down to the business of cataloguing. Only this morning, he'd thought he'd leave the best for last, but he simply couldn't wait. Blake Upton, the archeologist in charge of the expedition, had written to him about his momentous find. It was an almost perfectly preserved painted wood sarcophagus, complete with a mummy. The sarcophagus had been discovered in the Valley of the Kings in a tomb that Upton and his team had found, a previously unopened chamber filled with grave goods and wall paintings.

Having studied the images painted on the walls and the papyrus found inside the tomb that had been painstakingly translated by the two archeologists on the team, Blake had concluded that the tomb belonged to an important nobleman who'd lived during the New Kingdom, which encompassed the eighteenth, nineteenth, and twentieth dynasties of Egypt. The find was an absolute triumph, and the sarcophagus would be displayed in a glass cabinet in pride of place, the lid stood up vertically to be more clearly seen by the visitors, while the coffin itself would be low enough so that they could gawk at the mummy within.

Mason carefully lifted the lid of the appropriately marked crate, removed the padding used to keep the sarcophagus intact, and drank in the gorgeous colors and workmanship of the coffin. It really was breathtaking, the image of the occupant depicted in golds, reds, and blues, the kohl-rimmed eyes staring as if they could see him, their painted expression condemning Mason for what he planned to do. Mason looked away from the painted face. He didn't think displaying a mummy was quite the same as laying out an Englishman's corpse for everyone to see. That would be inappropriate and disrespectful to the deceased, but this person had died thousands of years ago. He no longer deserved consideration or respect, only interest.

Sniffing experimentally, Mason leaned forward, bringing his face closer to the sarcophagus. There was an odd smell, but he supposed it was to be expected, given its contents. He couldn't wait to see the mummy. Blake might have liked to be present during the opening of the crates, but since the ship had only just docked that morning, he wouldn't be making an appearance until tomorrow afternoon at the earliest. He'd be tired after the voyage and would probably wish to spend a few hours with his wife before setting off.

Mason held his breath as he carefully lifted the lid of the sarcophagus. It was heavier than he had expected, but he was able to lift it high enough to get a good look inside. Mason stared in horror at the contents, gripping the lid so as not to drop it from sheer shock.

There was a corpse within, but it wasn't a dusty old mummy. It was Black Upton, his face pale, his eyes closed as if he were merely taking a nap, his arms crossed over his chest just like the depiction on the lid.

"Blake?" Mason whispered, praying this was some sort of joke and Blake would open his eyes and sit up, but no such miracle occurred.

Mason Platt couldn't see any signs of violence, but it was painfully clear to him that Blake Upton was very dead.

"Mr. Howe," he said softly to the hovering watchman, as if afraid to disturb the dead man. "Alert Scotland Yard that we have a suspicious death."

Chapter 1

Tuesday, March 31, 1868

Jason Redmond yanked open the door and stepped aboard the London-bound train just as it began to move out of the Brentwood station, the passengers who'd just disembarked becoming blurry shapes as the locomotive picked up speed. Settling by the window, Jason set down his medical bag, then removed his hat and gloves and unbuttoned his coat, glad he had the compartment to himself and could make himself comfortable. It would have been a shame if he'd missed the train, but he'd stopped off to send a wire and hoped Daniel Haze would receive it before the train arrived in Charing Cross station. If not, Jason would simply take himself to Scotland Yard in the hope that Daniel would be there.

The telegram from Daniel had been brief and utterly lacking in information, but it was a plea for help, and Jason was only too happy to lend a hand. It'd been more than three months since they'd worked on a case together, and much had changed in the interim. Daniel had moved to London in January after accepting a position as a detective inspector at Scotland Yard. The offer had been as flattering as it was unexpected, since he hadn't been an inspector with the Brentwood Constabulary for long, but it seemed his reputation as a man who got results had spread as far as Scotland Yard, and he'd be a fool to pass up the opportunity.

Daniel would have been a happy man had Sarah agreed to join him, but she had chosen to remain in Birch Hill with their infant daughter, Charlotte, and her mother. Jason could understand Sarah's reluctance to return to London after the accident that had claimed their son's life but suspected there was more to Daniel and Sarah's separation than just a question of location. Neither had taken Jason into their confidence these past months, so Jason had kept his distance, not wishing to intrude on what was clearly a private matter.

He'd spent most of his time at home, keeping Katherine company as they awaited the birth of their first child. Jason's face split into a happy smile as he thought of Lily. She'd turned one week old yesterday, and already he was so besotted, he could barely believe he was leaving her, even if only for a day. Had Katherine not encouraged him to go, he might have refused Daniel's request for help, but Katherine understood him better than most wives understood their husbands. His desire to live a life of purpose and utilize his surgical skills prevented him from settling down into a life of lord of the manor. He wasn't cut out for idleness, nor did he feel that using his skills to help the police was beneath him. The work also kept him from losing his edge and reminded him of the frailty of human life.

Daniel hadn't described the case in the telegram, and Jason wondered why he hadn't simply trusted the postmortem to the Scotland Yard surgeon. Surely they had a competent man. Either way, Jason was glad Daniel had sent for him. He missed working on a case and hadn't held a scalpel in months, a situation that he hoped to rectify in short order. Before Lily's birth, he and Katherine had talked of moving to London so that Jason could either volunteer his time at a hospital or possibly teach. He liked the idea of shaping young minds and sharing his knowledge and expertise with a future generation of surgeons.

The move would have to wait until Lily was at least a few weeks older, but it was time to start making plans, and this trip to London could be a start. He'd stop into his lawyer's office and check on the status of the Kensington townhouse he'd inherited from his grandfather. The house had been let, since Jason wasn't using it, but perhaps now would be a good time to speak to the current residents about moving on. Katherine had yet to figure out who in the household would be coming up to London and for how long, which could mean either hiring new staff or making room for the staff they already employed at Redmond Hall. And then there was Micah. He'd been boarding at the Westbridge Academy since the start of the academic year, but Micah would be coming home for the summer holidays and wouldn't want to remain in Birch Hill when he could be in London.

Jason missed the boy, but he was doing well in school and making new friends, his fear of being ostracized for being an American Irish Catholic no longer dominating his decisions. Micah was happy, and Jason was happy for him and hoped Micah might take an interest in medicine once he was of an age to decide what he wanted to do with his life.

Greening fields and homey cottages were left behind as the train approached London, the rookeries coming into view, with their air of decay and dejection. Jason looked away, saddened by the poverty that seemed to hover over the slums, the residents either resorting to petty crime to survive or dead-eyed with utter loss of hope. He wasn't naive enough to think he could make a difference, but maybe someday these people would have access to medical care, and some of the surgeons he helped to prepare might be the ones to offer it.

Jason put on his hat and gloves as the train pulled into Charing Cross station, the doors slamming along the length of the train as the passengers began to disembark and head for the exits. He pushed open the door and stepped onto the platform, where young boys yelled themselves hoarse trying to sell the day's papers, and vendors sold hot pies and fragrant oranges to passersby who might wish to fortify themselves before continuing to their destination. He scanned the area for the familiar profile of Daniel Haze, spotting him further down the track, his spectacles fogged up with the steam from the engine, his face anxious. Daniel hadn't seen him yet, so Jason had a moment to observe the tense set of his shoulders and the pallor of a man who'd spent the winter amid the smog and chill of the city. Jason bypassed a matron with several large cases who nearly blocked the entire platform and strode purposefully toward Daniel. He couldn't wait to hear about the case.

Chapter 2

It had rained earlier, but the sky had cleared, and a fresh breeze that caressed Daniel's face felt almost springlike as he recalled that Easter was less than two weeks away. He hated to admit it, but he'd felt a childish sense of relief when Jason's cable had been presented to him as soon as he'd arrived at Scotland Yard this morning, ready to begin the investigation in earnest, whether Jason had agreed to come or not. This was his first high-profile murder case since joining Scotland Yard a few months ago, and he was unsurprisingly nervous. It was one thing to investigate a knifing in Spitalfields or a shooting in Seven Dials, but this victim was a prominent archeologist, whose name had been on everyone's lips when the last Egyptian exhibit opened at the British Museum, Blake Upton's contribution to the display unequalled by any other scholar of Egypt.

It would have been standard procedure to have the body sent to the morgue last night, as soon as Daniel had arrived on the scene and conducted a preliminary investigation, but he'd decided to try his luck and summon Jason, since he didn't quite trust the police surgeon attached to the Yard. Dr. Fenwick was a fine fellow, if one wanted to go for a pint at the local pub or discuss the latest developments in politics, but after working with Jason, Daniel found Dr. Fenwick to be crude in his methods and too quick to pronounce a verdict, often basing his conclusions on the obvious instead of taking the time to look for that which could be hidden.

Dr. Fenwick didn't usually make an appearance before ten o'clock and probably wouldn't begin the postmortem until he'd finished with the one he'd already had scheduled for this morning, so Daniel could afford to wait. He'd left Constable Putney to stand guard over the scene and keep the night watchman company. Between the two of them, they'd keep the evidence and the body secure until Jason either arrived in London or replied in the negative.

Daniel's face split into a grin when he saw Jason striding toward him, his gait brisk, his medical bag in hand. He was here to help, and Daniel felt a surge of gratitude toward his friend, secure in the knowledge that if there was anything untoward to find, Jason would find it and help Daniel solve this puzzling case.

Daniel raised a hand in greeting, and Jason gave him an answering smile.

"Daniel," he said as he clasped Daniel's hand in a firm handshake. "Pleasure to see you. How have you been?"

"Well, thank you," Daniel replied. "And you? How's Lily?"

Jason had sent Daniel a note announcing the birth of his daughter, and Daniel secretly hoped he'd be asked to be the child's godfather, but he didn't dare presume, given his current domestic situation. If he were to be asked, Sarah would have to be asked to be godmother, and Daniel wasn't at all sure either Jason or Katherine would want Sarah to hold such a responsible position, given past events.

Jason's smile grew wider. "She's perfect. It was difficult to leave her, even for a day."

"I'm sorry to tear you away for your family. I know what it's like to have a new baby."

"Katherine is already planning the christening. It will be sometime next month at St. Catherine's. She has asked the squire and Mrs. Talbot to stand up as Lily's godparents. I do hope you understand, Daniel," Jason added apologetically. "The Talbots are Katherine's only family, besides her father, and given their recent loss, she thought it would be the right thing to do."

"Of course, I understand," Daniel hurried to reassure Jason. "Sarah and I are hardly in a position to take on such a weighty role just now."

"Thank you. I was worried you'd feel slighted."

"Not in the least," Daniel said and knew it to be true. It was right and proper that Jason and Katherine should ask a respectable, middle-aged couple, who would honor their obligations to Lily and be a steadying presence in her life.

"I do hope you and Sarah plan to attend," Jason said.

"We wouldn't miss it."

The two men walked out of the station, where several boys were selling newspapers and penny dreadfuls to passengers who'd passed up the opportunity to purchase a copy inside. Daniel was relieved to see no mention of Blake Upton's death in the papers. The press hadn't gotten wind of the story yet, so that bought him at least a day until public opinion and external pressure to solve the case became a factor. The public was mistrustful of the police and expected them to solve every case within twenty-four hours to prove their mettle. Some cases were straightforward and required a minimum of investigation, but this wasn't one of those cases, and Daniel had to brace himself for the outcry that would follow if he didn't apprehend a suspect soon.

The crowd had thinned, so Daniel had no difficulty finding a cab.

Jason settled into the hansom and set his medical bag on the floor, looking like a man on a mission. "I'm glad you sent for me, Daniel. As much as I love my wife and daughter, I need something to occupy my mind. I haven't worked on a case since you left the Brentwood Constabulary. There's a new police surgeon, a Mr. Norton, who's perfectly capable of dealing with any corpses that come his way."

"So, you find yourself at a loose end?" Daniel asked, thrilled that Jason was eager to help.

"Indeed, I am." Jason laughed. "I'm starting to sound like a real Englishman."

"Don't worry. You've a ways to go yet," Daniel replied, referring to Jason's American accent.

Jason's wife privately called him 'Yank,' an apt description, since Jason had been in England less than two years and had previously resided in New York. He'd attended medical school there and had later spent time there recuperating after his imprisonment in a Confederate prison, where he'd almost starved to death along with his ward, Micah Donovan, whom Jason had brought to England with him when he inherited his late grandfather's estate.

"How's Micah?" Daniel asked.

"Fine. Enjoying school. But tell me about the case. I'd like to know what you've been able to learn before I see the deceased."

"Well, Jason, this one is a corker," Daniel said, pushing his spectacles up his nose.

"Do you know the identity of the victim?"

"Yes. His name is Blake Upton, and he's a well-known archeologist. He arrived home from a six-month dig in Egypt just yesterday. His body was discovered yesterday evening by Mr. Mason Platt, a curator at the British Museum. The body was hidden in an ancient sarcophagus, which had been delivered to the museum in the late afternoon. There are no signs of violence that I can see."

"Might it have been an elaborate suicide?" Jason asked.

"I really don't think so. According to Mr. Platt, Mr. Upton was very excited about a burial chamber his team had uncovered during the dig. He was coming back to accolades from the Archeological Society, numerous newspaper write-ups, and an exhibition of the artefacts at the museum. There would be no reason for a man in his position to take his own life, but anything is possible, so the first thing we must do is determine the cause of death."

"Has his family been informed?"

"Not yet. According to Mr. Platt, Mr. Upton is married but has no children. His wife wouldn't have known definitively that the ship was coming in yesterday, so she probably doesn't realize anything is amiss unless a member of the expedition has called on her. I thought it prudent to wait until the cause of death has been ascertained."

"Where can I perform an autopsy?" Jason asked.

"You may use the mortuary at Scotland Yard. I cleared it with my superior as soon as I received your telegram. He's heard of you and is very eager to make your acquaintance."

"Is that where the body is?" Jason asked, already in pathologist mode.

"No. I thought you'd want to see the body in situ before having it moved to the mortuary."

Jason nodded. "Yes, thank you. I would like to examine the sarcophagus as well, once the body has been removed."

"I left a constable guarding the crate, and he'll assist with moving the body to the mortuary. I'm afraid the sarcophagus must remain at the museum. It's a priceless artefact."

"I really see no reason to move it," Jason replied. "I simply wish to look at it and see if there are any traces of blood or tissue."

"I'm sure Mr. Platt can be persuaded to let you do that," Daniel replied. He handed a few coins to the cabbie, who was perched on his elevated seat behind the cab, and the two men walked the short distance to the museum, which had just opened to the public for the day.

The museum was vast, built in the Greek Revival style that made Daniel feel as if a temple had been erected in the heart of London. There was something grandiose in the design, and he supposed it was appropriate to the treasures housed within, but the sheer size of the place intimidated him. Sarah had suggested a few times that they visit the exhibits, but he'd always found an excuse, not really interested in the dusty relics found within. He was more interested in modern inventions and scientific discoveries, like photography and fingerprinting, than bits and pieces of old tombs and statues that had lost their noses and limbs centuries ago.

This morning, Daniel was glad that he didn't have to pass through the echoing exhibit halls to get to his destination. Mr. Platt had given him leave to use a back door that led directly to the storage area for the Egyptian exhibit, so he led Jason around the back of the building and knocked on the door, glad to see Constable Putney was still alert after spending all night with a corpse for company.

"Good morning, Inspector," the constable said. He was a young man of about twenty-one with reddish hair, wide pale blue eyes, and sparse facial hair, a sad attempt at growing a beard.

"Good morning, Constable. This is Lord Redmond, who'll be performing the postmortem. Please ask Mr. Platt to join us and then see about a wagon. We'll need to transport the body to the mortuary as soon as possible."

"Yes, sir."

"All was quiet?" Daniel asked as the much-relieved constable turned to leave.

"Yes, sir."

"Thank you, Constable," Daniel said, but his attention was no longer on the young man.

Chapter 3

Jason pulled off his gloves, removed his coat and hat, and placed his things on a nearby bench before approaching the crate. Nothing had been touched since Daniel had been called to the scene, the lid of the crate closed but not nailed down.

"Good morning," a middle-aged man who could only be Mr. Platt said as he hurried through the door that led into the museum.

"Mr. Platt, this is Lord Redmond," Daniel said.

Mr. Platt looked mildly surprised, but his concern seemed to be for the sarcophagus rather than for Jason's unexpected rank. "Do be careful," he pleaded after greeting Jason absentmindedly. "It really is very delicate."

"Please don't worry, Mr. Platt. I will be most careful," Jason assured him. He studied the crate, then ran a hand along the top. "Tell me, Mr. Platt, do you use your own wagons to pick up the crates from the port?"

"Yes, we do. The museum has a fleet of wagons that we use to transport artefacts and various supplies."

"I'd like to speak to the driver of the wagon," Jason said.

"Of course." Mr. Platt turned toward the guard, who was watching the proceedings, and motioned with his head. "Get Eugene Moore."

The guard left, and Jason turned his attention back to the crate. "Daniel, help me lift the lid."

Mason Platt stood off to the side, nervously wringing his hands. "When do you think you'll be removing the body?" he asked Jason. "It really is rather..." He let the sentence trail off, probably because he was about to say the remains were an inconvenience and prevented him from getting on with the business at hand.

"Within the hour," Jason assured him.

"This sarcophagus is a very rare find. It's so beautiful, so well preserved." Mason Platt sounded as if he were about to cry with frustration. "Once word gets out that it held a corpse, the exhibit will be tainted by scandal."

"It's a coffin, Mr. Platt," Jason pointed out. "It's meant to hold a corpse. I have no doubt your exhibit will be a great success. People will flock to it all the more because it's part of a murder inquiry."

"Do you really think so?" Mr. Platt asked, instantly brightening.

"I have no doubt of it. Now, if you don't mind—"

Jason braced his hands on the sides of the crate and leaned forward as much as the side would allow, his face mere inches from the victim. Blake Upton was around forty, with thick fair hair, sun-bronzed skin, and an athletic build. Had he been taller or huskier, he wouldn't have fit into the narrow coffin designed for someone short and slender. Blake's arms were crossed over his chest, his eyes closed as if he were taking a nap. At first glance, there were no signs of violence, just as Daniel had suggested.

Having studied the body for a few moments, Jason carefully turned the man's head to the right and then to the left. It wasn't easy, since rigor mortis had set in, but he was able to move it far enough to see if there was a wound on the back of the skull.

"Well?" Daniel asked impatiently. He was eager to begin the investigation, but for that, he needed something to go on.

"Give me a moment," Jason replied. He unfolded the man's arms with some difficulty and unbuttoned the jacket, running his hands along the torso, then down his legs, before carefully rolling the body onto its side so he could examine the back.

The door opened, and Constable Putney walked in, followed by two men. One of the men was introduced as Eugene Moore.

Jason turned away from the corpse to greet the man. "Mr. Moore, were you the one to collect this particular crate from the port?" he asked.

"I was, sir."

"And was the crate in good order? Was it sealed?"

"I didn't check, but the lid didn't shift or nothin' when the crate was loaded."

"Did you come to the museum directly from Southampton?" Jason asked.

"Aye, sir. Didn't even stop for a piss, beggin' yer pardon," he added. "Too valuable a cargo to leave unattended."

"Was anyone with you?"

"Not on the bench, but there were two other wagons followin'," Mr. Moore said. "We came straight back 'ere."

"Thank you, Mr. Moore," Jason said. "You may carefully lift the body out of the coffin onto this board," he indicated the lid of the crate, "then cover it with a length of canvas and deliver it to the morgue. Constable Putney will direct you."

"Yes, sir," the men replied in unison.

Jason oversaw the removal of the body, then turned to the coffin. He'd seen a sarcophagus once before when visiting the museum with Micah, but not this close up, and he was mesmerized by its beauty. This was no pine box to bury the dead; this was a work of art that had survived thousands of years. The paint looked as fresh as if the box had been painted just recently, the face of the deceased so skillfully depicted, Jason almost felt as if the kohl-painted eyes were following his every move. The hair, or headpiece, was painted black, and there were numerous images on the lid, possibly telling the story of the man's life. Or perhaps it had been a woman. It was difficult to tell just by looking at the facial features.

Tearing his gaze away from the lid, Jason turned his intention to the interior. There were several strands of fair hair, possibly having fallen out when the body was placed in the coffin, but other than that, Jason couldn't see anything that might resemble bodily fluids or tissue. Not even a broken nail. The inside of the coffin had an unpleasant smell and was a bit dusty, but that was partly due to the contents it had held for centuries and the more recent body that had lain inside. There were no other odors that aroused Jason's suspicions. He briefly wondered what happened to the mummy but decided not to ask since its whereabouts had no bearing on the task at hand.

Mr. Platt hovered at Jason's elbow, clearly terrified Jason would inflict damage on the artefact. Having examined the interior carefully, Jason turned away from the sarcophagus, Mr. Platt's exhalation of relief almost comical.

"Is there anywhere we can talk?" Jason asked.

"Of course. Follow me."

They adjourned to Mr. Platt's office, which was large and comfortable. There was a walnut desk, studded leather chairs, a glass-fronted cabinet stuffed full of well-read books and small knickknacks, and a decanter of something that might have been whisky or brandy on the sideboard. Jason and Daniel took the guest chairs, while Mr. Platt sat behind the desk.

"Mr. Platt, what can you tell me about Mr. Upton?" Jason asked.

"What do you wish to know?"

"How long have you known him? How well? Was he prone to bouts of melancholy? Did he perhaps have a fondness for opium?"

Mr. Platt looked astonished, as did Daniel, but he remained silent, allowing Jason to take the lead. Daniel had spoken to Mr. Platt last night, so this was Jason's turn to ask questions.

"Mr. Upton has had an association with the museum for the past five years. He's been instrumental in expanding our Egyptian exhibit and providing us with background information on the artefacts he's unearthed. The museum does organize its own excavations, but Mr. Upton's efforts were sponsored by Lord Belmont, who's a long-time patron of the museum. He donates all the finds to the museum and allows us to display them for as long as we care to. I must tell you that the burial chamber Blake Upton discovered on this dig, the sarcophagus, and the grave goods inside, is the most important discovery since John Turtle Wood uncovered the Temple of Artemis at Ephesus. The temple is fourth century B.C., but according to Blake, this burial chamber dates further back, to the New Kingdom, which we believe to have been at its peak in the seventh century B.C."

Jason nodded, not really interested in a history lesson. The only history he needed was that of Blake Upton. "Was Mr. Upton given to bouts of melancholy?" he asked.

Mr. Platt paused, clearly surprised by the question. "I really wouldn't know. Perhaps he was, and maybe he had a fondness for the opium pipe, but I'm not the right man to ask."

"Did you spend time with him socially or only in your professional capacity?" Jason inquired.

"We saw each other at several museum functions, but we weren't friends, if that's what you're asking."

"Do you have Mr. Upton's home address?"

"I already gave it to the inspector."

"Very good," Jason said, rising to his feet. "Thank you for your help."

"Can we display the sarcophagus now?"

"I don't see why not."

"Oh, thank you," Mr. Platt gushed. "And I hope you find whoever did this terrible thing. Mr. Upton's death is a great loss to archeology."

"What do you think?" Daniel asked as soon as they were outside again. He looked around for a hansom, but there wasn't one in the vicinity, so they started to walk, hoping they'd find one on the way. "Is there any possibility this could have been an elaborate suicide?"

"I really don't think so, unless someone else was in on it. Even if the man had taken a lethal dose of poison, he'd still need someone to close the lid and then seal the crate. He could hardly have done that himself. Besides, why go to such lengths?"

"Perhaps he wanted to be forever linked to the sarcophagus he'd found," Daniel suggested.

"He'll be forever linked to it anyway, if it's as great a discovery as Mr. Platt said it was. Seventh century B.C.," Jason said, shaking his head in wonder. "I can't even wrap my mind around that. To think that there was a thriving civilization in the sands of Egypt all those years ago, and they were such skilled craftsmen."

"Yes, it really is amazing. I can certainly understand why there's such a fascination with all things Egyptian. I read an article quite recently that suggested the ancient Egyptians and modern-day Englishmen have much in common."

Jason turned to look at Daniel. "What could they possibly have in common?"

"The Egyptians had the utmost respect for death. They planned for it and those who could afford it spent a fortune to bury their dead. Those tombs took decades to build, and they needed a large amount of goods to send their dead well prepared for the afterlife."

"Are people now burying pots and candlesticks with their dead?" Jason said, a smile tugging at the corner of his mouth.

"Not yet, but there's been a mummification right here in England," Daniel said, his eyebrows lifting with the incongruity of that statement.

"What? Really?" Jason asked, turning to gape at him.

"This happened long before you arrived on our shores," Daniel replied, "so you wouldn't have seen it in the papers, but I remember reading about it and discussing it with my father, who'd been absolutely horrified by such an unchristian treatment of the body. The tenth duke of Hamilton had requested that he be mummified according to all the rules and traditions of the process and be buried in an Egyptian sarcophagus that he had purchased for that very purpose in a tomb he'd built in his native Scotland."

"And who mummified him?" Jason asked.

"Thomas Pettigrew. He was a surgeon," Daniel added.

"The eccentricities of one wealthy man don't account for the tastes of an entire nation," Jason said.

"No, but you must admit that our society on the whole is fascinated with death. We have elaborate funerary and mourning traditions. When the average lifespan is no more than forty years, to spend two years in mourning for a loved one is a lot, don't you agree?"

"I agree that a person should mourn for as long as they see fit. No one should impose a timeframe on grief. Not everyone handles loss in the same way, and some people could benefit from distraction whereas others prefer solitude. I do feel sorry for the poor woman whose life we're about to change forever," Jason said, referring to Blake Upton's widow.

"As do I. Losing a spouse is nearly as bad as losing a child," Daniel said softly.

"Yes." Now that Jason had a child of his own, he could understand only too well what Daniel was referring to. The thought of anything happening to Lily was so acutely painful, he couldn't bear to contemplate it for even a moment.

"Jason, we have some time before the body gets to Scotland Yard. What say you to a spot of lunch? I don't want you to get lightheaded while you're working," Daniel added solicitously.

Normally, Jason didn't eat before performing an autopsy, but lately, if he didn't eat every few hours, he grew lightheaded and shaky. As a doctor, he knew these were symptoms of hypoglycemia, and he suspected he was at risk for diabetes mellitus, a condition that might have been brought on by his lengthy incarceration at Andersonville Prison. Some men were able to recover with no long-term ill effects, but Jason hadn't been so lucky. Almost a year of near starvation had taken its toll, and now his body was letting him know that it would never be the same. Jason had curbed his sugar intake and tried to eat protein with every meal, since he found it kept the bouts of hypoglycemia at bay.

"A steak and ale pie or a sausage roll will do," Jason replied. "I can't eat a full meal before performing an autopsy, but I would very much like to take you out to supper this evening, if you're free."

"I would like that very much," Daniel replied.

"Excellent. Would you like one?" Jason asked as they approached a street vendor who had about a dozen steaming pies laid out on a tray slung around his neck with a leather strap. They must have just come out of the oven, and they smelled divine.

"Why not?" Daniel said. "I can never say no to a hot pie."

By the time Jason had purchased the pies, Daniel had secured a hansom, and they ate their impromptu meal on the way to Scotland Yard.

Jason had been curious to visit the Yard, and he enjoyed a brief tour and a warm welcome from the policemen Daniel introduced him to.

"Let me introduce you to Superintendent Ransome," Daniel said. "He's head of Detective Branch. He's eager to meet you. He's something of an admirer." Daniel knocked on a glass-fronted door and was bid to enter.

"Sir, may I present Lord Redmond, lately of the Essex Police," Daniel said, beaming with pride.

John Ransome got to his feet and held out his hand. "It's an honor to meet you, sir. I've heard a lot about you."

"Thank you," Jason said, glad the superintendent didn't resent his presence. At first glance, John Ransome was nothing like Superintendent Coleridge, who had been Daniel's and, by extension, Jason's superior at the Brentwood Constabulary. For one, John Ransome was much younger, possibly in his late thirties. He wasn't very tall, but he had a lean, wiry frame and intense dark eyes beneath finely shaped eyebrows. His hair was very black, and his handlebar moustache was waxed into neat points. He smiled, but his gaze was watchful, appraising.

"I appreciate you helping us out," John Ransome said as he resumed his seat and gestured for the two men to settle themselves in the guest chairs. "We have our own police surgeons, of course, but this is going to be a highly publicized case, and your expertise certainly won't hurt. And, of course, you will be compensated for your time," the superintendent added.

"I'm not doing this for the money," Jason replied.

"Nevertheless," Ransome replied, dismissing the issue of money. "Have you come to any conclusions after examining the body?"

"I would prefer to wait until after the postmortem to share my findings," Jason said.

John Ransome smiled widely, as if Jason had just passed some unspoken test. "Good man," he said. "A good detective never rushes to conclusions. Please, share your findings with me once you have them."

"Of course, sir," Jason promised. "Now, if everything is in readiness, I would like to begin."

"Inspector Haze will take you to the mortuary."

The mortuary at Scotland Yard was like every mortuary Jason had ever worked in— sterile, cold, and utterly without character. He could have been anywhere in the world, including the hospital where he'd worked in New York before the war.

The body of Blake Upton was laid out on the granite slab, still fully dressed, as Jason had given express instructions not to touch anything. Jason dropped his walking stick in a metal stand by the door, removed his coat, hat, and jacket, and hung them up on a coat rack, then reached for the leather apron hanging behind the door. From his medical bag, he extracted the linen cap he wore when working to keep the hair out of his eyes.

Checking that he had everything he needed to begin, Jason approached the corpse and began to slowly undress him, not an easy task given that his limbs were as stiff as wooden planks. Jason sniffed the clothes before folding them and putting them aside, just in case there was any telltale odor of poison, but he would have smelled it back at the museum had there been anything to detect. Once the corpse was naked, Jason performed a thorough examination, checking everything from the scalp beneath his thick hair to the toenails before picking up a scalpel. He wouldn't have minded a bit of company, but Daniel was squeamish and never attended postmortems, preferring to wait outside and hear the results afterwards.

More than three hours later, Jason washed his hands with carbolic soap, removed the cap and the bloodstained apron, and donned his jacket before draping his coat over his arm and retrieving his hat, gloves, and walking stick. He was ready to share his conclusions with Daniel and John Ransome.

Printed in Great Britain
by Amazon